Tenacity
One Man's Unrelenting Drive Links Past to Present

J H MARSHALL

Published by Segue Press

Edited by JoEllen Claypool

For more information or to order additional copies of this book, please contact:
James H. Marshall, Sr.
seguepress@gmail.com
Tenacity is also available on Amazon.com

First printing 2017

ISBN – 978-0-9996961-0-1
Library of Congress Control Number: 2017918541

DEDICATION

I dedicate this book to our dear friends, both American and Chilean, who were with us in Chile. They are way too many to name them all, because so many made significant impacts on our lives. Two American couples stand out, namely Marian and the late Lynn Hoppie as well as Jane and Leon Leavitt. Two Chilean couples took us in as family, Raúl Vilugron and Maria Soto as well as Sergio Gutierrez and his late wife, Denisse Urzua.

CONTENTS

ACKNOWLEDGMENTS

My wife, Annie, for her consistent encouragement and great ideas over more than 54 years.

My daughter, Stephanie Campbell, who was my perpetual supporter with this book.

Duane S. Crowther, whose earlier editing sent this book in an effectively different direction.

JoEllen Claypool, whose editing gave me constant encouragement and the path to publication.

Carol M. Green for helping me enter the world of authorship.

Nina Lindbloom Wheeler, who was my proofreader in high school and again on this book.

PROLOGUE

Because of the stifling heat in their bedroom and the expected excitement of the next day, sleeping had been sporadic. The two boys, ages five and ten, had been elated to have their father home from the mine for a few days. They were especially excited to open the gifts he brought, and they were looking forward to the professional soccer game they would attend with him later in the day at the *Estadio Nacional*. Perhaps it was the heat, or perhaps they heard activity out on the street, but they both awoke about the same time.

They were trying to go back to sleep when they heard a terrible commotion. The front door of their home crashed open as six uniformed men rushed in shouting. Both their mother and their father screamed in protest as their father was dragged away without having the opportunity to put on his clothes. They watched the black van speed away carrying their father and the uniformed men. The whole process took less than two minutes, leaving their mother huddled on the floor sobbing hysterically.

For ten days, their mother searched frantically for their father, contacting every official she could think of. She heard rumors of others who had been picked up by Pinochet's secret police. There were stories of beatings and torture. Some of those who had been tortured were released weeks later, after receiving terrible beatings. There were reports that some died at the hands of their tormentors. Many were never heard from again.

A neighbor brought their mother home, supporting her as she could barely walk. At first, the boys thought she too had been beaten. Again, she was sobbing hysterically as she screamed, "They have killed him! They have killed him because of Alonzo Sandoval and his cursed mine."

She never talked of the event again, but the two young boys vowed they would get even with Alonzo Sandoval for what he had caused to happen to their father. The revenge they sought was delayed more than thirty years when their benefactor showed them documentation listing their father as the owner of the *Esperanza* Mine. He presented them with a plan to destroy Alonzo Sandoval and regain possession of the mine.

CHAPTER 1

The multicolored trees of the suburban valley gave way to the golden hues of the foothills and finally to the deep emerald blend of the evergreens. They didn't get very many opportunities to enjoy a day like this, which was a beauty. The gradual climb from the valley to the top of the foothills covered about sixteen miles. Before descending the next four miles to the river, Paul and Janet dismounted from the perches of their new Honda Gold Wing touring bike to enjoy the view.

"Look, Paul. Look at this view!" From the top of Horseshoe Bend hill, they could gaze behind to Boise Valley and ahead to the mountains climbing alongside the Payette River. They could imagine how the view continued to Cascade Reservoir and then to Payette Lake. As they gazed down into Horseshoe Bend, they could see the horseshoe curve of the river as it began its descent into Emmett.

Generally, both Paul and Janet were so busy they seldom had the time to loaf or roam, so this adventure was a treat. It started days earlier when Paul sent Janet an email. "I don't have anything on the docket for Thursday afternoon. How does yours look?"

She'd answered, "If I can spend time with you, I can

empty it very quickly. What do you have in mind?"

Paul was a muscular but distinguished looking man of thirty-eight. He was 6'2" and weighed just under two hundred pounds. He kept his dark, wavy hair well groomed. His sister-in-law called it the eighth wonder of the world. Janet found him equally attractive in a dress suit or hiking gear. His business kept him in front of people, but he loved to be in the mountains with Janet.

Paul answered, "I was thinking of a ride up to McCall and back on the Gold Wing before it's too late in the season. We might scope out the North Fork for a kayaking trip next summer. I just have one appointment in the morning. We could leave the house about noon and maybe could grab a bite somewhere along the way."

"Why don't I pack a lunch, and we can eat by the river?"

So, through emails, their trip was planned in detail. Mother Nature was very accommodating, blessing them with beautiful clear skies and a warm, Indian summer day.

The traffic was sparse on Highway 55, as it should be this time of the day and week. On a Friday evening or early Saturday morning, the highway would be filled with people leaving the valley for the mountains one more time before the weather turned cold. The revelers didn't usually begin on Thursday afternoon. As Paul and Janet looked back down the highway before starting their descent, there was just one lone pickup truck parked on the side of the highway back half a mile or so.

The bike handled nicely on the drive. The intercom in their helmets gave them the opportunity to carry on conversations as they traveled.

"Let's stop and pick up a cold soda or juice to go with our lunch," suggested Janet.

"I think there is a small market here in Horseshoe Bend."

Paul steered the touring bike into a parking place, and they both dismounted. He smiled as Janet pulled off her helmet and shook her long, blond hair. She was gorgeous at 5'10" and her athletic shape had not varied from when she played volleyball for Brigham Young University. Currently she was a triathlete who worked out in at least one of the three activities, running, biking or swimming, four or five days per week. She preferred the biking. She flashed him a big smile of white teeth and blue eyes before handing him her helmet and entering the store.

Paul locked the helmets to the bike before following her into the store. He looked around as he entered but couldn't see her. *She must have gone into the restroom*. He decided that was a good idea and entered the men's restroom.

Exiting the restroom, he quickly scanned the room for Janet and caught the eye of a customer speaking in Spanish. The speaker's companion also looked his way, and then they both turned away.

Paul generally paid attention when he overheard people conversing in Spanish. Having served a mission for the Church of Jesus Christ of Latter-day Saints in Peru, he prided himself on his linguistic skills. He liked to try to determine the geographic origin of the accent. He tried to listen, but the closer he got to them, the softer they talked.

Noticing they were being observed, the two men quit talking and picked up beer and potato chips before moving to the check-out counter.

Janet tapped him on the arm, breaking his concentration as she asked, "Did you find anything to drink?"

"No, I was waiting for you."

"Let's get some fruit juice and some water," Janet

suggested.

Paul could've guessed she would choose fruit juice and water, because even though she had suggested they stop for cold sodas, she never bought soda for herself and really preferred he not drink it either.

As Janet began loading their purchases into the storage compartment of their touring bike, Paul looked around the parking lot. He noticed the two Hispanics crawling into a new, dark blue Dodge Ram covered with mud. The truck was wearing the mud like armor. Paul wondered about that because the weather had been dry for a number of days. *Where could they get their truck covered in mud like that?* He tried to get a look at the license plate, but it too was covered in mud.

As Janet put on her helmet, she asked, "Can you remember where we stopped for lunch on our company rafting trip?"

"I think so."

"Do you think we can find it from the highway? That would be a great place to eat our lunch."

"Well, if we both keep our eyes peeled, we should be able to find it."

Neither of them had any trouble locating the lunch stop. Paul and Janet removed their helmets but left their leathers on. Janet carried the lunch she had prepared as Paul locked the helmets. Janet chose a table near the river removed from the view and sounds of the highway and next to a table with an animated family with teenagers.

"I'm glad you prepared lunch. It's so much better than fast food."

She smiled sweetly as she commented, "This is such a peaceful spot here by the river." Janet spread a blue and white gingham cloth on the table. "No telling what little beasts have left prints on this table. Paul, don't you just love the sound of the river?"

"You don't really notice it until you listen," responded Paul. "Watch the power of the water pushing over and around those boulders."

"I wonder where all of that water comes from. It's time for the new snows to come, and yet, the river just keeps on flowing. It's lower now than it was when we floated through here, but there's still a huge quantity of water passing by every minute."

"It seems to be part of something much bigger than itself," suggested Paul. "The river, the trees, the wind, the animals; they all seem part of an overall plan."

"I wonder if we are part of its overall plan," Janet continued.

Paul wrinkled his brow wondering, "What do you mean? We're just passing through."

"Maybe that deer across the river is just passing through, too. All the people driving up and down this highway are just passing through, but everything is still part of this huge scene."

"That's way too deep for me. This fried chicken and potato salad are important to what's happening here, but the rest is way beyond me. By the way, I love your cold, fried chicken, and I hesitate to eat anyone else's potato salad. If you don't make it, it doesn't taste right."

She grinned in pride and then continued, "I wonder if we're doing all that we should to be part of the overall plan."

"You mean the overall plan for this picnic area?" he questioned mischievously.

"No," she replied indignantly. "I mean Heavenly Father's plan, His plan for you and me."

"You don't think it is important to Him that we are eating fried chicken and potato salad beside the powerful Payette River?"

"Perhaps it is," she shrugged in frustration. "Don't you ever wonder if that is enough?"

"I really don't think much about it. I just try to do my job and take care of my church assignments and let everything else take care of itself."

"I don't believe that for a minute," she retorted. "You're always thinking of ways to please me or do something for me. You're always trying to make life better for Jeff and his family. Back to my original question, do you think we are doing all we should be doing?"

"In what regard?" He knew she was trying to tell him something but was having a difficult time getting to the point.

"Well …" Janet looked embarrassed, as though she were discussing a topic off limits. "Well, I wonder," she paused, looking at Paul with her big, blue eyes, "I wonder if it's time for us to start our family."

Paul and Janet married older than most of their friends. They were both successful in their own careers before taking on the responsibility of marriage. They'd put all of their free time into each other, and even though there'd been a few discussions about children two years earlier when they were dating, the subject hadn't been discussed during the last few months.

"Is this something you've been thinking about?" asked Paul.

"Yes," she replied, "especially when we're around Jeff and Michelle and their girls. I want to be a mother, and you would make a wonderful father. I see how you are with Sonia and Shelly."

"Well, remember, we decided a long time ago that when you're ready, we should go ahead." He grinned as he added, "We certainly aren't getting any younger."

"Don't remind me," she scolded. "I'm glad you remember it that way because I quit taking the pill six weeks ago." She gave him a look that asked, *Am I in trouble?*

"You did? Without discussing it with me?"

"Well, you said, 'When I'm ready.'"

He reassured her. "Of course it's OK, but it is a moderately important decision to make unilaterally. I just wish I'd been involved."

"I'm quite sure you were involved, but you're right, Paul. I should've talked to you before. I was just afraid it might not work. My Aunt Alice was never able to get pregnant, and I didn't want you to be disappointed until we knew for sure."

"And now … you know for sure?"

Janet reached across the table and took Paul's hand in hers. She smiled and announced, "I am sure because," Janet stood up and posed for the grand announcement, "I am pregnant."

Bubbling over with pride and joy, Paul rushed around the table and took Janet in his arms. He gave her a big kiss, and then they bowed to the applauding people at the next table.

***

The river wasn't nearly as high as earlier in the year. Still, it was violent with the white water rushing around the huge boulders. The river had been on their left, but after crossing a bridge, it was now on their right. The highway was excellent but was still only two lanes, one lane going north and the other going south. There were very few stretches in which passing was possible as the highway was marked with a double solid line.

A little past the sign indicating Big Eddy on the river, they came to a sharp left turn in the highway. Huge rocks hung down from the west side of the mountain, making passing impossible. Reliving the previous conversation with Janet, Paul was driving the motorcycle a little faster than he should have been. As he entered the sharp left curve he was musing, *I'm going to be a father.* The thought elated him.

At that instant they both noticed a large, dark pickup truck passing them on the left. Janet screamed, "Paul!" as the truck slammed into them on the side.

Paul scowled as he glanced up and recognized the muddy truck from the market. He applied his brakes immediately, but by that time, the truck had forced them off the pavement onto the loose gravel. He tried to turn the handlebars to the left, but the truck was right beside them pushing them toward the river. Paul glanced up in complaint as the passenger looked right at him, grinning and waving evilly.

Paul applied the brakes with all his strength, but the bike was too heavy to stop the momentum in the loose gravel.

"Paul, Paul, we are going over!"

CHAPTER 2

The weight of the Gold Wing carried Paul and Janet over the edge of the embankment into the white, swirling waters of the Payette River. Paul tried to lay the bike on its side to slide down next to a large boulder. There was just too much weight and they ended up nose-diving right onto the rock. The momentum carried the back of the bike over the top. Janet's weight pushed Paul forward, and he slid out of the saddle into the shallow water while she was catapulted out into the rapids. The bike landed in the deep water on its back.

Paul glanced up in time to see the rapids carry Janet backwards around a boulder in the middle of the river and out of sight. Frantically, he searched hoping to see her, but she didn't reappear.

Climbing out of the shallow water as he watched for Janet, he quickly removed his helmet, leathers and boots. *Please, Heavenly Father, make her come to the top.*

Noting the current swept by the rock around which Janet had been carried, Paul jumped in. He swam with all his force so as not to be carried around the boulder where she had disappeared. He was able to grab hold of an edge of the rock and pull himself up onto it.

Paul looked intently into the swirling river for any sign of Janet. He thought he could see her blue helmet down in the white foam. Without another thought, he jumped into the water and reached down for her. Her hand was up, stretched as if reaching for help. When he took hold of her hand, she fastened a grip on his. He pulled with all his might, but she wouldn't budge.

Paul slid around to get more leverage to pull. She still had a firm grip on his hand, and they both struggled to no avail. *Her feet or legs must be wedged under a log or something. Please, God, do something.*

"Come on, come on!" screamed Paul. "Push out of there."

Paul ran his hand down her body to where he found her leg bent around and wedged under an underwater log. He tried to dislodge it but couldn't. The force of the water worked against him. As he tried to move into a better position, he became caught in the current which washed him away and down the river.

Paul flipped over on his back with his feet downstream so he could see where he was going. He looked up and swam with all his force towards the western bank of the river. Just as he arrived at the edge, the current caught him again and washed him around another big rock and back out into the middle.

Oh no! I can't let this current carry me away. I have to get back to Janet and our baby. Dear Heavenly Father, please help me get her out. Please help her get out.

Again, Paul used all of his force to swim to the edge of the river. Exhausted, he pulled himself free of the water and looked up the river. He was probably fifty to seventy-five yards downstream from the boulder where Janet was trapped. *Time is running out.*

He climbed the river bank to the highway and was running up the highway when a car with a family stopped.

"Do you need help?" cried the young mother.

"Yes, my wife is in the river under a rock. I can't get her out."

The man shouted that there was some rope in the trunk. The woman tried to use her cell phone, but there was no signal.

"Gil, you help him. I'll drive to where I can get a signal and call for help," she screamed.

Her husband threw one end of the rope to Paul and held on to the other. Paul jumped into the river, just like he had before and swam to the boulder in the middle of the river. His arms were tired and felt like jelly. He was able to pull himself back onto the rock behind which Janet was stranded. Lying on the top of the rock, he tried to reach down to her hand. He couldn't reach it from that position. He risked being swept away by jumping back in beside her.

Quickly, Paul lowered himself into the water, being careful not to get caught in the current. When he reached out for her hand, she didn't respond. Wrapping his own leg around the same log that had Janet entrapped, he held himself in position as he tied the rope around her waist. He knew how to tie a bowline rapidly but not under these conditions.

After tying the rope around Janet's waist, he tried to pull himself back out of the water, but there was no place to get a foothold. As he maneuvered for position, the current caught him again, and he was washed away. He let go of the rope hoping, *Oh no! I hope that guy has hold of that rope.*

He prayed again as he struggled up the edge of the riverbank and staggered back to where the stranger was trying to pull Janet from where she was lodged behind the big boulder. Paul could see him pulling with all his might. About this time, another car with two men stopped. After a quick explanation, they too pulled on the rope. Even with the four of them pulling, they couldn't dislodge her. Pulling that hard, Paul knew they were doing irreparable damage to Janet, but they had no other choice.

***

It took the rescue crew more than an hour and half to remove Janet's body from the river. They pulled her to shore and began CPR, but even Paul had lost hope that Janet could be revived.

Lucy Stafford, Gil's wife returned after calling the county sheriff and did her best to comfort Paul. He gave her the phone numbers of Jeff Harkin, his partner and best friend, and Janet's parents, Ralph and Christine Wilson. He asked her to return to a place where she could receive a signal and notify them of what had happened. He didn't want to leave Janet's side.

Finally, the deputy approached Paul, "What happened here?"

Paul explained how they had been riding their motorcycle when a truck tried to pass them on the curve. He described the fiendish look on the passenger as the truck pushed them over the edge. Deputy Robinson listened very patiently as Paul explained as best he could how these were the same two Hispanics he had seen in the store in Horseshoe Bend.

Deputy Robinson and Paul could see the obvious slide marks of the braking. They could also see the skid marks of the pickup as it returned to the pavement.

An hour later, Janet's body was finally loaded into the ambulance. By then, Janet's parents, Ralph and Christine Wilson, and Paul's friend, Jeff, had arrived.

Christine Wilson broke into sobs when Paul explained to her what had happened to her daughter. None of them could help but ask, "Why?" The explanation of the dark pickup truck didn't make any sense at all. Perhaps it was just stupid people doing stupid things.

"Where do you want us to take her?" asked the ambulance driver.

Paul was startled by the question. He hadn't even given it a thought. Questioningly, he looked at the Wilsons and Jeff for help. Ralph Wilson frowned as he suggested Grandley's Mortuary and Christine concurred. The driver looked up at Paul, who also nodded.

Once the ambulance left and Deputy Robinson finished asking questions, the crowd of people quickly dispersed. Again, Paul thanked Gil and Lucy Stafford after writing down their address and phone number.

"Come on, Paul, let's go home." Jeff Harkin took charge and ushered Paul to his own Land Rover.

As Paul started to get into the SUV, he thought of Ralph and Christine and returned to them. "Are you going to be all right?" he asked.

"No," Janet's father answered. "We'll never be all right again. Children should never die before their parents and what a terrible way for her to suffer."

Paul started to add that it was even worse knowing that Janet was pregnant but decided it was already bad enough for her parents. They didn't need that burden too.

On the way back to the valley, Paul recounted the day's events, returning often to the dark blue Dodge Ram pickup truck. The question kept coming up, "Why?" Neither of them could suggest a logical answer.

Neither of them could think of anything more to say until they arrived in the valley.

"Why don't you come home with me and stay at my place," suggested Jeff.

"No, I want to go home."

"Do you think you should be there alone?"

"No, but she's gone, and I don't want to be with anyone else right now."

Except for calling his grandparents, Paul left the calls to everyone else to Jeff and the Wilsons. He entered his home and shook off the emptiness. He unplugged his phone and sat down on the floor in the dark with his back to the wall and moaned.

***

Within just a few seconds, the computer screen lit up with the face of the man who was to bring riches back to their family, riches which had been stolen years earlier. "Our mission was successful," reported Roberto Contreras.

"Tell me about it," urged the benefactor.

"As you instructed, we followed their motorcycle. They stopped at a convenience store to use the restroom and buy refreshments. We followed them into the store."

"Did they see you?"

"Yeah, but he didn't know us or who we are."

The benefactor frowned to himself. *Why did they let themselves be seen?* "Then what happened?"

"We followed them until they stopped to eat lunch and waited where they couldn't see us. They took almost an hour to eat; they didn't seem to be in a hurry. After they finished their lunches, they continued up the highway. As we were getting closer to the sharp curve we had discovered, we crept right up behind their motorcycle as though we were waiting for an opportunity to pass. As they started into the curve we pulled up beside them and pushed them into the river."

"Yeah," interjected Esteban, "I waved at him as they went over the bank into the river. It was great!" Causing pain to the man who had stolen their property by killing his son was worth almost as much as regaining their fortune.

Their benefactor shook his head and frowned. "He saw you?"

"Oh yeah," bragged Esteban, "his eyes were as big as saucers."

"Are they dead?" He wanted no survivors.

"They must be," replied Roberto. "The river was raging wild. They were dressed in leather with boots and helmets. We don't see how either of them could have survived, but we didn't dare hang around. We drove north to the car wash and quickly washed off the mud and then continued north returning to the valley by a different route. We're now on our way back to California."

"That may not be wise just yet. We want to make sure that both of them are dead. When you know for sure, get back to me."

"Si, Señor," replied Roberto before he broke the connection.

***

Even though Christine and Ralph Wilson had watched as the EMTs inserted their daughter's lifeless body into the ugly, yellow body bag, they still couldn't grasp the fact that she was dead. The whole process had been disgusting, but the worst was watching them zip up the body bag and close it over her face.

"I should never have let her marry him," he screamed.

"What?"

"When he requested permission to ask for her hand in marriage, I should have said NO!"

"Ralph, you couldn't have stopped that marriage. Paul was being courteous and respectful when he asked you for her hand in marriage. You wouldn't have stopped that marriage by saying no."

"She would never have married him if I had refused," he professed without conviction.

"You are just trying to find a reason to blame yourself for Janet's death."

"I don't blame me," he protested. "I blame Paul!"

"For what happened to Janet?"

"Yes! He should never have put her on that blasted motorcycle."

CHAPTER 3

Paul couldn't believe how slowly his car seemed to move as he traversed the same route he and Janet had covered a day earlier. The scenery had lost all of its beauty and serenity, revealing only distress.

He automatically reached for his cell phone and then remembered it had been ruined by water when he was thrown into the river.

Arriving at the store in Horseshoe Bend, Paul was pleased to see the same clerk who had served him yesterday. Paul waited until he was alone and cautiously approached.

"Hi, my name is Paul Merrick. I came in here yesterday with my wife."

Defensively the clerk looked up in question. "Was there a problem?"

"Yes, er … no. Not with you but with some people that were here in the store when we were. Do you remember us?"

"Yeah, I think so. Weren't you wearing motorcycle leathers, both of you?"

"That's right. Do you remember anyone else in here at the same time?"

"I'm not sure. Say, what's this all about?"

"There were a couple of other guys in here at the same time, speaking Spanish. They were driving a muddy truck."

"Yeah, maybe I remember. What's this all about?"

Paul hadn't wanted to go into details but guessed it would be necessary to get the information he needed. He told the clerk the story of the two in the pickup running them off the road into the river and finally Paul blurted out how his wife, Janet, had been killed.

"Oh yeah," responded the clerk, now ready to help. "I heard about that. News like that carries quickly. So, you were the ones. I'm really sorry, man. You must be sick. How can I help? Were they the ones who ran you off the road?"

"Do you know who those guys were?"

"No, I've never seen them before in my life. They just bought some beer and stuff and took off."

"Did they pay with a credit card or a check?"

The clerk looked up and thought for a moment. "Nah, they paid cash. Sorry. The sheriff's deputy stopped by a while ago asking questions about the same guys, but he didn't say what it was all about."

Paul was startled that the police had not arrived until today. "You say the deputy came in today asking about them, not yesterday?"

"No, it was about an hour and a half ago."

Paul was seething. *How could the police hope to catch the murderers if they didn't even start looking until today? They're probably in the next state by now.*

"Do you know where I could find the deputy that talked to you?"

"He's probably down at Lola's having a cup of coffee about now."

"Lola's?"

"It's a little coffee shop on the other side of the road

about a half mile north of here."

Paul was out the door in a second before he realized he hadn't thanked the clerk. Returning, he said, "Thanks so much for your help," as he pulled some bills out of his pocket.

"Hey, that's not necessary, man. You've already gone through enough, and I didn't have anything to help you."

Paul dropped one of his business cards on the counter as he turned to leave again.

"If you think of anything that will be helpful …"

"Sure, but I don't know what that would be."

Lola's wasn't difficult to find, and luckily there was a county sheriff's car parked in front.

As he entered, Paul noticed the deputy talking to the waitress. Paul waited until she walked away to serve another customer.

"Excuse me, sir," he started, "may I talk to you for a minute?"

Deputy Stewart was a husky, dark-haired man in his mid-forties. He had a drooping mustache and dark glasses were sticking out of his breast pocket. He turned to face Paul and replied, "Sure, take a seat. How can I help you?"

Paul tried to remain calm as he explained who he was. He wondered why the sheriff's office had only begun today looking for the two men who ran him off the road and killed his wife.

It was obvious that Deputy Stewart was weighing whether to take offense or try to calm Paul down. He chose the latter.

"Well, son, this isn't our case, and we weren't asked to help until this morning."

"I don't understand, not your case?" questioned Paul.

"Well, your accident didn't take place in our county. We

weren't the first responders."

"Accident? The accident didn't take place in your county? My wife was murdered. There was no accident." Paul wanted to hit someone or something.

"Calm down. I can understand how you feel."

"Really, how?" He had hoped the sheriff's office was well on its way to capturing the murderers.

"If something like this happened to me, I would be upset." Deputy Stewart seemed to be sincerely interested in helping. "Now, let's see if I can help you. I got a call from Valley County this morning asking if I could check out the people who sup … the people who ran you off the road."

"What did you discover?"

"You said your name is Paul? Paul, you know I couldn't tell you anything even if I found out something, but I guess it won't hurt to tell you I didn't find anything that will help us find these two guys. I guess the only thing I did was verify your statement that you'd seen two such men, and they were driving a truck that you described."

Paul felt a little calmer though still frustrated. "Was it Deputy Robinson who called you?"

"No, it was Deputy Garcia. I think he's the investigating deputy."

"Where is this Deputy Garcia?"

"He works out of the Valley County sheriff's office in Cascade."

Paul thanked Deputy Stewart, thought about ordering some breakfast and decided he wanted to get to Cascade immediately to talk to Deputy Garcia. Even though he was hungry, he didn't feel like eating.

As he left Lola's, he noticed a pay phone hanging on the wall and dialed his office hoping Jeff would be in early. Jeff answered the phone on the second ring.

"Hey Paul, where are you? I called your home and your cell and got no answer."

"I left early, and my cell was destroyed by the water. I'm on a pay phone in Horseshoe Bend on my way up to Cascade to talk to the county mounties."

"You should have called me, and I would have gone with you."

"Sorry, I didn't even think of that. I just felt I needed to be doing something."

"You're still in shock, Paul. You shouldn't be out there driving around by yourself. You know we always work better as a team. Just wait there, and I'll catch up with you. We'll go to Cascade together."

"No, you have plenty to do. I'll be fine."

"What about planning Janet's funeral? Shouldn't you be helping with that?"

"I probably should, but I left that to her parents. I told them to call you if they have any questions."

"Don't you think they need you right now?"

"Don't use the guilt trip on me, Jeff, not now. Of course, they probably need me, but this is something I need to do. Give them a call and ask if there is something they need. I'll check back with you."

Paul hung up without giving Jeff a chance to respond and walked back to his SUV. *Sometimes there are advantages in not having a cell phone.* The hardest part of the trip to Cascade was driving past the curve where the murder – he hated calling it an accident – had occurred. He stopped to look around.

Except for some skid marks, there was nothing about the curve to give notice of the dreadful event of the previous day. He looked into the water, and his motorcycle was gone. Then he studied the rapids and the rock where Janet had been caught. *Why didn't God help? What could I have done differently?* He couldn't think of anything. He paused for a second to watch the traffic passing, everyone but him functioning as if everything in the world was normal. *Nothing is normal. She was with me yesterday and now, she's gone. It hurts so bad I can't stand it. Nothing will ever be normal again. Dear God, why did you let us down? I promise to find the two who killed her no matter how long it takes or wherever it leads me.*

Still agitated, he walked into the Valley County sheriff's office.

"I'm Garcia," responded the friendly investigating officer. He was a medium height, trim, athletic type wearing his uniform too tight and had an inviting smile. He appeared to be about Paul's age. "How can I help you?"

Everyone keeps asking that, but I'm not getting any help at all. Paul introduced himself and asked if there had been any success in finding the men who drove him and Janet off the road.

Garcia explained that when the crash happened, Deputy Robinson had called it in, and a search had begun. He also explained that in Valley County there were numerous pickup trucks fitting the description. The only distinguishing characteristic was the mud.

No mud-covered vehicles had been located.

"What can you tell me about the men themselves?" asked Garcia.

Paul described them as best he could, again calling them Hispanics. Deputy Garcia glanced up with a frown on his face. "What does an Hispanic look like?" he questioned.

"I don't know what Hispanics look like, but the two I saw were speaking in Spanish."

Garcia smiled and asked about what Paul had heard,

asking many of the same questions that Deputy Robinson had asked the day before. Paul asked if he could check in every few days to check on the progress.

CHAPTER 4

Leaving the sheriff's office, Paul had driven just a couple of blocks when he noticed a self-service car wash on the east side of the highway. *Of course, that's the answer. They washed their truck. Once they ran us off the road, they needed to quickly change the appearance of the truck, and the best way to do that was to wash it.*

Paul tried to remember if he'd seen any other car washes between Cascade and Horseshoe Bend. *Where could they wash it, at a car wash or at their own place? If at their own place, they were from around here.*

Paul approached the car wash, got out and walked around. There were three washing stalls. Paul carefully looked for a sign that mud had been washed off of a vehicle. He found it in the middle stall. He picked up a clod of mud and put it in a plastic bag he found in his SUV.

There was no one near except for two young boys throwing a football around in the adjacent park. *What can I lose?*

"Hey, you guys are good. Do you practice often?"

One of them replied, "Yeah, we practice every day."

"Who is the QB?" asked Paul.

"I am!" they both replied at once, and then they both

grinned. They appeared to be between twelve and fourteen years of age.

"Were you here yesterday? By the way, my name is Paul Merrick."

"I'm Steve and he's Derek. Like he said, we're here every day."

"If I give you five bucks each, can I have some of your time?"

"Five bucks? Sure," replied Steve.

Derek wasn't so sure. "Wait, what do we have to do?"

"Just answer some questions," replied Paul, "about yesterday. Did very many vehicles come in to wash their cars?"

"Nah, not many," answered Derek. "It's getting cooler. Soon they will shut this place down for the winter."

"How many did you see come in here?"

"Maybe two or three."

"Can you remember anything about them?"

"Well, there was a man driving a really dirty white car. He was still dressed in a white shirt and tie," Steve said.

"And there was that guy who brings his car in every week, a Beamer," Derek added. "And there was that really muddy truck."

"A muddy truck?" questioned Paul.

"Yeah," replied Derek. "Two guys were in and out so fast. One minute they pulled in covered with mud and the next minute they are driving off without the mud."

Paul experienced hope for the first time since Janet's murder. He listened as the two boys described the two men and the dark blue Dodge Ram. He asked if they noticed the license plates.

"Of course," replied Steve. "We always want to see where the strangers are from. They were from California."

"You're positive?"

"Sure," they both cried in unison.

Paul peeled off a five-dollar bill for each of them. Then he pulled off another two bills and said, "If you'll take a few more minutes and repeat what you just told me to Deputy Garcia, here's another five bucks for each of you.

Again, they both cried, "Sure," in unison.

The three of them walked back to the sheriff's office. Again, Paul asked for Deputy Garcia.

"Paul, back so soon? How can I help you?"

"Do you know Derek and Steve?"

"Sure do."

"They have something to tell you." Paul handed Deputy Garcia a plastic bag filled with mud and walked out of the building, smiling.

***

Pilar knocked lightly and then opened the door to Sr. Sandoval's office. He looked up at his administrative assistant and smiled. "What can I do for you, My Dear?"

"I'm afraid I have bad news for you, Señor. As you've requested, I was checking the local news for Idaho and came upon this article."

She started to hand him the printout of the news article, but he brushed it away. "Just tell me what it says," Sr. Sandoval commanded, his face turning pale.

"Your son, Pablo, was in an accident, and his wife was killed."

"Oh, no!" replied Alonzo Sandoval. "What happened?"

"The two of them were riding together on a large motorcycle when they were run off the road into a river."

"Was it an accident then?"

"The newspaper article doesn't say but calls it a 'hit and run.' It says the truck that bumped them off the road didn't stop and the authorities haven't found it. Her death is being investigated."

Sr. Sandoval reached for the printout so he could study it carefully later. Reading in English was not difficult for him, but for Pilar it was even easier.

"Pilar, please make travel arrangements so I can attend the memorial services."

"Do you want to travel alone or do you want to take Security with you?"

"Have Security assign two men. I'd like it to be Miguel and Gaston, if they are available."

"I'm sure they will be available, but I'll check first."

"Thank you, Pilar."

Alonzo dialed his wife's number and waited for her to answer. "*Mi Amor*, I am so pleased that you are home."

"Remember, you told me to stay home, that it was too dangerous for me to be out without Security."

"I know I told you that, but I also know how frustrating it is for you to stay in when there are so many things you could be doing."

"I am not happy about it, but I know it is important to be safe."

"Maria Isabella, I have some sad news."

"What is it, Dear?" she asked.

"I just received word that Pablo and his wife were in a serious accident, and Janet was killed."

Maria Isabella gasped, "I'm so sorry, Alonzo. How difficult this must be for you. You must go there and be with him."

"I want to, but he really doesn't even know me. I don't know what his reaction will be if I show up."

"It doesn't matter what his reaction will be. You must be there to support him. Even if he doesn't want to see you, he must know that you will always be there for him."

Alonzo smiled to himself. "How lucky I am to have such a supportive and understanding wife. Please tell Jorge?"

"What will I tell him?"

"He is a very intelligent young man. Just tell him the truth."

Alonzo picked up the phone again and called Carlos on the intercom. "Carlos, can you come in for a moment?"

"Of course, Señor, I'll be right there."

In less than a minute, Carlos knocked lightly on the door before opening and entering. He could see the distress on the face of Sr. Sandoval. "Is something wrong?"

"Yes, Carlos, something is wrong. I need to travel to the United States." He briefed Carlos on Janet's death.

"That is understandable, Sr. Sandoval, but what about the board of directors' meeting of *Banco República* scheduled for the day after tomorrow?"

"As my executive vice president, you'll represent me there, Carlos. You know everything I know. You should be able to handle it fine."

"There will be questions about the security of the bank."

"I know there will be. Julio Batley is prepared to give a report to the board. He should be able to answer all of their questions. I trust you to do what needs to be done."

"I will do my best, Señor, and I'll keep you abreast of what is happening while you're gone."

"Will you call my attorney and remind him that I would like to peruse my latest will and testament before I leave. I would hate to have an accident on this trip before the correct codicils have been completed and notarized."

Wondering what changes had been made, Carlos responded, "I will see that it happens before you leave."

CHAPTER 5

Paul had been so busy trying to track down those who had murdered Janet that he hadn't given much thought to Janet's funeral. He didn't want to think about it either. Somehow, deep in the confines of his mind, without a funeral, Janet wasn't truly gone. He couldn't adjust to the thought of her not walking into the room or looking up and smiling when he came into her presence.

"Grandleys are sending a car," Grandmother Merrick mentioned as she entered the dining room.

Paul was seated at the dining room table immersed in the files he'd created. "I'm sorry," responded Paul, "what did you say?"

"I said that Grandley's Mortuary is sending a car to pick us up. They should be here in the next fifteen minutes. The viewing starts at 9:00 AM at the Stake Center."

"Isn't that awfully early?" asked Paul as if it were the first time he heard it, which it wasn't. "The service doesn't start until 11:00 AM."

"The bishop says he is expecting a huge crowd. We hope to finish the viewing at 10:30 AM for the family prayer."

"I don't know if I can do this, Grandma. Janet was always the one who was good at greeting people. I just feel empty. How can I help them?"

Grandmother Merrick smiled and gave Paul a hug. "That's not your job, Dear. They're not coming to feel good. They're coming because they love Janet, and they want to say good-bye."

"I don't understand. I surely don't want to say good-bye, not now, not ever."

"I know, dear. The Lord will give you strength. He will support you. He will help you through this."

"Grandma, I'm having a hard time with the Lord right now. It's difficult to not blame Him. Why couldn't He have helped me save her? I'm not sure I want His support or help."

"You've been through hell, dear; you mustn't talk like that. You deserve to feel some relief, but you have to allow it to happen."

"I don't want to allow it to happen."

They were interrupted by Grandfather Merrick shouting from the living room. "The car is here!"

Paul picked up his suit jacket from the back of his chair and threw it over his shoulder. Grandmother Merrick picked up her purse and put her arm through Paul's as they joined Grandfather Merrick in the living room.

"Before we leave, I think we ought to have a short family prayer here, just the three of us," suggested Grandfather Merrick. Without waiting for their response, he knelt down in front of the sofa. Paul and Grandmother Merrick glanced knowingly at each other as they joined him. Paul nodded at Grandfather Merrick, who bowed his head and began praying. Paul felt empty and resentful.

The driver, dressed in a plain, dark blue suit, greeted the three of them and opened the door to a late model, dark blue, luxury Cadillac. It wasn't a stretch limousine, but there was ample room for the three of them in the back seat. In a few minutes they arrived at the Westview Stake Center.

The driver opened the door and ushered them through the back door of the church. They turned right into the Relief Society room where Janet's casket was in position, surrounded by floral bouquets and arrangements. Except for mortuary workers, no one else was there.

Janet looked beautiful, but somehow, Paul felt it wasn't her. Something was missing. He had the feeling that she was in the room but not in the body. It seemed empty. He wanted her to get back in her body and crawl out of the casket.

Paul felt a hand close into his and looked up to see Christine Wilson, Janet's mother. Her tear-filled eyes were full of love for her departed daughter and for him.

Janet's brother, sister and their families soon entered and there was another round of hugs. Many had red eyes from much crying. Except for the first night, Paul hadn't felt much like crying; he felt like screaming. He was much too angry to cry.

Within minutes the Relief Society room filled to capacity with family and friends and there was one hug or handshake after another. Paul knew most of the people, but there were also many he didn't recognize. Some he'd seen only once before at their wedding reception years earlier. Many were young women from the stake who'd known Janet in her capacity as Stake Young Women's president. They also knew her from youth conferences or stake girls' camp. It was obvious they all loved her and missed her terribly.

It seemed but a short time when Arthur Grandley, from the mortuary, came into the Relief Society room and whispered into Ralph Wilson's ear. Ralph looked up at the crowd in the room and then followed Mr. Grandley out into the hall. In a short time, he returned and whispered to Paul. "There's a line of people out into the parking lot waiting to get into the viewing. We have to cut this line off someplace or we'll never get the funeral started."

Paul didn't care if it ever started but realized that what his father-in-law said was true. "What does he suggest?" asked Paul.

"He suggests they cut off the line somewhere, perhaps at the end of the sidewalk, and tell the people there isn't enough time for all of them to come through the viewing."

"I hate for anyone to be cut off who wants to see her, but I guess we have to do something."

"Well, there was a viewing last night and another this morning ..." Ralph Wilson stopped in the middle of his sentence. Paul nodded.

It was almost 10:50 AM when all but family were ushered out of the Relief Society room so those remaining could hold family prayer. Of course, Jeffrey and his family were considered by all to be family. Janet's brother, Brad, offered the family prayer. Paul and Christine said their last good-byes to Janet. Janet's mother adjusted her daughter's clothes and hair one last time, kissed the end of her finger and touched it to Janet's forehead and then helped Paul close the lid of the casket. The family was ushered into the chapel where the middle section had been reserved.

Paul was surprised to note that the Stake Center was filled to capacity with well-wishers, friends and family. The chapel was full and the cultural hall behind was filled with folding chairs. Even the stage at the other end of the cultural hall was filled with people.

From the looks of the crowd in the Stake Center, every young woman from the stake and her friends from the neighboring stakes were in attendance with their families. Not only had Janet served in her own stake, but she'd spoken and sung in most of the local stake youth conferences of the area. She'd been the idol of many of the young women and now she was gone. The tragic way that she was taken from them shocked the young women. They wanted and needed some answers.

Paul knew how he was feeling but was surprised at the outpouring of love and appreciation from others. Gradually, he realized he was not alone in his feeling of emptiness. He sensed many others were also sensing tremendous loss.

Jeff, the bishop and the stake president spoke. Later, Paul couldn't remember what any of them said. He knew they'd talked about the atonement of Christ and God's plan of happiness for his children, which gave him little comfort. He could remember the peaceful feeling when the Stake Laurels sang "Where Can I Turn for Peace." He wasn't prepared for the last song. It was a recording of Janet and Paul singing.

The two of them often sang together, and they'd been asked to sing in various funerals. Just a few months previously they'd been asked to sing "Going Home." At first, Janet was reluctant to sing it thinking that song not appropriate for a Mormon funeral, but after singing it together a few times in practice, they decided the family could choose any song they wanted. Without Janet or Paul's knowledge, the family had recorded that entire funeral service and had given them a copy. Janet's parents had decided that no song was more fitting and no singers more appropriate for Janet's funeral than Janet and Paul.

Paul was positive that this part of the funeral hadn't been discussed with him. He would never have approved it. As he heard the two of them sing together, he began to sob.

His body shook, and he couldn't stop. His grandmother held him and let him cry and cry.

Soon, Paul and the others were ushered from the church as Janet's brother and cousins hoisted her casket into the hearse, which was a station wagon version and same color as the Cadillac that carried Paul and his grandparents to the service.

Close family members were escorted to other Grandley cars. Paul and his grandparents were ushered to the same car that had brought them. As they settled back into the soft leather seats, Paul sighed in relief.

His grandmother, obviously concerned, took his hand in hers and said, "Paul, I think I saw your father in the congregation."

CHAPTER 6

"What did you say?" Paul thought he had heard his grandmother correctly but wasn't prepared for what she had said.

"I'm almost positive I saw your father in the congregation," Grandmother Merrick reiterated. "It's been many years since I've seen him. He is obviously much older, but I'm confident it was him."

When was the last time I saw him? Alonzo Sandoval had shown up at Paul's graduation from Harvard's MBA program. Paul had never been close to his father. He'd been raised by a single mother and then, after her death, by his maternal grandparents.

Kathleen Marie Merrick met Alonzo Pablo Sandoval Muñoz at a reception in the Chilean Embassy in Washington, D. C. when she was serving as an intern for Senator Peterson of Idaho. Alonzo Sandoval had aggressively pursued her and even joined the Mormon Church in Chile so she would marry him. They'd been married by her local bishop in Idaho and then, to the chagrin of Edward and Mary Ann Merrick, the young couple made their home in Santiago, Chile.

Alonzo Sandoval was a wealthy and powerful young

man in Chile. There were many who were surprised when he brought home a North American wife. Kathleen, skilled at charming people, was comfortable in powerful circles in Washington, D. C. To her, Chile was similar, just a different language.

She was college educated in Spanish and after the customary six months of adjusting her ear to the sounds of Chilean Spanish, she was able to entertain in a manner befitting the spouse of a young Chilean aristocrat.

The pampered lives of Kathleen and Alonzo Sandoval were delightful in Chile. She was able to return to the States two times every year to visit her family and do the shopping necessary for things not available in South America. Those things not available became even more prevalent in the last year or so.

After three years of marriage, Kathleen became pregnant and began to worry about the birth of her child. She knew that medical care in Chile was excellent, but she wanted her mother near for the event. She was relieved when Alonzo suggested that when she went home to visit her family, that she stay in the States until after the birth of their firstborn. She never returned to Chile.

After Paul was born, every time she thought it was time to return home, Alonzo suggested she wait a little longer. He made trips to the States to see her every few months but still discouraged her returning to Chile. When she finally stated she was coming back to Chile, no matter what, Alonzo confessed that he had a mistress and she'd be uncomfortable in Chile. She was heartbroken and never considered returning to Chile again.

Paul and his mother never suffered for lack of money. His father bought a home for Kathleen and Paul and provided them an ample allowance each month. Within a short time, she was dead. Paul was only five.

Alonzo made no attempt to have his son come to live with him in Chile. Paul was raised by his maternal grandparents, Edward and Mary Ann Merrick. The monthly allowance continued to arrive from Chile, most of which wasn't needed. What wasn't used was invested for Paul's education and mission, but that also was not necessary because Paul always found his expenses were paid, and he still received an ample allowance. His savings account grew and grew.

As Paul became older and learned more about his father, he began to blame him for his mother's unhappiness and her untimely death.

At Paul's MBA graduation, his father had suggested Paul might want to come to work for him in Chile. Paul hadn't been interested. Alonzo handed his son an envelope with an indecent amount of cash as a graduation present.

***

Alonzo Pablo Sandoval Muñoz was a distinguished, well-dressed aristocrat from old money. His family dated back to the time of Pedro de Valdivia when an ancestor had received a land grant. Of slender build with a height of five foot ten inches, he was tall for a Chilean. His family had been involved in banking and mining back ten generations. It was Alonzo who decided that engineering fit in well with their mining operations, and it was Alonzo who began buying into additional businesses when he felt they too would be complimentary to the ongoing operations.

For generations, the Sandoval family had been careful to marry into and with other powerful families of Chile. There were many political and financial ties in the family history. It had long been assumed that Alonzo would marry Maria

Tereza Bustos Carrera, who also came from an old-money family with similar political ties. Even he expected to marry Maria Bustos until he met Kathleen Marie Merrick. The Bustos family was shocked and humiliated and from that time on, did everything they could to destroy the promising political career that Alonzo faced.

Alonzo was expected to excel in both business and politics. His father, Pablo Alfonzo Sandoval Carasco, was a personal friend, and some said distant cousin, of Eduardo Frei Montalva, president of Chile from 1964 to 1970. Alonzo was one of the young men expected to go far in politics because of his connection with Frei.

***

Many who attended the funeral didn't follow the entourage to the cemetery. Even so, there was still a large crowd gathered for the dedication of the grave, which was offered by Janet's uncle.

Trying not to be obvious, Paul scanned the crowd. He found his father standing outside the circle of friends and family with two men dressed in dark suits. Alonzo Sandoval waited to approach Paul until most of the family and friends had wandered off.

"I am so sorry about your loss, Pablo." His father was the only person who called him Pablo.

"Thank you. How did you know?"

Alonzo ignored the question and suggested they walk. The two men, followed by Alonzo's associates, began a walk around the cemetery. It was a long time before either of them spoke.

"What will you do?" questioned Alonzo.

"I really haven't thought about that." Paul knew his father wanted to visit, but he really was uncomfortable as they'd never had a father-son conversation. There had been many times growing up he would have loved to have been able to ask "Why?", but this wasn't the time, and frankly, Paul doubted there would ever be.

As they walked and made small talk, they were followed at a distance by the two body guards. Finally, Alonzo stopped, looked Paul directly in the eyes and asked, "Pablo, would you consider coming to Chile for a time?"

Paul was shocked at the question. He'd not considered going to Chile and certainly not now when he was so eager to find Janet's killers. He didn't answer; he just looked at his father in awe.

Alonzo continued, "This hasn't been easy for you. Perhaps a time away from your usual surroundings, away from your usual associates, family and friends would be helpful to you."

Paul studied his father. The suggestion seemed to be sincere and well meant. He considered carefully his answer.

"Right now, the only thing I want to do is find my wife's killers."

"Killers," questioned Alonzo. "I thought it was an accident."

"No, it wasn't an accident. We were forced off the road. I don't know if they were personally trying to kill us or just wanted the thrill of hurting someone."

Alonzo turned pale. He was shocked. He wondered if his own personal enemies had somehow expanded their objectives to his family in the United States.

After walking for a few more minutes without talking, Alonzo returned to his request that Paul come to Chile for a time. "When you are ready, Pablo, I'd like you to come to Chile and be with me. I want us to get to know each other. I want you to know your Chilean family. This may not be the time, but when you feel it is, please come down."

"I'm not ready for that now. Perhaps I'll never be ready. I appreciate the offer and perhaps we can reconsider down the road."

"There is another thing, Pablo. I know you have been very successful in turning around businesses that find themselves in difficulty. Our family business is struggling and could use your help."

Paul frowned and was disturbed at what he was hearing. He had no idea that his father even knew what he did for a living. He knew nothing of his father's business and certainly, his wife's funeral was no place to receive a job offer.

"This is probably not the time nor the place," Paul began.

"No, it isn't. I apologize," replied Alonzo.

Paul looked up and realized that they had walked a great distance from Janet's gravesite. He turned to start back in that direction. Alonzo gave a look to his associate, "We can continue our talk. Gaston can return for the car." Gaston immediately commenced in the direction of the car while Miguel remained nearby.

Other than the fact he knew his father to be wealthy and powerful in Chile, Paul knew very little about his father. "I don't even know what your business is."

"Well, we are involved in an abundance of things." Alonzo shared with Paul a brief synopsis of the family business.

"Tell me about your business," Alonzo inquired.

Paul smiled and talked about what all had happened in his business life since he had last seen his father. Alonzo smiled and exposed a look of fatherly pride and appreciation. "How do you find these businesses?"

Suddenly, Paul caught a flash of light out of the corner

of his eye, followed by an ear-splitting explosion. Alonzo immediately dropped to the ground, pulling Paul down with him. From his hands and knees, Paul looked up to see Alonzo's car engulfed in flames. As they turned to look at each other, Paul and Alonzo both knew the explosion was meant for them.

CHAPTER 7

In the months following Janet's funeral, Paul still hadn't spent any meaningful time in his office. He wasn't concerned because Jeff Harkin was a skillful partner who could easily run the company in Paul's absence.

For the first few weeks, Paul had either driven to Cascade to visit personally with Deputy Garcia or he'd called him on the phone. Garcia tried to be friendly at first, but after a few weeks, it became less easy for him to welcome Paul's interference. Investigating Janet Merrick's death was his responsibility. He wasn't even convinced that a crime, other than fleeing the scene of an accident, had been committed.

Now that a full year had passed, there was little likelihood that Janet's killers would be caught and held accountable. Paul wondered what, if anything, he personally could contribute to the tracking down of the two culprits. In his search for possibilities he thought of the only clue he had, the California license plate that Derek and Steve had seen. After an entire year, Paul wondered if there was a way to match such a license plate.

He quickly realized he didn't have the personal capacity to discover that information. Perhaps a detective agency could. Searching online, he discovered the Rodriguez Investigative Services of Los Angeles. Paul dialed the 800 number.

After Paul gave her a brief description of his needs, the receptionist connected Paul to one of the investigators. "This is Roland Williams. How can I help you?"

Mr. Williams listened carefully as Paul briefed him on his wife's murder and volunteered they had very little to go on. He wondered why Paul was calling a California detective agency instead of one in Idaho.

"First, the pickup truck I'm looking for was licensed in California. Second, I've heard that yours is the best international detective agency in the Western United States. There's a possibility this investigation could lead us to South America." Paul continued by telling about the bombing of his Father's car.

The conversation continued for more than an hour, with Paul sharing as much information as he could. Mr. Williams explained that such a search could become very expensive. After a discussion of their rates, Paul reassured him that cost wasn't an issue.

"I'll put together a contract and fax it to you this afternoon," explained Roland Williams.

"After getting my attorney's approval, I'll wire you the retainer's fee," replied Paul.

Paul sat back in his chair and seriously considered the contract he was about to sign. He sensed someone standing in the doorway of his office. He looked up to see his partner, Jeff, leaning against the doorpost.

"Hey, Jeff," Paul quipped with a forced smile.

"Hey, Paul, I'm surprised to see you here."

Paul's attempt at humor was unsuccessful. "What, surprised to see me in my own office?"

"Well, this office isn't occupied much lately."

"Yeah, I know, and I apologize. Even when it is occupied I can't keep my mind on the work."

"I know, Paul; I understand. You probably wouldn't see me coming near this place if the situations were reversed. Anything happening on the investigation?"

"Everything of significance was discovered in the first two weeks. I suspect they have filed Janet's case away. The FBI is still working on the car bombing, but they aren't telling me anything."

Jeff quipped, "You know what they say, if you really want something done, do it yourself."

"That is right. Come on in and sit down. You don't need to hold up the wall."

"Thanks," Jeff said as he moved toward the leather couch. "I really was surprised to see you here and just stuck my head in."

"I apologize for making you do all the work this past year."

Jeff responded, "I'm not concerned about Segue Dynamics. The business is doing fine. Paul, it was your money that started Segue. The strength of the company came from your personal work. You didn't need me, but you brought me on as a partner. You have made me a wealthy man. Michelle and I appreciate what you have done for us."

"I couldn't think of anyone with whom I'd rather work. You were always a big help to me, and you've done a great job of keeping Segue profitable during my absence."

"Paul, you could retire completely, if you wanted to. We have a great staff. Some ask for you personally, but, as you said, your mind is elsewhere, and I am worried about you."

"Don't worry about me. I'm fine."

Jeff knew he was skating on thin ice. "Really? When was

the last time you went to church?"

Paul looked at his friend quizzically before answering, "Janet's funeral."

"Michelle and I can't get you to come over for dinner. You and I haven't even gone to lunch together. I suspect you haven't been to the gym. I suspect you aren't even praying anymore."

His ire building, Paul felt the strong urge to flee. "Jeff, you know you are the only person in the world I would allow to speak to me this way."

"I know. That's why I'm the one who has to do it."

"Why does anyone have to do it? Just leave me alone."

"I just can't see Paul Merrick leaving me alone if the roles were reversed. When Janet died, you died too."

"Janet didn't die, Jeff, she was killed."

"When those two thugs killed Janet, they killed Paul Merrick too. Do you want them to win? Paul, it's been over a year. It is time you rejoined the living."

Paul leaned forward to get up from his chair. He gave Jeff a look that bordered between anger and hurt. Then he slumped back down and looked at the floor. "I don't want to live."

Jeff paused for almost a full minute before asking, "What's that got to do with it? If God wanted you dead, you would have been killed in the Payette River with Janet. He had His opportunity."

"Jeff, I don't much care what God wants."

"Paul, will you listen to yourself. You used to be the most diligent, faithful person I knew. There was nothing you wouldn't do to help someone find their place in God's plan of happiness. Now you're wallowing in self-pity."

Again, for Paul, the urge to jump and run was almost overpowering, but he didn't. Jeff had been his best friend since age twelve. He knew Jeff wouldn't be telling him these things if they weren't absolutely necessary. "I feel God let me down, Jeff. I'm not very pleased with His plan of happiness for Janet and me."

"Have you ever thought that God's plan for you and Janet might be better than your own plan?"

"No, there is no plan for Janet and me. The two who shoved us off the road thwarted God's plan for us."

"So, this is all about those two?"

"I guess it is."

"Paul, you know what you always ask people when they have an important decision to make: 'So, what are your choices?'"

Paul allowed just a hint of a grin to shine through his eyes. "OK, you're right. What are my choices?"

"Are you asking me?"

"No, I'm asking me." He paused for a time to consider his options. Then he said, "I can either drop the obsession I have to find the culprits who killed Janet and let the police succeed or fail, or I can take it upon myself and make sure they are caught."

"So, which is it."

"I don't think I can do the former. I just got off the phone with an investigative service in California. They're going to try to trace the truck that ran us off the road."

"That sounds like a great idea. Paul, I know all of this is driving you crazy. I'm sure my thousands of questions aren't helping either. I'm concerned about you."

"I know you are and as uncomfortable as it is, I really appreciate it. Yeah, it is driving me crazy. I should be sad about Janet's death, but, even now after all this time, all I feel is anger. I don't know what I'd do if I was ever in the same room with those two guys."

"It seems logical to me that Janet's murder and the car bombing are connected."

"There was something that happened in that short time I was with my father at the cemetery that suggests you are right."

"What was that?"

"When I told him that Janet's death wasn't an accident, his face turned ashen. He didn't say anything, but there was definitely a sign of awareness."

"Maybe you need to go talk to him about it."

"What do you mean, go talk to him? It's not like he is in Portland or Salt Lake City. I can't take a quick trip to visit with him."

"Why can't you? Paul, until you get this resolved in your head, you're not going to be able to do anything else. It's been over a year and you can't lay this aside. A little trip to Chile would be nothing in comparison to what you have gone through this year."

"My father did invite me to go down there."

"He did?"

"Yeah, when we were walking at the cemetery. He said he wants to get to know me, and he said he would like my help with his businesses."

"What kind of help?"

"He didn't say, but he seemed to know all about Segue Dynamics. He seemed to think that I could help him some way."

"He didn't tell you what kind of help?"

"We didn't get that far. About that time, his car blew up."

"Paul, I think you should check into that. You have the time and we're doing fine here."

"I think you are right. I'll consider going to Chile."

"Do that."

"If I do, no matter what, I will not stop until those two are behind bars."

"With your tenacity, they don't have a chance." Jeff couldn't hide the grin as he slipped from Paul's office.

CHAPTER 8

Roberto Contreras is almost a head taller than his brother, Esteban. Although he is only forty-eight years of age, he appears older because he is prematurely graying on a very sparse head of unruly hair. He is fairly lean and very strong. He can appear very intimidating when he wants and he has constantly intimidated his younger brother. He is the smarter of the two and obviously the boss, always has been, from the time Esteban was born when Roberto was five.

Esteban is softer, pudgier and very impulsive. He doesn't think things out very well and often doesn't follow the plan his brother gives him. He's constantly trying to please his brother but knows that's impossible. He knows he'll always screw up anything they have planned.

They live with their mother in a shack of a home in a dangerous part of town. It's not uncommon to walk down the small street in front of their home and see a neighbor selling drugs on the street corner. Roberto intimidates them and they leave the Contreras brothers alone. He also intimidates his mother just as he does Esteban.

He never discussed with her his plan to get the mine that Sr. Sandoval stole from their father. She'd never mentioned that they once owned a mine. She never talks about their father. Whenever his name comes up, great fear shows in her eyes.

Both men can remember back in 1973 when they came home to find her sobbing, "They have killed him, they've killed him."

When their benefactor informed Roberto that his father had been the owner of a copper mine and on the verge of riches, he got angry, and when he discovered that the reason his father was killed was so Alonzo Sandoval could secure that mine, he became livid. Again, as he had as a young boy, he vowed that someday he would get revenge.

Their benefactor, Pedro Velasquez, explained that he could prove that Rodrigo Julio Contreras Mora had been the owner before the coup, and Sandoval S.A. became the owner after the death of Rodrigo Contreras.

"How can we get the mine back?" Esteban had asked.

"We just have to convince Sr. Sandoval that it's in his best interest to return your property to you."

Esteban asked, "How do we do that?"

"We let him know that it would be cheaper for him in the long run to return the mine to you than it would be to hang onto it."

"I can see a number of accidents happening at that mine," suggested Roberto.

"That could happen and those accidents could also happen to other companies owned by Sr. Sandoval. We already know that Sr. Sandoval owns *Banco República*."

"Roberto began to smile, realizing how Sr. Sandoval himself could bankroll their quest."

***

"I'm glad you came," Christine Wilson greeted her son-in-law. "It's been so long. I was afraid that if we didn't get you back soon, you'd never want to come again."

Christine Wilson was usually a diminutive ball of energy. For the first few months after the death of her daughter, there'd been little energy for anything. For months, she worked hard to escape the dark den of depression and achieved some success. Hoping to also help Paul escape, she suggested they invite him for dinner and begin their lives without their daughter.

Ralph was strong and stoic. He was a full foot taller than his wife and much huskier. He was built like a wrestler but was actually a dentist. His immediate reaction to his daughter's death was anger. He wasn't even sure to whom he should direct that fury. Sometimes he was bitter with Paul for not taking care of his daughter as he had promised. Sometimes he was annoyed with himself for giving them permission to marry. Sometimes he was resentful towards God for taking away the light of his life, and he was always furious with the scum bags who had run her into the river to her death. He knew what he would like to do to those men if he came across them.

Christine opened the door before Paul had time to ring the bell. "Hi, Mom, you can't know how hard it was to come. Even though I told you on the phone I would, I almost didn't. On the way over here, I thought of a million reasons that this is a bad idea."

"Thank you for coming, Dear. It's bad enough to lose Janet. We were afraid we'd lost you too."

"You won't lose me, but even after this much time, it still feels terrible coming here without her." Paul couldn't help himself. Christine put her arms around him and cried with him as the two of them stood holding each other up. Ralph entered the room and started to extend his hand, thought better of it, so he also gave Paul a loving hug.

"We are so glad you are here," spoke Ralph Wilson. "I

can imagine how hard it is for you. You are a brave and strong man."

Paul didn't feel very brave or strong, but he was grateful for the vote of confidence.

After dinner they retired to the living room to visit. Ralph couldn't hold back any longer. "What have you heard about the search for Janet's killers?"

Paul was almost relieved to get that topic out in the open. He told them about his visits with Deputy Garcia up in Cascade as well as his visits with Detective Nelson and Agent Escobar in Boise. He explained that they were no closer to finding the killers than they were at the end of the first week. Finally, Paul explained about his own search and what Rodriguez Investigative Services had discovered.

The dark blue Dodge Ram pickup truck that had been used to force him and Janet off the road into the Payette River had been rented to two men from Chile. Roland Williams was able to get copies of their driver's licenses so he could see their photos.

Paul quickly recognized them as the two he had seen in the store in Horseshoe Bend. The fake licenses didn't discourage Paul as that was expected.

"So, like we suspected, Janet's death and the car bombing at the cemetery are probably the same men?" questioned Mr. Wilson.

"I think they are," replied Paul. "I think they were both done by men who have some axe to grind against my father in Chile."

"What are the police going to do about it?" asked Mrs. Wilson.

"There is an FBI agent in Chile who is carrying on the investigation down there."

"Are the police close to finding them?"

"Not that I can tell. I worry that nothing more will happen unless I do it. Only when I'm working on her case do I feel I'm trying to make up for letting Janet down."

"You didn't let her down, Paul," said Christine Wilson. "You had no way of knowing."

"No, I didn't, but I keep thinking that I should have. I also feel I need to continue the search to find them."

"How?" asked Ralph Wilson.

"Since the fake driver's licenses place the murderers in Chile, I've decided to go there."

"Oh my," exclaimed Mrs. Wilson. "When?"

"Immediately."

***

Paul awoke to the sun peeking over the tips of the Andes and under the dark clouds above. The view was spectacular as he cast his eye off to his left. The wing behind him was pointing toward the snow-capped peaks. The bed of soft clouds beneath formed a pillow on which the plane seemed to be resting.

He was surprised to realize that he'd slept through most of the flight, having not slept well since Janet's death. His first-class seat on his flight was very comfortable and made rest easier.

Once the decision had been made to fly to Chile, events transpired very quickly. He'd made a telephone call to his father, who was jubilant. Alonzo Sandoval tried to sound calm and contained, but Paul could sense his father's excitement over the phone.

His father informed him that Pilar Flores, his administrative assistant, would arrange everything. She'd email his itinerary and pick him up at the airport. Paul responded that he could obtain his own ticket, but Alonzo was unrelenting. Paul knew they were talking about $4,000-

plus for air fare. Alonzo treated it as if he were paying for a $40 lunch.

In less than an hour, Pilar sent him his itinerary with the confirmation number. All he had to do was show up at the airport in Boise two days later and board the plane. Paul worried that he might be going off half-cocked until he checked with Deputy Garcia and Detective Nelson. He realized that after all this time, if he wanted Janet's case solved, he'd have to do it himself.

Garcia had seemed irritated when Paul faxed him a copy of the rental car agreement and the two driver's licenses wanting to know how Paul obtained them, hinting that he may have done something illegal.

Detective Nelson and Agent Escobar showed more gratitude, as if this new information could prove helpful. They might have wondered how Paul obtained the information but didn't seem concerned, not even surprised the two were Chileans. When Paul told them he was flying to Chile to continue the search, Agent Maria Escobar supplied him the address of the FBI office in Santiago and the name of the agent assigned to the case, Victor Riquelme. Even though Paul asked, she didn't reveal much except that perhaps the bombers were trying to get to Paul's father. Why they were making the attempt in Idaho rather than in Chile didn't make any sense unless Paul was also a target.

Paul's flight took him first to Salt Lake City and then to Atlanta. From Atlanta, he flew nonstop to Santiago, Chile arriving at 7:35 AM. Paul was quickly ushered to the front of the customs line. When he removed his wallet to pay the entrance fees, he was told they had all been paid. When he passed through customs, he found Pilar Flores waiting for him.

Pilar was about thirty with straight, long, brunette hair

and sparkling, blue eyes. Even though she was only five feet four inches tall, she walked with an air of authority. No one challenged her command. She dressed in bright colored clothes which reminded him of a gypsy. Her height would seem undersized in the United States, but Paul noticed she was taller than many of the Chilean women. She quickly commanded her driver, who had gathered Paul's bags, to follow them to an SUV which was parked near the entrance of the airport. While the driver was putting Paul's bags in the back, Paul attempted to open the car door for Pilar, but she quickly opened it for him. They both sat in the back seat, leaving the driver alone in front.

Though it seemed longer, the drive took only about a half hour to forty-five minutes from the airport to his father's office. Pilar talked the entire time they were traveling acclimating Paul to Santiago, instructing him where they were and pointing out landmarks. She pointed to a statue of the Virgin Mary on a hill they were passing. For a number of minutes, they were in a tunnel and she explained that they were driving underneath or near the river. She explained that they wouldn't be going through the downtown district of Santiago as Sr. Sandoval's office was on the outskirts of Providencia, heading toward the *barrio Las Condes*.

They arrived at a very modern, glass-covered building of twenty-plus floors. The driver drove them into the underground parking facility then quickly came around and opened their doors for them. Pilar suggested they leave Paul's bags in the car as she would be taking him to his hotel a little later. First, they needed to present themselves to Sr. Sandoval.

CHAPTER 9

Paul had only spoken with his father a few times in his life and really knew nothing about him. He was anxious as they approached the office, which was on the twenty-sixth floor. It presented a feeling of being open, welcoming and lush. With the wave of her hand, Pilar ushered him past the receptionist and past Sr. Sandoval's personal secretary. She knocked lightly on the door. She didn't wait for an answer before opening it and signaling for Paul to enter.

Paul's father, with a huge smile on his face, was already rushing around the edge of his immense walnut desk. He swept past the outstretched hand and gave Paul a massive Chilean hug (*abrazo*). He was obviously pleased to have his son in his office in Chile. Pilar slipped quietly away to leave the father and son to themselves.

"How was your trip?" his father asked him as he studied him up and down. He'd last seen his son at Janet's funeral, but in a way, he seemed to be looking at his son for the very first time.

"It was really uneventful," replied Paul. "The flight was comfortable, and the view this morning was spectacular. Pilar moved so quickly to arrange my flight that I'm here days before I expected."

Paul's father frowned slightly. "I hope we gave you enough time to prepare."

"Oh, you gave me plenty of time. Once the decision was made, I was antsy to get down here quickly."

"What made you change your mind about coming?" questioned the father.

"There were a number of reasons. First, you invited me, and second, I've discovered that the two men who ran Janet and me off the road were from Chile. One of the reasons I'm down here is to find them and make sure they face justice."

For the second time, Paul watched his father's face turn ashen. Then crestfallen he suggested, "So, it is true, my enemies were the perpetrators of the death of your dear wife."

"I don't know whether they are your enemies, but they are certainly mine. I might ask, why do you have enemies?"

"My enemies go back a long time. We will have plenty of time to talk about them, but now that I know the truth, I'm worried about you. We must take proper precautions.

Perhaps the place I'd planned for you to stay is not the safest."

"Why do you say that?"

"Well, everyone knows I own the hotel. All my out of town guests stay there. If there are people here eager to do you harm, that may be the first place they'll look. Perhaps it would be better if you stayed with me and my family in our compound, which is well guarded."

Paul was stunned by this statement. He'd frankly never considered his father might have a family. His mother passed away thirty-three years ago, when he was only five, so it was only logical that his father would have remarried. He tried not to frown as he thought that perhaps his father had married the mistress that had caused his mother so much shame and pain. "No, I don't think that would do," replied Paul. "Let's think of another alternative."

Alonzo didn't argue and looked off to the side as if in deep thought. "I own an apartment building that was built in the forties. It's in Providencia, where many of the old mansions have been raised to make way for high-rise apartments. I've always loved that old building and haven't had the heart to tear it down. I doubt that anyone even knows I own it. It is not modern and may not be up to your standards, but perhaps you'd not be noticed there."

"You might remember I served my mission in Peru. The place you describe sounds very much like the apartments in which I stayed. I'd like to have a look before we make a decision."

"I'll have Pilar check on it for you. In the meantime, let's check you into the hotel for tonight. I'll have Security watch over you until we can get you better situated. Let's give you a chance to rest up. I do want you to come to the house for dinner tonight so you can meet Maria Isabella and your little brother, Jorge."

This time, Paul couldn't hide the wonder in his face. He had no idea that he even had a brother.

"I know," apologized Alonzo, "I never told you about my family here. Your mother has been gone a long time. I married about eighteen years ago, and Jorge is fifteen.

Even though you know nothing of him, he knows and has always known about you.

He's more excited to meet you than I was to have you come to Chile. We'll have dinner about ten. Pilar will pick you up."

Paul nodded realizing that he needed to meet his brother sometime. This was as good as any other. *It might be fun to get to know a brother,* thought Paul.

Alonzo picked up his phone and asked for someone to come in. A moment later, Pilar returned with a young man who appeared to be about five years younger than Paul.

"Paul, these are the two people I rely on most to help me coordinate my business affairs. You have already met Pilar. She is my administrative assistant, and she takes care of the details in my business life and many in my personal life. Carlos is my executive vice president. He has full authority to represent me in all the Sandoval businesses. He will acquaint you with our different companies and what all we do. These two make my business life pleasing. They also know where all the ghosts are hidden and what we need to watch out for."

Then he turned to Carlos and Pilar. "This is my son, Pablo. He's come down to be part of my family, both my personal family and my business family. I want you to treat him even better than you'd treat me. He will help me with our business problems as he tracks down the men who killed his wife. He thinks they may be in Chile, and I think they may be connected to the troubles we're having here. Please provide him everything he needs, no questions asked."

Paul noticed a little cringe in Carlos' face when his father mentioned that Paul would be helping with the business. The recoil was immediately replaced with an enthusiastic smile. Pilar didn't react at all. Paul supposed she wasn't hearing for the first time the reasons for Paul's visit.

"We're so pleased you're here," spouted Carlos. "Your father talks about you all the time."

That startled Paul. He spent very little time thinking of his father and was surprised to learn his Father spoke of him.

***

The same driver who drove them from the airport also drove them to the hotel. While they were traveling, Pilar handed Paul a cell phone. "This is yours. I've keyed in Sr. Sandoval's, Carlos' and my numbers. Feel free to call any of us at any time.

Paul showed her the address for the FBI office. "I'd like to stop by there tomorrow or soon to talk to the agent who is trying to track down my wife's killers."

"Sr. Sandoval, I'm so sorry about your wife. We all are. I promise to give you all the help you could want," replied Pilar. "Finding the FBI office will be easy. It is only fifteen minutes from here."

Paul was startled to hear himself addressed as Sr. Sandoval. Technically, in Chile, his name was Pablo Sandoval Merrick. So, his surname in Chile would be Sandoval. However, in the United States, it would be Merrick. He'd always used his mother's maiden name, Merrick, as his surname, and he'd have to get used to Sandoval here.

Pilar frowned when he suggested, "Why don't you call me Paul?" So, he quickly changed that to "Pablo." Then he asked, "You know where the FBI office is?"

"No, I just know that address and it isn't far away."

"Where can I rent a car so I can get around?"

"You don't need to rent a car, Pablo. This is your car. This car and the driver are assigned to you and are always at your disposal. He will drive you anyplace you want to go."

"What if I want to go someplace by myself?" Paul asked.

"That may not be wise. The same men who tried to kill your father may try to kill you."

"You mean the ones who blew up his car in Idaho?"

"No, I mean the ones who ambushed his car here in Chile and killed one of his bodyguards."

CHAPTER 10

As Paul showered, shaved and dressed for dinner, he thought about the last comment Pilar had made. Someone had ambushed his father's car and tried to kill him. That was the second attempt on his father's life of which Paul was aware. He wondered if there were others. Then there was the attempt on his life and the murder of Janet. Paul wondered what it all meant. He was convinced that one way or another all these events were connected but how, and what was more important, why? He knew he was in the right place. Now if he could manage not to get killed himself. Paul really didn't care. Living without Janet was unspeakably agonizing. He'd either make sure her killers were brought to justice or he'd die trying.

The phone in his hotel suite reverberated, jolting him out of his weighty thoughts. It was Pilar in the lobby informing him she'd arrived to ride with him to his father's home for dinner. He found her dressed in a stunning, blue, silk evening dress instead of the bright colored office attire from earlier in the day. Paul was thankful he'd changed into a blue blazer and grey slacks as he suspected, based on her apparel, dinner would be more formal than those to which he was accustomed.

"Is it common to eat dinner at 10:00 PM here in Chile?" asked Paul as they traveled.

"Yes," she answered, "we generally dine quite late. I know that isn't your custom, but that's the way we do it here. When a family has small children, the children eat much earlier, and they are usually in bed before the adults have their meal."

Starting to worry about his appearance, Paul asked, "Should I have dressed more formally?"

"No, you are dressed exactly the way you should be."

He wondered if she would have said the same thing even if he'd been dressed in jeans and a T-shirt and surmised she probably would have. They continued to discuss some of the customs of Chile. In most cases, he wasn't surprised. He tried to steer her into a discussion regarding the attack on his father she had mentioned, but she avoided that subject.

In a little less than an hour, the driver was announcing himself at a locked gate. Immediately and automatically, the gate began to swing open. There appeared to be two uniformed men stationed at the gatehouse. During the drive from the gatehouse to the large home of Alonzo Sandoval, a distance of approximately a quarter of a mile, Paul spied an additional six armed, uniformed security officers. He imagined there were many more around the compound that he didn't see. He wondered if this was normal, if it was because of his presence or because of the attack that Pilar had mentioned earlier.

The driver stopped immediately in front of the large, four-story, stone house. They faced a stone staircase that began as a semicircle and culminated, after twelve or thirteen steps, on a large veranda, which encircled the house. Another guard waited at the massive double entrance doors.

The Sandoval estate had been in the Sandoval family for more than two hundred years. This particular house, called *El Castillo Sandoval* by the locals outside the compound walls, had its origin over a hundred fifty years previously. It hadn't always been this large but had been added to by each succeeding generation until it reached its present size and magnificence under the guidance of Alonzo Sandoval's father in 1932. The depression, which had curtailed most businesses in the thirties, wasn't enough to hinder construction on the Sandoval estate. When many couldn't find jobs, the neighbors of *Castillo Sandoval* always found work. Since the late thirties, the only changes that had taken place were due to modernization and making the house earthquake proof.

Paul's driver stopped at the bottom of the steps and quickly came around to help Paul and Pilar out of the car. Paul was nervous as he climbed the steps to the entrance of the elegant home. From what Paul could see from the front of the house, it had to be over 10,000 square feet.

They were ushered into a living room where Alonzo and his wife were waiting. Paul noticed that their son, Jorge, wasn't waiting with them.

"Pablo, this is my wife, Maria Isabella."

She was a beautiful, elegantly dressed, slim gentlewoman with jet black, shoulder length, wavy hair. She was slightly taller than her husband in her three-inch heels. She seemed reserved as she moved gracefully to kiss Paul on each cheek. In English she said, "Pablo, welcome to your home in Chile. Your father has told us so much about you." She turned and whispered to a woman of about fifty, dressed in what appeared to be a domestic uniform, who was standing off to the side, seemingly awaiting instructions.

Within a short time, a gangly teenager, who Paul surmised to be Jorge, quietly entered the room. He looked at Paul waiting to be introduced. Alonzo, smiling broadly, introduced the two brothers.

Jorge was slightly taller than his mother and, therefore, taller than his father. He was thin with thick, dark, curly, unruly hair. He gave a shy smile, stuck out his hand and said in English, "I'm pleased to meet you, Pablo."

Throughout the dinner, Alonzo tried to maintain a continuous conversation. Maria Isabella complied and so did Paul, but Jorge only responded when he was asked a direct question or if prodded by one of his parents.

Paul had a million questions but decided this was not a good time. He hadn't come to Chile to be included in the family. He came to find the fiends of hell who had killed his precious Janet. He assumed that when that was accomplished, he'd board the next plane and return to his life in the United States and the Sandoval family would return to their normal lives in Chile.

As he looked around the table, he also wondered about the presence of Pilar. She'd been warmly greeted by Maria Isabella, and it was obvious that Jorge knew her also. She seemed comfortable to be eating with the family, and yet, she was the only non-family member in attendance. *Was she often invited to dine with the family or was she there as dinner partner for Paul?* Paul hoped that wasn't the case because he was certainly not ready for female dinner partners even after a year, not now or not ever.

Even though Paul had been greeted by both Maria Isabella and Jorge in English, he supposed familial conversation was usually in Spanish. So, in Spanish, Paul asked Jorge about school. Jorge seemed to pause a moment, even glancing at his father, before answering. Alonzo didn't seem to give any kind of signal. Jorge answered, in Spanish, that he'd attended a private school until recently but had begun to study at home with private tutors.

Paul wondered if the reason for private tutors was to better keep Jorge safe from those who had already made attempts on Alonzo's life and possibly on Paul's life as well. He thought it might be indelicate to ask that question yet, so he asked if Jorge preferred school or private tutoring. Again, Jorge glanced at his father before answering and again, Alonzo made no attempt to guide him one way or another.

"I prefer attending school with my friends, but I'm probably learning more and faster with tutors here at home."

"Do you still get to see your friends?" queried Paul.

"Yes, two or three of them often come here to the *Estancia* to see me and we often text."

"So, this is a cattle ranch, not just a home?"

"Yes," interrupted Alonzo. "One day, when you're here during daylight hours, Jorge will show you around on horseback."

"That would be wonderful. How big is the ranch?"

Again, it was Alonzo who answered. "It is not a large ranch, only a few thousand acres. It's mostly a place to live quietly and ride our horses."

Paul was a little startled to learn that the family home was a cattle ranch and not just a well-protected compound. *A few thousand acres must be much harder to secure than a smaller compound,* thought Paul. With so many questions on his mind, he again turned his interest toward Jorge. He discovered that Jorge wasn't that interested in sports. His interests turned more towards the scholarly pursuits, but his hot button seemed to be the computer.

***

As they were getting ready for bed Maria Isabella commented, "I'm impressed with your son, Pablo, *Mi Amor*."

Alonzo smiled. "I was hoping you would like him. I haven't been able to spend any significant time with him, but he's a good man. You don't resent his being here?"

"Of course not, he's part of your family. Your family is my family. Jorge seems delighted to know him. He's thrilled to have an older brother. I think we should do what we can to include him in all family gatherings. He needs to come out and spend some time with Jorge."

***

Pilar hadn't participated in conversation at dinner other than answering specific questions. On the return trip to the hotel, she said, "I could tell you had some additional questions but decided not to ask them yet."

"How could you possibly know that?" Paul thought her statement a bit presumptuous.

She smiled and answered, "Maybe I didn't know for sure, but I certainly would have had many more questions had I been in your situation."

"Yes, I did, but my questions might have stirred up more than my father wanted."

"I'm sure your father knew, when he brought you here, that much would be 'stirred up' as you say."

"Are they safe on the *Estancia?*"

"Your family? We really aren't sure anymore who is safe and who is not. I'm sure that's the reason that Jorge was pulled out of school. He's much safer on the *Estancia* than he would be at school."

"Do we have any idea who is attacking my father?"

"Not really," she answered. "Only recently have the

attacks become personal."

"You mean there have been other attacks that were not personal?"

"At first there were accidents in one or another of the family businesses. No one connected them at first. We are even starting to wonder if the bank robberies are connected."

"Do you have many bank robberies?"

"*Banco República* has many branches. It is expected to have a bank robbery occasionally."

"What about the ambush of my father?"

"He was up north to inspect one of the mines. They had turned off the main highway headed towards the mine. Because of the accidents and threats, he was traveling with bodyguards, two of whom were in the lead car and one who was in the passenger seat of his car. As they rounded a curve, gunfire hit your father's car killing the guard. The other guards returned fire, and the attackers fled. At first, the bodyguards pursued the attackers, but they were worried about leaving your father unprotected, so they returned. The attackers have never been identified."

"So, you suspect the attack on my father is connected to the accidents at his businesses?"

"Yes, we even believe the bombing of his car in Idaho was done by the same people."

"Who are these people? Are they the same people who killed my wife?"

"We don't know. We suspect they are."

"Why are they doing this?"

"We don't know for sure, but a warning Carlos Mendocina received might give us a clue. It said, 'If Sandoval does not give us back what is rightfully ours, you are next.'"

"Who are they and what is rightfully theirs?"

"We don't know but Carlos is really scared. That's why he wasn't here tonight. He and I often have dinner with the family. He's terrified to go anywhere he might be exposed."

"Have you been threatened?"

"No, though I suspect it is only a matter of time. That's why we are concerned about you. They've already made one attempt on your life. We worry there may be more. That's why your father assigned a bodyguard to you."

"I have a bodyguard?" Paul asked incredulously.

"Yes."

"I haven't seen him."

"Yes, you have. He was with you at the cemetery in Idaho. He's Miguel, your driver. He's right in front of you."

CHAPTER 11

Discovering that Miguel Ortega was not only his driver but also his bodyguard motivated Paul to become acquainted, but he found Miguel reluctant to share personal information. Paul soon discovered that he had more than one body guard as another one was stationed in the hall in front of his door all night. Miguel was ready and available first thing in the morning.

Miguel was a little taller and more athletic than most of the other Chileans Paul had observed. He was of husky build, perhaps a weight lifter. His brown hair was cropped in a military cut.

Paul wanted to know, "Where do we go for breakfast?"

"We can go anyplace you like. There's an excellent breakfast buffet here in the hotel, but it would be easier to protect you if you ordered from room service."

"Well, Miguel, I'm not hiding in my room. You're welcome to join me for breakfast, but I'm going to the breakfast buffet." Paul thought he noticed a flicker of a smile or perhaps it was a smirk. In any case, Miguel didn't protest, but he didn't join Paul for breakfast.

The breakfast buffet was well stocked. He might have still been in the United States considering the breakfast.

There were scrambled eggs, waffles, all kinds of pastries, fruits, juices and coffee. Other than the fact that the meal wasn't as hot as he would have chosen, Paul found it very palatable.

He studied the other guests who were using the buffet and decided he wasn't the only American in the room. He observed Miguel and another well-built man eating and seemingly visiting at a table near the window.

When Paul finished eating and stood up from his table, both Miguel and the other man also rose. The other gentleman left the restaurant area. When Miguel joined Paul he asked, "Where can I take you today?"

Paul pulled a piece of paper from his pocket with Victor Riquelme's office address.

"I want to go here first thing, and then we need to find an apartment. I can't stay here."

"This is?"

"The FBI office."

"Have they contacted you since you arrived yesterday?"

"No." Paul thought of telling him more but decided, *If Miguel is not going to be open with me, perhaps it is better if I return the favor.*

Miguel nodded without adding another word. He followed Paul back to his room and waited in the hall.

* * *

Agent Victor Riquelme wasn't nearly as helpful as Paul had hoped. He had an open file and had communicated with Agent Maria Escobar in Idaho. She'd forwarded a copy of the driver's licenses that Paul had provided her. As Paul had expected, they were fake. He had requested help from his Chilean counterpart, but so far they didn't have actual names to go with the driver's license photos.

"How helpful have the Chilean police been on this investigation?" asked Paul.

"My Chilean contact is playing me close to the vest."

"What is the status of the FBI here in Chile?"

"We're here as guests of the Chilean government. We have to be careful not to step on any toes. I tried to attach the word 'terrorism' to this case and my contact just rolled his eyes. 'There are no Chilean terrorists in the United States,' he said. When I mentioned that you'd been run off the road by men using false Chilean documents, he said anyone could have done that, not necessarily Chileans. I finally got his attention when I reminded him that Alonzo Sandoval's vehicle had been bombed. He wanted to know if the same men had done the bombing. I told him we thought so, but so far we have no evidence. I'm afraid that's all I have to report."

"Can we rely on them?"

"Do you mean, are they corrupt like some other Latin American police departments?"

Paul allowed a slight smile and responded, "Perhaps that's what I mean."

"No, they're not corrupt. Years ago, some of the local police departments were corrupt, but they don't exist anymore. The local, rural and national police are all combined into one force. They are the *Carabineros de Chile*. It is one unified institution under the direction of the national government. Besides, the *Carabineros de Chile* is an investigative force called *Polícia de Investigaciones de Chile.* This is the group with which we're working. My contact is part of the *P. I.*"

"Would it be helpful for me to meet him?"

"I don't know. It might at some point. For now, let me be the front man on this." Paul didn't like that idea, but he didn't say anything.

They ended their conversation with a warning from Riquelme that Paul allow the FBI and PI do the police work and a promise to keep each other informed.

***

"Let's go find an apartment," suggested Paul as Miguel opened the door to his SUV.

"There's no need to hurry," replied Miguel. "We have a plan to keep you safe in the hotel."

Ignoring Miguel's comment, Paul instructed, "Let's look at that apartment building Sr. Sandoval mentioned." Paul watched for any reaction from Miguel. There was none.

They drove to the apartment house, where Miguel circled the block once so Paul could inspect the exterior of the building. It was in a quiet section of Providencia. Paul could see many old mansions as well as apartment buildings, some old some new.

The Sandoval apartment house had an antique pink, stucco finish and was five stories high. Each of the windows opened to a small balcony, large enough to contain pots of flowers and nothing else, surrounded by decorative metal. The glass windows were protected by wooden shutters.

The building was definitely attractive and reflected the best of the era. He could see why his father hadn't wanted to replace it with a more modern building. One approached the building on foot from the front through a large ornate metal gate. A wide, stone path, splitting a beautiful garden, led to the front entrance. It must've been most elegant in its time. Miguel and Paul didn't enter by the front pedestrian gate but through a side gate for vehicles where they could park in back.

They were met at the back door by a spry, spindly, grey-haired, smiling gentleman who would have to stand on tip toes to reach five feet of height.

"Buenos dias, Sr. Pablo."

Paul shook the extended hand and smiled. Then he glanced at Miguel with a quizzical look on his face which questioned, *Who is he? Why does he know me? I thought we were trying to keep my whereabouts unknown.*

"This is the *gerente* of the apartment building. Obviously, he has been forewarned of your coming. I don't know by whom."

"Pilar Flores called and told me to be prepared for your arrival," responded the manager of the apartment building. "No one but me knows you are here or knows that you are coming. We have just the apartment for you," he gushed. "I'm honored to have the son of Sr. Alonzo Sandoval staying in one of my apartments. He and I have been dear friends for forty years. I am called Vicente Troncoso."

Paul was impressed with this spry, little man. He still wasn't sure this was the best place for him to stay, but he hoped it was. "Let's have a look at that apartment, Sr. Troncoso," suggested Paul.

"Oh no, you must call me Vicente, Sr. Pablo."

"Let's make a deal. I'll call you Vicente if you will call me Pablo."

"Yes, yes, let's make a deal, Sr. er … uh Pablo." Vicente looked a little uncomfortable, but when Paul winked at him with a smile, he was suddenly put at ease and tugged on Paul's arm as he led him to the elevator.

Vicente, Miguel and Paul all entered the small but modern elevator. It took no time at all to rise to the fourth floor. Vicente led the way down the hall to two apartments in the East Wing of the building. "The apartment on the left would be best for Sr. Pablo," Vicente said as he looked at Miguel. "You and your men could use the one on the right."

The apartment Vicente had suggested for Paul was larger and more modern than Paul expected. There were three bedrooms, one of which was furnished as an office, a kitchen, two bathrooms and a living room. The apartment was already comfortably furnished. There was a king-sized bed in the master bedroom with two twin beds in the other bedroom. The third bedroom was furnished with a beautiful walnut desk, with matching supportive furniture. The living room had a large couch, an easy chair, some end tables and lamps and a large flat screen TV. Paul was surprised to find the kitchen not only conveniently laid out but already stocked with prepared foods and drinks. Vicente grinned from ear to ear at Paul's surprise and approval.

Next, they explored the apartment across the hall that Miguel and his men would use. It was furnished, though not as elegantly as Paul's. It, too, was stocked with food. After checking the internet and telephone connections, Miguel shrugged that it would be adequate.

"Well, I guess this is where I'll be staying. Perhaps we should return to the hotel to retrieve my bags."

"That won't be necessary," replied Miguel. "Hector will need to bring over our equipment. He can bring your things at the same time. Would you like me to drive you back to the office now?"

"Not just yet," replied Paul. "I have an address I want to check out first."

It took approximately forty-five minutes to navigate the traffic. They pulled to the side of the street across from the address listed. One could see a ten-foot high, white, metal fence covered with graffiti. The tracks in the driveway indicated that many trucks had passed through the portal. There was no indication of living quarters. A large, open structure appeared to cover lumber of all sizes and shapes.

Near the structure was a dilapidated cement truck which looked like it hadn't been used in years. The fence was too tall to see anything else behind the walls.

They approached the gate on foot and rang a doorbell attached to the fence. After ringing the bell twice more with no response he tried the gate and found it unlocked. As he started to push it open, Miguel reached out and held his arm. With hand signals, Miguel motioned for Paul to stand behind him as he pushed the gate open enough for the two of them to enter.

They both slipped inside and stood scrutinizing the yard. It appeared to be a lumber or building supply yard. Besides the building sheltering the lumber, there were large bins which held different types of rock, gravel, sand and soil. There was a small front-end loader which had seen better days and which appeared to have been used recently. Finally, a scrappy looking man of approximately fifty years of age exited a small office near the back of the lot. He hesitantly approached Paul and Miguel who had begun moving towards him.

"May I help you?" he asked.

"Is this a building supply depot?" asked Paul.

"Yes, many of the local contractors have their supplies delivered here. Are you contractors?"

"No, we're looking for a couple of men who used this as their address."

"Many contractors do that."

"These two weren't using this as a drop address but as their permanent address."

Cautiously the warehouse manager offered, "Well, we do have one or two that pick up their mail here as well. What are their names?" Paul read their names off the copies of the driver's licenses. "No, I don't recognize either of those names," replied the manager.

"Perhaps if you looked at their photos, you would recognize them?"

The warehouse manager looked at the photos and too quickly blurted out, "No, I have never seen them before in my life."

Paul and Miguel couldn't help but notice his terror-filled eyes. They excused themselves and the manager was only too happy to see them go. They heard him slip a padlock on the gate when it closed behind them.

CHAPTER 12

Pilar guided Paul to his beautiful, deluxe office with a high-rise view of the magnificent, snowcapped Andes Mountains. It was spacious and beautifully decorated with mahogany wood and burgundy leather.

Concerned, Paul turned to Pilar, "Was someone removed from this delightfully furnished office so I could use it?"

"No, it's been vacant for some time. Your father had it furnished for you when he came back from your wife's funeral."

"That was more than a year ago. I didn't decide to come down here until just a few days ago. How could he have known I was coming?"

"Maybe he didn't. He's been talking about your joining us all that time. Until you really came, it was perhaps wishful thinking. Some of us guessed it would never happen."

"This office is much too luxurious for a short-term consultant."

Hesitantly, Pilar suggested, "That is a personal issue between you and your father. In the meantime, this is your office. I will double as your administrative assistant as well as his. Anything you need, ask me, and I will see that it is done by the proper people. "

Confused, Paul blurted, "I don't even know what I'm doing yet. Who would be the logical person to bring me up to speed on the companies involved and their problems?"

"That would be Carlos," replied Pilar. "He's been waiting to brief you on APS and the companies it holds."

"What's APS?"

"APS is the holding company for all the Sandoval businesses." When Paul didn't ask more questions, she continued, "I'll let Carlos know you are available."

"Before you have Carlos come in," interrupted Paul, "I'd like to learn a little about him and even before that a little about you."

There was a brief flash of a blush before Pilar replied, "Well, Carlos has been around for a long time, even before he finished school."

Paul laughed, "Wait, wait, wait, I said before I hear about him, I need to know a little about you."

'Oh, sorry," she replied.

"No need to be."

"I came to APS as an intern while working on my MBA at the university."

Paul was interested. "How did that happen?"

"Well, honestly," began Pilar, "Sr. Sandoval paid for my education, and working for APS as an intern seemed a good way to help repay him while preparing myself for the real world."

Paul was visibly taken aback by the thought of his father paying for someone else's education. He'd always found his own tuition and fees had already been paid before he had the chance to pay them. He was shocked to find out his father financially supported others.

"If it is not confidential," Paul asked, "why did he pay for your education?"

"Well, I grew up in a very poor family. My parents couldn't afford to pay for private schools, and the public schools aren't very good. Someone in my church, a friend of my parents, knew I loved school and was advanced in my abilities to learn. He talked to my parents and told them he knew someone who might be willing to provide me with scholarships. Soon, I was moved from public to private schools and the tuition was always paid. I thought that would end after secondary school. I didn't think I would be able to attend the university, but I received a notice in the mail offering me a full-ride scholarship. A few years later, the same school also notified me that I had been admitted to the MBA program with another full-ride scholarship. I've always suspected that all this was arranged and probably paid for by your father."

Remembering the philandering tales that he'd heard about his father, Paul began to wonder about this rich man providing scholarships to an attractive young woman. His face must have given him away because Pilar quickly added, "Before your mind starts inventing things, I never even met your father personally until I came here as an intern during my MBA studies. We've never discussed what he's done for me financially. He's never made any untoward advances to me or to anyone else that I know of. The friend of my parents once said, 'Sr. Sandoval always supports three or four good students all the way through school.'"

This was a notion completely contrary to what he'd imagined of his father. "You say he constantly supports three or four students every year?"

"That's what our friend told us."

"Do all those other students my father financed work for

APS?"

"No," replied Pilar, "the only ones I know of are Carlos and me. Perhaps there are others in some of the other companies. However, some of those he helped became dentists or doctors. Our companies don't hire many of those."

"He paid for Carlos' education as well?"

"Yes, I think he has supported Carlos since infancy."

Paul wanted to know why and blurted out, "How is that?"

"I don't know, but when we have dinner with the Sandoval family, there seems to be an almost familial intimacy that goes way back. In some ways, he seems to be part of their family."

That brought other questions to Paul's mind. He remembered that his father hadn't wanted Paul's mother to return to Chile because he had a mistress. Paul wondered if Carlos' mother was that other woman. He didn't want to ask such a blunt question of Pilar as she didn't think Sr. Sandoval acted improperly towards any woman. "How did he come to know my father?"

"I don't know for sure," answered Pilar thoughtfully, "so you'll have to ask one of them."

"How long has Carlos worked here?"

"I think he, too, started right out of school. He seems to know everything happening anywhere in APS much sooner than anyone else. He can carry innumerable details of multiple businesses around in his head and is rarely incorrect. He's very friendly and submissive to your father, though he can be very aggressive and demanding of employees and the leaders of Sandoval businesses. He seems to be very efficient."

"He sounds like the kind of person I'd want working for

me," offered Paul.

"There hasn't been anyone between him and Sr. Sandoval in the line of command for years. As the executive vice president of APS, he represents Sr. Sandoval in negotiations of purchases of new companies, in board meetings, and he oversees the presidents of the companies owned by APS. Everyone knows that an order from Carlos must be treated as though it were coming directly from Sr. Sandoval. Unofficially, he's the heir apparent to be the next president of APS when your father retires. Some think that may not happen now that you're here."

Paul mulled over what Pilar had said. Perhaps Carlos was considering Paul a threat to his progression at APS. Paul thought he'd do well to treat Carlos as the head of the business with himself as a consultant, not the other way around. "He needn't think of me as his competition, I won't be here that long. I'm just a hired consultant, not even one who expects to get paid. Will he be resentful of my coming in as an outside consultant on these company problems?"

"First, I can't imagine Sr. Sandoval not paying you. Second, Carlos is usually the first person to see a problem in a company, even before the president of that company, and the first to come up with solutions. These current problems have seemed to be beyond his fixing. He may resent requiring assistance, because I can never remember him feeling the need for it before. I think he was shocked to realize Sr. Sandoval was bringing you in to help."

"Pilar, you've been very accommodating. Is it possible that I could meet with Sr. Sandoval for a few minutes? Then I'd like to visit with Carlos."

"Sr. Sandoval usually goes home before now but he may be waiting to talk to you.

I'll see if Carlos can see you when you finish."

Pilar led Paul to his father's office and opened the door without knocking. Sr. Sandoval looked up from his desk and immediately smiled. "I was hoping you'd have time to come in and visit with me today. Sit down, sit down."

There was an arrangement of two leather couches facing each other over a beautiful walnut coffee table which matched the huge desk. Paul and Alonzo took their place on opposite couches. "Are you settled into your new apartment?"

"I've seen it. Miguel told me not to worry about moving in as Hector would take care of my things."

"Miguel isn't much of a talker, but he is very efficient."

"Is he head of your security?"

"No, but I have a great deal of trust in him."

"That is one of the things I wanted to talk to you about. I think I'd rather do the search for Janet's killers on my own. I think it may be too intimidating to people when I show up with Miguel as my enforcer."

"I was hoping that is what they would think so you would be safe."

"Miguel probably is making it safer for me, however, when I show up in a big expensive SUV with a bodyguard, I might not get much information. I'd like to try it on my own for a while."

"What do you mean, on your own?" asked Alonzo.

"Well, I'd like to do it without Miguel."

Alonzo frowned. "He could stay in the car and just be nearby," offered Alonzo.

"I'd really like to do it without Security nearby at all. They could still watch from the apartment across the hall when I'm home but I'd like them to have a much lower profile while I'm here at work or out investigating."

"It would seriously worry me, but as you wish. I'll give

Miguel the word."

"Sr. Sandoval," Paul began again awkwardly.

"Is it too uncomfortable for you to call me father?"

"No," Paul carefully considered. "I can do that; it's just that we really haven't had that kind of relationship."

"I hope we can remedy that."

"Father, exactly what is your hope that I can accomplish with your business?"

"What would you do if you were hired by a holding company in the United States?" asked Alonzo.

Paul chuckled. He was in a much different situation in Chile with APS than he'd ever been with Segue Dynamics. "We usually buy a company before we try to improve it. Owners have more authority to make the changes necessary."

"Pablo, couldn't you treat APS as if you owned it? You are my son, and I've put out the word to treat you exactly as they would treat me."

"Even though you've put out the word, no one really expects me to be here more than just a short time. To them, I am a consultant for his father's business."

"Earlier you asked me what I hoped so I'll tell you exactly what that is. I hope you will become part of my business on a permanent basis. You and your brother, Jorge, will inherit this business, and you will take over as president of APS when I retire."

This was a bombshell for Paul, and he knew that many in the business would be equally shocked, especially Carlos. "Don't you know that Carlos is planning to replace you as president when you retire?"

"Well, he may, if you choose not to accept it. However, you are family and are more qualified. My first choice is to have my two sons take over."

Filled with consternation and considering the conversation he had with Pilar, Paul wondered about the possibility of there being a third son whom Sr. Sandoval wasn't acknowledging.

CHAPTER 13

Paul showed Carlos to one of the two leather, wingback chairs in the corner where they had a spectacular view of the mountains. He sat in the other. "Thanks for taking time for me, Carlos."

"We're so happy to have you with us. Your father has spoken so much about you and sings your praises," gushed Carlos. "You and Segue Dynamics have been very successful."

"Well, I wish I could say I'm happy to be here, but it's a result of a terrible disaster in my family. In response to my father singing my praises, I don't know how he knows that much about me."

"I offer my condolences on the loss of your wife. If I can be of any help in apprehending those terrible men, please accept my assistance. As for your father, he knows much about you. He's followed your career and your life very carefully. I know your father wants you to help us somehow in our business, though I'm not sure how."

"First, I'd like to know a little about you and your responsibilities at APS, and second, I'd like to hear about some of the problems my father may be concerned about."

"Why do you need to know about me?"

"From what I have heard, you are the implementation of what Alonzo Sandoval wants done in APS. Is that correct?" questioned Paul.

"I'm your father's executive vice president by title but really no more than the messenger boy," Carlos replied modestly. "When your father wants something done, I make sure it happens."

"Aren't you the contact person with the presidents of each one of the companies owned by APS?"

Carlos and Paul continued to talk about Carlos' roll in directing the business affairs of APS. Carlos' assertion that he was no more than a messenger boy obviously wasn't true. He often made decisions on the spot and expected the presidents of the companies to follow his direction. For the most part Carlos had free rein. It was obvious that Sr. Sandoval had great confidence in his executive vice president.

"How did you become connected with APS?"

Carlos wondered if Paul wanted to know how he became connected to APS or to Alonzo Sandoval. "I have always known Sr. Sandoval. He's been a close friend and benefactor to my family since I was a small baby." Carlos was careful not to reveal the relationship between his mother and Alonzo Sandoval.

"When did you come to work for APS?"

"When I finished school, I began working for *Banco República*. I'm sure Sr. Sandoval kept track of my progress and about seven years ago I was transferred to the holding company. Eventually I was appointed executive vice president. I've been here ever since."

"You've risen rapidly. I'm sure you've been a tremendous asset to Sr. Sandoval and APS."

"I hope so. He's been such a help to my family and me. It's important for me to do all I can for him."

There were so many more questions that Paul wanted to ask, but he thought better of it.

"Carlos, tell me about the problems with the business. Are these accidents that I've been hearing about part of them?"

"Yes, I'm sure that is part of what your father was hoping to solve."

Realizing that the business was experiencing more than problems caused by accidents, Paul asked, "Those aren't the only problems?"

"Well, profits are down in a number of the businesses. We believe much of that is related to the economy."

"So, what do you think Segue Dynamics could do to help APS?"

"Frankly, I really don't know what a consultant, who doesn't really know our business, could do. Most of the problems will take care of themselves as the economy stabilizes. That being said, your father seems to want your opinions on correcting the loss of profitability."

"What about the accidents that have plagued the APS companies?"

"Well, we started experiencing incidents in the various companies over a year ago. At first, there was an isolated problem in one company and then later in another. I was the one who began to suspect the problems might be connected because I work closely with all APS companies," replied Carlos.

"What kinds of incidents are we talking about?"

"At first, they weren't anything that would be noticed. There was a belt on a motor in a mine that was cut. At the time, the operations manager of the mine thought one of the workers wanted the motor to stop so he could take the rest of the day off. There were numerous occurrences of that level of seriousness, such as: sugar being put in gas tanks of vehicles, air removed from tires, oil drained from motors, or a piece of metal being placed in a gear cog. These episodes happened over a period of months. Since they were in different Sandoval companies, they weren't noticed."

"So, these were events which slowed down or stopped production for periods of time," stated Paul. "Were they serious enough to affect profitability?"

"Not noticeably, but to a certain extent they were because in each case, production stopped while repairs or corrections were made," replied Carlos. "Sometimes parts and even new motors had to be obtained. Because they were the kinds of things that happen normally in business, no one gave them much thought. I finally realized there was a correlation of things happening throughout APS companies, slowing production."

Paul wrote a couple of notes on a pad. "From what you said, it sounds as though these occurrences gradually became more serious."

Carlos glanced at the notes that Paul was making and then continued. "That is true. We had an elevator sabotaged so that it fell. We were very lucky. You can imagine what would've resulted if someone had been on that elevator and it had fallen numerous floors."

"So, the elevator had no passengers?" asked Paul.

"That one didn't, but then it happened again in another APS company. This time there were two employees riding the elevator. When the elevator fell, they were seriously hurt. As a result of more than one elevator being sabotaged, our insurance rates increased and numerous employees began seeking other employment. Some employees were superstitious and others worried that someone was out to destroy APS"

"Did you begin to think that someone had an axe to grind against APS?" Paul wanted to know.

"Axe to grind?" It was obvious that Carlos didn't recognize that expression.

"Someone had reason to try to damage the company. On any of these incidents, have any culprits been identified?"

"No, as I mentioned at the beginning, at first we thought it was workers trying to slow down their work so they could rest. Then we thought maybe it was disgruntled employees with an axe to grind, as you say, against the company. Now we're not sure."

Paul continued to write down the information that Carlos provided. "These incidents could also have affected profitability. Repairs, parts purchased, rapid turnover and down time; all of those affect production no matter what kind of work it is. Were there more dangerous sabotages where lives were endangered?"

"Yes," replied Carlos, "some of our trucks have had their brake lines cut. A dangerous gas was released in the duct work of one of our central air conditioners. We even found poison in some of the food prepared in one of the cafeterias. Luckily, that was discovered before anyone ate the food. We have had a few armed bank robberies."

The problems that Carlos described seemed very serious. "Certainly the police must have become involved," mentioned Paul. "Have they come up with any suspects who might be behind all of this?"

"Not really," answered Carlos, "and recently various leaders in our companies have received personal threats. The police are studying those threats, and hopefully they will discover something useful."

The more Carlos talked, the more Paul realized how serious these incidents were.

"What is the nature of those threats?"

"Until recently they've been on the line of, 'things are going to get worse for you if you continue working for Alonzo Sandoval.'"

"The notes mention Sr. Sandoval directly?" asked Paul incredulously.

"Yes, some of those who have reported such threats have left us to work elsewhere. It is possible that others who have left received threats and didn't report them. There are probably others who would like to leave APS but can't because of the economy. There are no other jobs out there."

"Carlos, I was informed that you, too, received a threat. Is that true?"

Carlos seemed relieved to talk about his threat. "It came right after the elevator fell with employees."

"How did you receive that threat?" asked Paul.

"It was in a text message to my phone."

"Couldn't the police trace the phone to its owner?"

"No, it was traced to a disposable phone," replied Carlos. "They weren't able to determine the owner."

"What exactly did the message say?"

"It said, 'If Sandoval does not give us back what is rightfully ours, you are next.'"

"You took that to mean that you would be killed?"

"Or severely injured."

"What did they mean by 'what is rightfully ours'?"

"I really don't know. They must think that Sr. Sandoval has something and they want him to give it back."

"Sr. Sandoval or Sandoval companies?"

"It could be either."

"You don't have any idea what they want back?"

"No, I don't. It wasn't mentioned in the message."

"How do they expect to get it back if no one knows what it is?"

"That was our question exactly."

Paul was deeply concerned. "Doesn't that make you apprehensive?"

"Of course it does. I wonder every day if a bomb is going to go off in the next car I enter, or I wonder if an elevator is going to fall the next time I am in it. I'm very nervous."

"You're not tempted to leave APS for your own protection?"

"Paul, I've been led to believe that when Sr. Sandoval retires, I'll become the president of APS. That is a great honor. However, even with that, I'm seriously tempted to leave APS and hope that will be the end of my worries." Carlos paused, then looking directly at Paul asked, "How do I know this isn't some grand plot just to get rid of me so I can't lead APS?"

CHAPTER 14

Vicente was ensconced in his glassed-in office concentrating on his computer screen. He spied Paul through the huge window and waved for him to enter.

"Vicente, could you help me?" began Paul.

"Well, good morning to you, Sr. Pablo."

Paul smiled as he remembered that the American way of getting right to the point was considered bad form in Latin America. There needs to be a certain amount of small talk and friendly conversation before approaching the business purpose of the conversation.

Paul grinned as he replied, "Good morning, Vicente. You have a pleasant office here."

"It is comfortable. I like it."

"It seems more modern than I would have expected for this building."

"Even though the exterior of this building is much as it was when it was first constructed, the interior has been renovated and modernized. I'm proud to be the *gerente* of such a delightful building. Now, Sr. Pablo, how may I serve you?"

"Vicente, I need to learn how to use public transportation here in Santiago."

"I thought you had a driver."

"Today is Saturday, and I thought it would be well to give him the weekend off. Everyone else seems to manage without a driver, I thought I'd try."

Vicente frowned, "Is that wise? Is that safe?"

"Why would you ask that?"

"There have been so many terrible things happening to people who work for your father. I worry that you may be putting yourself at great risk."

Showing an air of confidence, Paul responded, "There is a possibility of risk, but my father has been attacked twice while guarded. Perhaps I'll be safer if I don't draw attention to myself with a power car and a muscular driver."

"That may be true, Sr. Pablo, but still I worry. Well, to answer your question, first you need to buy a *Bip* card. That is a smart card which is the payment system for *Transantiago*. You use it to travel on any bus or the metro. You pass your smart card across a reader which extracts the fare for your ride. Any subsequent rides you take during the next ninety minutes will be on that same fare."

"Where do I buy the *Bip* card?"

For the next twenty minutes Vicente explained where to buy *Bip* cards and how Paul could use the various local bus lines, the main bus lines and the metro. Vicente handed Paul a handful of pocket-sized maps, one for each section of the city, showing all the public transportation in that section.

"You need to be careful, Sr. Pablo. There are many pickpockets on *Transantiago*. They like it best when it's crowded."

"One more question, Vicente. I'd like to go to church tomorrow. Do you know where I can find a Mormon Church?"

"Of course I do, Sr. Pablo. You must come to church

with me."

Paul was astonished. "You're a Mormon?"

"Of course I am, Sr. Pablo. That's how I met your father."

This news was even more baffling. Paul had heard from his grandparents that his father had joined the church so his mother would marry him. "You met my father at church?"

"Yes, in actuality, I met him at his baptism. We were both baptized the same day. We've been close friends ever since."

Paul really didn't know how to process this information. Paul encouraged Vicente to tell the rest of the story.

"I heard about your father when the missionaries were teaching me. They were really excited because a member of the rich and powerful Sandoval family was being taught the gospel by another set of missionaries. It was as though his baptism would open up the whole of Chile to the church and perhaps it did.

"I was surprised when I showed up at my baptism and saw that Sr. Alonzo was being baptized in the same meeting. I guess I expected them to have a special baptismal service just for him and his guests, but that isn't what happened. He had a few friends there, including his beautiful fiancé."

"You met my mother too?"

"Yes, your parents and my wife and I became quite close through church activities. Even though we were from very different worlds, we were often together."

For the next half hour, Paul listened as Vicente described how his parents and the Troncosos had attended church and activities together. He learned how his mother, Kathleen, and Vicente's wife, Claudia, had become close friends. She was saddened that Kathleen never returned to Chile. They were both saddened that Alonzo quit coming to church.

***

Just across the street from the local supermarket, Paul came across a line of people waiting to get into a *Transantiago* kiosk. The wait, which only took about fifteen minutes, gave him time to watch and learn. He noticed a large map on the wall which was a blowup of the combination of pocket maps Vicente had given him. In his mind, he rehearsed the buses and metros he'd have to board to reach his destination.

As Paul was buying his *Bip* card, he noticed various buses passing by going each direction. He checked the numbers of the buses with the large map on the wall. After he obtained his card, he crossed the street and walked one block east and boarded the bus. When he completed his mission in Peru a number of years previously, he'd promised himself no more buses. Now, here he was riding a bus in Chile.

He watched carefully for the location where the bus line intersected with the metro. After many stops, suddenly many riders on the bus arose. He looked out the window and, sure enough, he saw the signs for the metro.

Paul exited the bus and followed the crowd as they descended two flights of stairs into the subway terminal below. He learned he would need to descend another level to catch the metro going north or south. As he wanted to go south, he took the right stairway. The platform was lined with lighted billboards and advertisements. There were bright colored plastic seats lining the wall for those waiting, but he didn't have to wait long for his train. As the doors opened, the passengers quickly entered and took their seats.

Not having to compete with traffic, the subway traveled much faster than the buses above. A female's voice announced each station as they approached. He was so engrossed in listening to her voice that he almost missed his own stop. He exited the subway and climbed the three flights of stairs to the street. He took a minute to acclimate himself and then crossed the street to board the yellow local bus that would take him the rest of the way.

Paul still had the address, but the area seemed to look different from a bus than it had earlier from the SUV. Paul noticed the street he was seeking as they passed. He got off the bus at the next stop and walked back. He still had three blocks to walk before arriving at the construction yard.

He had no idea what kind of reception he would receive. The manager had shown great anxiety as he and Miguel had departed two days before. Paul rang the bell at the gate and waited. It wasn't long until the same man, the manager, slid open the gate. He must have been expecting a delivery because he looked surprised to find Paul standing there. He looked up and down the street as if searching for someone.

Paul tried to ease the tension by offering, "I sensed you were nervous in the presence of my associate the other day, so I came alone. I still have more questions I'd like to ask you."

"I told you all I know," replied the *gerente.* He immediately turned and started to walk away.

Paul had the feeling the warehouse manager knew more than he was revealing. He wondered, *How do I get him to talk to me?*

"Perhaps if I showed you the photos again. . ."

The *gerente* quickly interrupted Paul, "I told you, I've never seen those men before in my life."

"Are you the only one who works here?" questioned Paul. "Perhaps someone else has worked with these two men."

"That's not possible, I'm the only one here. I'm always

here. I live here." The manager pointed to what looked like a shed in the back of the lot which Paul realized was living quarters. Someone, perhaps the manager's wife, had planted flowers around the edge of the building. Looking closer, he noticed a child's bicycle leaning against the shed, probably his daughter's. Scrutinizing the home, Paul realized the manager was supporting his family with very meager means.

"I don't want to insult you," offered Paul, "but perhaps this will help you remember." Paul held up 25,000 pesos.

Too quickly, the manager blurted, "No, that will not help me remember more. There is no more to remember." Before starting to walk away again, his eyes lingered too long on the 25,000 pesos, which were worth about $50 in American money.

"Señor, I'm sure this will help with your little family. I know these are hard times." Paul doubled the ante to 50,000 pesos.

The manager started to shake his head, but his eyes were fixed on the pesos. He motioned for Paul to follow him as he led the way toward the living quarters and sat down at a table, which Paul suspected was where the family ate their meals. The *gerente* visibly shuddered. Paul wondered if he was asking this man to risk his life.

Paul sat across the table from the *gerente* and slid the 50,000 pesos toward him. He looked long and hard at the money before slowly sliding his hand toward the money and then snatching it quickly and slipping it into his front shirt pocket.

Resolved to earn the 50,000 pesos, the *gerente* shuddered again and asked, "What is it you wish to know, Señor?"

"What is your name?" asked Paul.

"I am Luiz Rossi, Señor, and you are?"

"I am Paul. Pablo Sandoval," replied Paul.

"You speak Spanish very well, even though you are not Chilean." It was a statement not a question.

Paul slid the photos which had been taken from the fake driver's licenses across the table. "Would you look at these photos again, Sr. Rossi?"

"Luiz," he corrected. He took the photos and looked at them carefully.

Paul knew that Luiz recognized the men in the photos immediately, but he was still trying to decide how much to reveal.

"These are very dangerous men, Señor," Luiz said in almost a whisper. "I fear what they would do to me or my family if they knew I was talking to you about them."

"There's no reason for them to know," assured Paul.

"What if they see you coming or going, Señor?"

"Luiz, let's make sure I have all the information I need today so that I have no reason to return."

Paul sat quietly and gave Luiz the time he needed to make the necessary decisions. Finally, Luiz looked up from the photos and looked straight into Paul's eyes.

"They are brothers, Sr. Sandoval, Roberto and Esteban Contreras. They are building contractors. They have used this location for years as a delivery site for their supplies. When their lumber or building supplies arrive, I let them know, and they come and get them. That is really all there is to it."

"How do you let them know?" asked Paul. "Do you call them on the telephone or send them a notice in the mail?"

"I call them. I have their phone number."

Paul slid his notepad across the table. "Please write that number for me, Luiz."

"They'll know I gave it to you." Luiz' voice was

quivering. For a moment, Paul thought the man might start to cry. It was obvious that he was terror stricken.

"I won't let them know how I got the number. I won't call them. I'll use the number to find an address," assured Paul.

Luiz hesitated just a moment more then wrote the phone number on his pad. He gave another shudder as he slid it back across the table.

"What have they done that frightens you so?" asked Paul.

Luiz Rossi paused for a moment before answering. "At first, they only had building supplies delivered here. I never suspected they might be receiving anything else. Sometimes their supplies arrive in crates. I never look inside, I just sign for the delivery and call them. One time, I received some wooden crates for them. I called, and this time, both Roberto and Esteban came with two workers. As one of the workers was using the front-end loader to place the crates on their truck, he swerved too quickly, and one of the crates fell and broke open. Señor Pablo, even though I didn't look long, I saw the crate was full of guns. I looked away quickly and pretended I didn't see. Both of the Contreras brothers jumped on that front-end loader operator and beat him something fierce. The other worker just watched with his head down. The operator was bleeding all over the place and fell unconscious. They threw him into the back of the truck like a bag of potatoes.

"Then Esteban Contreras came over to me and said, 'If you ever tell anyone what you saw here today, the same thing will happen, not only to you, but to your little girl. Do you understand?' Then they drove away."

"The next time they came to pick up a delivery, they acted like nothing had happened, but they handed me a box with a doll in it for my little girl. Esteban winked at me and gave the most evil grin I have ever seen. I am afraid, Señor, very afraid."

Paul then reached into his pocket and pulled out another 50,000 pesos which he slid across to Luiz. "I will be very careful not to let them know we talked, Luiz."

CHAPTER 15

What is all that noise coming from the kitchen? It's Saturday; I wanted to sleep in.

She arose to investigate and threw on a light robe before leaving her bedroom.

Her bedroom was in the back of the house owned by her parents, Fernando and Freya Flores, ages sixty-seven and sixty. The bedroom had been hers since she moved out of her sister's room at age twelve. She'd been happy sharing the same room with her older sister. However, Marcela had been delighted to finally have a room all to herself at age sixteen. Four years later, Marcela had married Orlando and the two of them remained in Marcela's room. As their children, Alejandro and Vanessa, were born into the family, they gradually took over the room that had belonged to her brother and eventually another room which had been added in back.

Every year, Marcela and Orlando schemed to obtain a home of their own, but Orlando's work had been inconsistent. So, they continued to live in three bedrooms in the back of the Flores home. Pilar's parents had the bedroom near the front of the house. By custom or financial condition, it was not uncommon to find three and even four generations sharing the same small house.

Pilar suspected Marcela and Orlando would never be able to buy a house of their own. This one would eventually become theirs and they would take care of Pilar's parents. Pilar would eventually move into her own apartment and, if her dreams came true, marry and have a house and family of her own.

The older she became, the more clouded became her dreams. She was already thirty. There had been opportunities to date and marry, but marrying someone with different standards was simply not an option. She enjoyed being close to her family, especially Alejandro and Vanessa, so she procrastinated looking for an apartment.

"What is all the racket in here?" Pilar wanted to know as she entered the kitchen to find Marcela and Vanessa grinning.

"We're preparing lunch," responded Vanessa proudly.

"Yes, we are preparing lunch, Sleepyhead," continued Marcela. "What gives you the right to sleep in so late?" she teased.

"I worked late last night, so I thought I'd sleep in," responded Pilar.

"Yes, I noticed you came home, dressed in your best party dress and left again in a very fancy car. You certainly didn't look like you were working to me." Marcela continued to poke fun at her with a pinch of envy in her remarks.

"I had to go to dinner at the home of Sr. Sandoval. You don't go there for dinner without dressing up."

"You had to go?" Marcela persisted in mocking. "After working all day, your boss made you go to his house for dinner?"

"Well, he didn't order me to go, but it was an invitation I

couldn't very well ignore."

"And why couldn't you ignore his invitation?"

Pilar didn't really know how to explain her circumstances to her sister. "His son, who has lived his entire life in the United States, is down here to help Sr. Sandoval with his company. Sr. Sandoval asked me to pick up his son at the hotel and bring him to dinner at the Sandoval *Estancia*."

Marcela couldn't help herself. With a huge smirk on her face she asked, "So you were his son's date? Your boss asked you to be his son's dinner date?"

Pilar blushed as she tried to respond to her sister's inquiries. "No, I was not his date. I was an employee picking up his son and making sure he got to the dinner safely."

"So, let me see if I have this right. You picked up Sr. Sandoval's son at the hotel dressed in your best party dress and drove him to the *Estancia* as his bodyguard?"

"Oh, Marcela! You are so exasperating. I wasn't his bodyguard, and I didn't drive the car. One of the drivers picked us both up."

Marcela wasn't ready to stop the kidding. It was way too much fun. "So, it was the driver who picked him up and made sure he got to the dinner safely. So, what was your role?"

"I give up. I don't know," replied a defeated Pilar.

"Well, tell me about him," pleaded Marcela.

"Who?"

"You know who. What is the son's name?" continued Marcela.

"Sr. Sandoval calls him Pablo Sandoval. He responds to that, but he calls himself Paul."

Half teasing and half curious Marcela persisted, "Is he married?"

Pilar made her best effort not to but began to blush slightly. "Why would you ask that? Never mind, I don't want to know. No, he's not married. He's a widower." Trying to convince herself, she repeated emphatically, "He's a widower!"

Marcela's eyes opened much wider as she exclaimed with a grin, "Woo! How old is he?"

"Oh, he's probably about thirty-five, and before you ask the next question, he is very handsome."

Seven-year-old Vanessa, who had been following the conversation very carefully, looked at her Aunt Pilar and asked, "Is he dreamy?"

Aghast, Pilar looked at her niece and asked, "What did you just ask me?"

Marcella giggled as Vanessa repeated her question. "Is he dreamy?"

"Where on earth did you ever hear a question like that?" Pilar asked Vanessa.

"On American television."

"What do you think 'dreamy' means?"

"It means, does he make you dream about him," Vanessa replied in all seriousness.

Both Marcela and Pilar laughed out loud as Pilar protested, "No!"

Marcela winked at her daughter as she remarked "I'll bet."

***

Paul didn't sleep well Saturday night. He could handle the daytime when he was busy, but at night, all he could think about was how much he missed Janet. Sometimes he was caught up in the sadness and other times he was so angry at the men who killed her that he personally wanted to torture them severely before killing them. He was so angry with God that he couldn't pray.

There hadn't been much personal interest in attending church since Janet's homicide. Perhaps attending today would help him put life back into perspective. He'd promised Vicente that he would accompany him and his wife.

Paul was waiting when Vicente called from the lobby. "Are you ready to go to church?"

As Paul exited the elevator, he was greeted not only by Vicente but also his lovely wife, Claudia. She was taller than her husband by almost half a head, and she probably outweighed him by forty pounds. Her dark eyes sparkled with animation. With great courtesy, Vicente introduced his wife. "Claudia, this in Señ … this is Pablo Sandoval, son of Alonzo Sandoval. Pablo, this is my wife, Claudia Espinoza."

"It is such a pleasure, Sr. Pablo. Your mother, Kathleen Marie, was such a dear and wonderful friend. I was so heartbroken when she didn't come back from North America after you were born. It is wonderful to see the son she went home to bear. I can see both your mother and your father, Alonzo, in your face." She gave him a familial hug and positioned her cheek for him to kiss as if he were a well-known member of the family.

"The pleasure is mine, Señora Espinoza, to meet a friend of my mother." Paul would have liked to stop right there and learn more about his mother, however, Vicente motioned with his hand toward the door. The three of them stepped out the back door of the apartment building where a tan Hyundai Santa Fe was parked. Vicente opened the passenger door and signaled with his hand for Paul to enter, but Paul escorted Claudia Espinoza to that seat. She beamed as he helped her into the SUV. Paul took his place in the back while Vicente entered to drive.

Claudia gushed about Paul's mother all the way to the church, which only took a few minutes. Paul wished the drive could have lasted longer.

Unlike the LDS churches in the United States, this one had a high, ornamental fence surrounding the grounds. A large, matching gate was open through which Vicente drove. The building was narrow across the front and extended deep into the lot. There was a driveway the full length of the lot beside the church which led to a parking lot behind. Vicente stopped beside the church and allowed Paul and Claudia to exit.

Paul noticed more members arriving on foot than entered the gate by automobile. They were arriving in groups of twos, threes and more, all visiting with each other with great animation. As each group of members entered the church, Señora Espinoza quickly introduced him. Occasionally, she introduced him as the son of Alonzo and Kathleen Marie Sandoval. Sometimes she responded to questioning looks to remind them that when their branch was newly organized, Paul's parents were part of the congregation. She reminded them of things that happened almost forty years previously, but there were only one or two who indeed remembered.

Just as Paul was beginning to join Vicente and Claudia on their pew, he was startled to see Pilar Flores enter the church with two children, a boy and a girl. She was equally amazed to see him. She paused for just a second before approaching. "Pablo, this is my niece, Vanessa, and my nephew, Alejandro. Children, this is Señor," she paused for a moment and then said, "*Hermano* Sandoval. He works with me."

Vanessa looked at Paul and then at her aunt before

starting to ask, "Is he the ..." Pilar quickly distracted her niece before she could complete her question and guided them to a pew on the other side of the chapel.

It hadn't occurred to Paul that Pilar was a member of the church. After the meetings were completed, as he was waiting for Vicente and Claudia to finish visiting with their friends, Paul approached Pilar, who was standing near the back of the chapel with Vanessa.

"It's good to see you here, Pilar. I had no idea that you were a member of the church," he commented.

"Don't you remember that I said an old friend of the family told my parents he knew a man who might help finance my education?"

"Yes," Paul responded. "I remember." She nodded toward Vicente Troncoso.

"Vicente?" exclaimed Paul. She nodded.

About that time, Vanessa's parents arrived with Alejandro in tow.

"Who is your friend?" Marcela asked.

Pilar blushed a little as she replied, "This is Pablo Sandoval. He's the son of Alonzo Sandoval, my boss. Pablo, this is my sister, Marcela, and her husband, Orlando." Indicating the older woman who came in with them and was still visiting with some of her friends near the front of the chapel, "That is my mother, Freya Donoso."

"I'm so pleased to meet all of you. What a pleasant surprise!"

"Pilar has told us so much about you," gushed Marcela, "but she didn't tell us you were a member of the church." Pilar, standing behind Paul was signaling "no" to her sister as Marcela continued, "We must have you over for dinner someday." She grinned at her sister as Pilar cringed behind Paul.

"That would be delightful," responded Paul.

Pilar threatened her sister with her flashing, blue eyes, however, quickly switched back to a smile as Paul turned to her. "I'll see you at the office tomorrow."

One of the two women who had acknowledged to Claudia that she remembered Paul's mother scurried to his side. "I've been thinking about your mother during the service today. She was such a lovely and friendly person. I was so sad when she had to leave. I wasn't surprised when she left. That was such a dangerous time and the lives of North Americans were in danger."

Paul was somewhat surprised. "You thought my mother's life was in danger? Why?"

Before answering Paul, the sister looked around, as if she were worried that someone might hear. In a conspiratorial whisper she replied, "Everyone was suspicious of his neighbor. Big business was at war with the unions. Many wanted socialism to succeed. There were lines to buy food everywhere. The government was taking over many businesses. North Americans were not trusted, and you know," she paused to look around again to see who might be listening, "it was your government that forced the ouster of our President Allende."

"No one would have thought my mother was involved in that," Paul interjected.

"No, that's true, but she was married to one of the most powerful men in government and business. Your father had many enemies."

"He had enemies?" Paul asked, trying to keep the sister talking.

"My, my, yes! Many wanted his businesses nationalized on one side and on the other. There were some saying that he'd stolen businesses from those who were not so powerful."

"Some thought my father had stolen businesses from others?"

"Oh, *Hermano* Sandoval, I really shouldn't be telling you all of this, but yes, there was talk that when Pinochet came into power, Sr. Alonzo was not only able to retrieve his companies that had been nationalized, he was able to confiscate a mine from a family without wealth."

"He confiscated a mine? From whom?"

"Oh, I don't know the details. It was probably a false rumor. That was a long time ago." Paul noticed the sister glance up as Vicente was moving in their direction. She quickly slipped away and out the front door. Vicente frowned in her direction saying nothing.

"Thank you so much for inviting me to your ward. Everyone seemed so friendly," commented Paul.

Claudia responded, "We have a good ward. Everyone is always friendly. The members were so happy to see you, especially those who knew your mother."

"Yes, there was one member who seemed to remember a lot about her. I was talking to her just as you approached. Did you see who she was?" Paul noticed Vicente frown again as he mentioned her.

"That was Albina Jimenez, the ward gossip monger. She was a member of the branch when your mother was attending. However, I don't remember them having much of an association. It worried me when I saw her speaking to you. What she says isn't always reliable."

Claudia interrupted as Vicente was talking. "Vicente, you shouldn't say things like that about *Hermana* Jimenez. She means well. Sometimes she embellishes her stories to make them a little more interesting than they really are, but you shouldn't call her a gossip monger."

Vicente didn't ask what *Hermana* Jimenez had said, and Paul didn't offer. However, he couldn't let go of the thought that his father may have cheated someone out of their business or mine.

"Pablo," interjected Claudia, "you must come to our apartment for dinner this evening."

"I'd love to, Claudia, but I promised my father that I'd join them for dinner tonight."

"Please pass on our love and best wishes to your father."

CHAPTER 16

When Paul returned from church, Miguel Ortega was waiting for him.

"Sr. Pablo," began Miguel, "your father informed me you'll be going to the *Estancia* for dinner. May I drive you?"

Paul suspected Miguel might be in trouble with his father if Paul showed up at the *Estancia* by bus. He wasn't even sure if buses were a possibility to that location. Since he was only trying to be inconspicuous when he was searching for Janet's killers, he responded, "That would be very helpful, Miguel. Thank you. Did my father indicate to you when he wanted me to come out there?"

"He said to bring you when you were available."

If Paul had been home in the States on a Sunday afternoon, he would have quickly changed to more comfortable clothing immediately following church, but the one dinner he'd attended at the *Estancia* had been fairly formal so he decided to remain dressed in his suit. "I'm ready whenever you are, Miguel."

Paul was becoming more familiar with the drive, and he was beginning to recognize more of the landmarks. Even though the traffic was sparse on Sunday, the drive still required almost an hour. Paul sat back, relaxed a little and enjoyed the scenery as they passed by.

Using his cell phone, Miguel called ahead to provide an estimated time of arrival so when their SUV pulled up to the closed gate, it began to open immediately.

Miguel stopped the SUV and immediately another uniformed guard opened his door and motioned for Paul to climb the steps to the front entrance. When he reached the top step, another guard rang the doorbell and without waiting for someone to answer, opened the door. His newly discovered younger brother, Jorge, was the first to greet him as he entered.

When they first met, Jorge appeared tentative but not today. He seemed to have been anticipating Paul's arrival. He invited Paul into the living room and showed him to one of two wingback chairs in the corner. Jorge took the other chair.

"Father tells me that you are a powerful man in the United States. He says you own many companies," gushed Jorge.

Paul was a somewhat amused with this opening and was careful not to grin. "I wouldn't say that I'm powerful, Jorge. Our company does own a number of businesses, but they're not all mine."

Jorge looked askance, "You don't own them?"

"My friend, Jeff Harkin, and I started a company a few years ago called Segue Dynamics. The two of us own most of the stock, and it owns a number of other companies."

"So, you do own them through a holding company," replied Jorge.

Paul was surprised that a fifteen-year-old boy would know about holding companies. "We search around for small to medium-sized businesses that are struggling. Because they're struggling, we can usually buy them at bargain prices. We analyze them carefully and implement the changes that are necessary to help them regain their potential. Once they are profitable again, we often sell them at a profit."

"How many employees do you have?"

"Do you mean at Segue Dynamics or including all the employees of all the companies?"

"Oh, that is right, each company you own probably has many employees."

"Some of them do."

"Do you fire them all when you take over their company?"

"Not usually. Sometimes the reason a company isn't profitable is because of some of the employees, but usually, when we take over a company, we try to keep as many of the former employees as possible. We don't want to disrupt their lives. Many of them have invested years in the business, and they are a great resource to making it profitable again."

"Don't you need to fire some of the people?"

"There are usually a small number of people we need to let go. They may be the cause of the loss of profitability or they may be trouble makers. We usually discover the trouble makers quite soon. They either get on board, or they need to find new employment."

Jorge looked troubled as if there was something he didn't understand. "What does 'get on board' mean?"

"It is a colloquial expression which originally meant 'get on the train' or 'get on the ship' that frankly means to become enrolled in our plan for the company."

"Can I come and work for you someday?"

Paul was shocked by the question. Paul assumed that Jorge would have much more responsibility running APS someday. "Why would you want to come and work for me?"

"Because you work in the United States, and my father… er, our father says you are the best at what you do. I want to learn from the best."

"How old are you, Jorge?"

"I'll soon be sixteen," he replied.

"Without looking at you, based on your questions I would have guessed your age to be twenty-five. I'm impressed." Jorge was obviously pleased with the compliment. Paul continued, "I'd think you'd have plenty to do here in Chile running APS."

"Someday, that may be true. However, I suspect you will run APS before I do."

Paul chuckled. "I have plenty on my shoulders with Segue Dynamics to consider taking on APS. From what I have seen of Jorge Sandoval in the last few minutes, I don't think you'll have any trouble taking over the reins of APS when your father retires."

Looking around to make sure no one was in earshot, Jorge almost whispered. "Pablo, he's your father, too. I don't think our father is in very good health. I don't think he is going to run APS much longer. If you don't run it for him, I'm afraid Carlos Mendocina will take over. I'm afraid of what will happen to APS when that happens."

"Don't you think Carlos would do a good job?"

"Oh, I think he'd do a good job, but he wouldn't want me working with him. That's why I want to come up to North America and work for you."

Alonzo Sandoval entered the room and, grinning, asked Jorge, "Aren't you a little young to go to North America and work for your brother?"

Jorge's face flushed realizing that he'd been overheard

and wondered what else his father had caught. "Oh, I don't mean now, Father, I mean after I get my MBA."

Still smiling, Alonzo asked, "You're planning to get an MBA?"

"Of course I am. If I'm going to be successful in business, I need an MBA like Pablo."

Smiling at that, Alonzo looked at Paul. "Are you hungry, Pablo? We probably won't have dinner for a few hours yet. Wouldn't you boys like a sandwich or something?"

"I would," interjected Jorge.

"You're always hungry." Alonzo laughed. "Let's have some sandwiches brought out to us on the veranda." Turning to Paul he added, "Don't you want to get rid of that jacket and tie. Jorge and I are dressed casually today."

The veranda overlooked a large swimming pool and gardens. Paul could see the water was crystal clear. He asked, "Isn't it too early in the season to be using the pool? The weather is fairly cool."

"Jorge and his friends use the pool year round. During the cold weather, the pool is heated to ninety degrees Fahrenheit, so it feels hot when you enter the water," replied Alonzo.

"Yes, we like to use the pool in the winter. It feels great," continued Jorge.

Realizing that Jorge was schooled by tutors and only left the *Estancia* under armed guard, Paul asked, "What else do you and your friends do besides swim in a heated pool?"

"We ride horses, ride four-wheeled ATVs, play soccer, but what we like to do the most is play video games."

"Ah, yes, video games," added Alonzo. "They can play video games for hours."

"Do your friends spend a great deal of time here?" asked

Paul.

"Not as much as we'd like, however, they're here a lot," interjected Alonzo. Jorge smiled at his father.

Paul didn't want to cause any apprehension so he didn't ask, but he wondered how safe Jorge and his friends were when they were playing on the *Estancia*. He knew it was heavily protected because of the many uniformed guards. When he was alone with his father, he would broach that question. Looking at Jorge, he asked, "I'm not very good with video games, so perhaps you could show me around on horseback if I come back out here one day this week."

The expression on Jorge's face let Paul know that he'd be very pleased to do just that. Alonzo was very pleased with the expressions of friendship between the two brothers. About that time, the uniformed server showed up with a huge platter of sandwiches, chips, cold vegetables and warm drinks.

After eating their fill, Alonzo decided to begin showing Paul around the *Estancia* using a Land Rover instead of horses. Miguel spotted the three of them heading for the vehicle and quickly came over and offered his services as driver. Alonzo declined and offered to let Paul drive, but Paul suggested that it would be better for Alonzo to drive since he knew where they were going. From the look on Jorge's face, Paul surmised that Alonzo didn't often take the wheel.

With great anticipation, Jorge interjected, "I'll drive."

Alonzo laughed and suggested again that Paul take the wheel. Calling to mind the expression on Jorge's face, Paul willingly slipped into the driver's seat with Alonzo in the passenger seat and Jorge in back. Paul was directed to the paved path which separated the horse barns from the paddock. Glancing in the rearview mirror, Paul noticed that

Miguel and three other uniformed guards followed behind in a black SUV at a constant distance of about a hundred yards.

Alonzo noticed Paul looking in the mirror. "They have instructions to keep us safe. I'm sure we would be safe anywhere on the *Estancia* anyway, but it doesn't hurt to have Miguel and his crew close by."

The three Sandovals took a leisurely ride around the entire ranch. There was a paved lane on which one could drive motored vehicles. Perpendicular to each paved lane was a dirt path for horses. Sometimes, there was a white wooden fence between the two paths, and sometimes there was not. Everyplace in which the paved road led to an exit from the Estancia, Paul saw another guard house with at least two armed guards.

There were paddocks and barns for many horses, more than were needed to man this ranch. They passed two separate herds of cattle. Alonzo explained that both herds were registered animals. The first herd was Hereford, and the second was Santa Gertrudis. Alonzo explained that Santa Gertrudis cattle had been bred to thrive on the brush country of Texas, and they were thriving here in Chile as well.

Simultaneously, Paul saw the black SUV behind them surge forward as he heard gunshots. At first, he thought the gunshots were coming from the SUV containing Miguel and the three other Security guards, but he quickly realized they were coming from the direction toward which Paul was driving. He pulled the Land Rover over to the right as Miguel leaned out of the SUV, which was now right beside them, and shouted, "We have a security breach at gate number 4. Please return to the *Castillo* where other guards are waiting to protect you."

One of the guards, who had been in the SUV, quickly transferred to the Land Rover beside Jorge. He had an AK-47 in his hands. Paul made a quick U-turn and drove as quickly as he could back to the *Castillo*.

CHAPTER 17

Paul had returned to his apartment in the city and Jorge had retreated to his computer. Alonzo and Maria Isabella were left to re-examine the events of the day. The security breach had been the focus of attention during dinner, but Maria Isabella knew that Alonzo would have revealed only what he wanted in front of Jorge. He wanted Jorge to feel secure and free from worry. Those wishes were slowly vanishing as the sun does as it slips below the horizon.

"So, what really happened, Alonzo?" asked Maria Isabella.

"You mean at the security gate?"

"Yes!"

"Miguel said the two guards at the gate were having a routine quiet Sunday when they looked up to see a large pickup truck moving rapidly towards them. They signaled for it to stop, but it hardly slowed down before crashing through the gate. The guards fired shots at the truck, and it stopped immediately. The two occupants of the truck screamed, 'Don't shoot! Don't shoot! It was an accident.'"

Maria Isabella was incredulous, "An accident?"

"That's what they shouted. Our guards held them until the *Carabineros* arrived and took them into custody. The guards then called a wrecker which removed the truck."

"How could it have been an accident?" asked Maria Isabella.

"According to Miguel, the occupants of the truck had been drinking. They were traveling down Avenida Mendoza much too fast when they realized the street ended at Avenida Bosque. They couldn't slow down in time and crashed through the gate.

Remember, this isn't the first time that someone driving too fast on Avenida Mendoza has crashed through our fences into the pasture."

"How about the shots fired?"

"One of the guards is young. He probably thought someone was breaking into the *Estancia* and fired his weapon before recognizing the real situation."

"With all the accidents that have been happening throughout APS and the attacks on you and Pablo, how can we be sure it was an accident?"

"I suppose we can't be."

"Alonzo, do you know the objective of this conspiracy? They tried to kill you twice! They tried to kill Pablo, and they did kill his sweet, innocent wife. I just have a hard time believing this truck crashing into the *Estancia* was an accident. What if there had been many vehicles? The first one could have broken through the gate, and the others could easily have entered. We could have all been killed."

"We're safe here, *Mi Amor*. We have many armed guards, and they're well trained. We'll increase their numbers. I'll also speak with the officer of the *Carabineros* and ask them to increase their vigilance around the *Estancia*."

"What is this conspiracy? Who are these people?"

"We don't know. Pablo's been able to trace Janet's killers here to Chile. He believes the attacks on me were connected to the attack on him and Janet. I believe he'll get to the bottom of it."

"Do we know what these people want?"

"When Carlos was threatened the message was, 'If Sandoval does not give us back what is rightfully ours, you are next.'"

"What is 'rightfully ours?'"

"I really don't know."

"You are such a good man, Alonzo. I can't believe for a minute that you could have taken something that rightfully belonged to someone else."

"I don't believe I have, but in business, people often think they have been wronged."

"When was this 'thing' supposedly taken from them?"

"I don't know that either. Many of the businesses, which make up APS have been in this family for many generations. Was this 'thing' taken from them last year or two hundred years ago? I have searched my brain for answers. I really don't know."

"Is this how it was back then?" questioned Maria Isabella. "Is this how it was when you had to send Kathleen away?"

Alonzo put his face in his hands and shook his head. "I thought this was all over years ago."

"Was it like this?"

"Not really, even though we were threatened then, too. We were trying to hold our businesses together. The government, under Allende, had nationalized some businesses and was threatening to take others. We were in a business war. We were trying to position our companies so the government wouldn't take them over. We were trying to negotiate with the government on others and there were other companies and individuals trying to take advantage of the situation. I didn't mind the threats when they were directed at me. I thought they were just that, threats, but when the threats suggested I might want to be more cooperative if I wanted my wife to be safe, I began to take them seriously."

"Did you know then who was making the threats?"

"Not any more than I do now. For all I know, after forty years, they could be the same people."

"What did you do?"

"Kathleen was expecting Pablo. She'd voiced some concern about bearing her child so far away from her mother. I encouraged her to return to the United States for the birth. I felt she was much safer there than she would have been here. We could have flown her parents down here for the birth, but I thought this was a good opportunity to remove her from harm's way."

Maria Isabella could tell that the direction of this conversation was causing emotional stress. She knew the love Alonzo had for Kathleen. Maria Isabella had known her personally, having visited her in this very home on numerous occasions, but she had always wondered why Kathleen didn't return after the birth of her baby. With all that was happening in their family, she thought it time for her to know the whole story.

"Why didn't she come back after Pablo was born?" she asked.

Alonzo grimaced slightly and said nothing for a minute or two.

Maria Isabella comforted him. "You don't need to tell me if you prefer. You know I have never asked you to tell about that portion of your life."

"No," he assured her. "It's time you knew. Kathleen had the baby, and I traveled to the United States to see them both. I stayed almost a month, but it wasn't good to be away from the business that long. My father was still the president of Sandoval S.A. which later became APS, but it was mostly titular. I made most of the decisions. He encouraged me to stay as long as I wanted, however, his phone calls became progressively more urgent. I finally decided it was time to return to my work. Kathleen wasn't quite ready to return.

"When I returned and realized how dangerous our situation was in Chile, I was gratified she stayed. As the months rolled on, she began to hint that it was time for her to come home, I continued to discourage her and suggested there was no rush. Then the wife of my cousin, Jorge, who worked for Sandoval S.A., disappeared. At first, we thought she may have been kidnapped, however, we never received a demand for ransom. We never found her alive or dead. Jorge, a broken man, later drank himself to death. Shortly after she was kidnapped, I received a phone call with the threat, 'Your American wife is next.'"

"They threatened your family?" asked Maria Isabella incredulously.

"I didn't know what to do. I hoped Kathleen and Pablo would be safe in the United States, but I wasn't sure. By this time, Kathleen was pressing me strenuously to allow her to return to Chile. She said our family needed to be together. I agreed but feared for her safety and the safety of Pablo. I kept encouraging her to stay in the United States longer, but she finally said she was coming home."

"What did you do?"

"I lied to her. I told her I had a mistress, and everyone knew about her. I told her it would be uncomfortable to have both her and my mistress around at the same time."

"That must have been terrible for her. It must have been terrible for both of you."

"It was, but it was the only way I could think of to keep her away and safe."

"Did you ever see her again?"

"No, never. Later, I tried to call her, but her father wouldn't summon her to the phone. Once I called, and she answered. When she recognized me on the phone, she hung up."

"Oh, M*i Amor*, I'm so sorry."

"It was the most difficult time of my life."

"How did you provide for her?"

"I hired an attorney in the United States. I had him set up a trust fund for her and Pablo. It bought a home for her and provided an income. She never asked for anything, but she never refused it either. The attorney kept me informed about anything that happened to her and to Pablo. She died of cancer about five years later. I knew I wouldn't be welcome at the funeral. I did drive to the graveside service. I stayed in the car, and no one saw me."

"What a heart break!"

"Later, I tried to contact Pablo. His grandparents wouldn't allow it. I knew I could force the issue and bring him to Chile, however, people were still disappearing, and I wanted him to be safe. So, working with my attorney, I made sure that all of Pablo's expenses were met. When he graduated from high school, from college and when he received his MBA, I was there. We had abbreviated conversations, but he really never knew me as his father. He didn't even go by the name of Sandoval. In the United States the surname is the last name, so there he is Paul Merrick.

"Here, he is Pablo Sandoval, and everyone knows he is your son. He lost his mother when he was so young, but now he is finally getting to know his father."

"Soon he will lose his father to the same disease."

"Maybe not soon," suggested Maria Isabella. "The doctor said you could have another two years."

"He said it could be as early as six months or as late as two years. That doesn't give me much time to get to know my son. I'd hoped that operation five years ago would have eliminated the cancer in my body."

"We thought it had. We thought they got it all."

"Then it was localized, but now it's everywhere. I don't think I have much time."

"Please don't talk like that. I'll take whatever time I can get. I'm sure that once Pablo knows the whole story, he'll take whatever he can get also."

"I regret that he doesn't want to take over the business."

"How do you know that?"

"He came down to find the ones who killed Janet. I think he will, and I think they are the same ones who are trying to kill me." Then Alonzo snorted in laughter. "Wouldn't that gall the fiends who are trying to kill me if I beat them to the punch by dying of cancer before they can kill me?" He laughed again.

"I don't think that's humorous. I still have hope that you are going to beat this. Why don't you think Pablo would want to take over APS?"

"He's built a strong and successful business of his own in the United States. He is the best at what he does. He plans to return to that business once he's uncovered Janet's killers."

"I hope he can be persuaded to run the Sandoval businesses. He'd be such an example and mentor to Jorge."

Alonzo laughed again. "Jorge has already asked him for a job. He wants to go to the United States and work for

Pablo."

"Now?"

"No." Alonzo laughed. "After he earns his MBA."

Maria Isabella laughed too. "That may be a while. He is only fifteen."

"Almost sixteen," corrected Alonzo, still laughing. "If we had enough time, we could easily get Jorge ready to be president of APS."

"Well, you hang on as long as you can, and perhaps Pablo will take over long enough to get Jorge ready."

They didn't notice Jorge standing just outside the door with his face in his hands.

CHAPTER 18

Alejandro and Vanessa had finally gone to bed. Marcela would have liked to lay down to rest but Orlando was on the bed reading, so she joined Pilar in the living room.

"You look worn out," exclaimed Pilar.

"By the time I get those two live wires to bed, I'm usually worn out."

"Why don't you lie down and rest?" suggested Pilar.

"I was going to, but Orlando is already on the bed reading. I didn't want to interrupt him."

"Then join me, I'd enjoy the company."

"I'm sure there is other company you'd probably rather have. I'm impressed with your friend, Pablo. He is very handsome and appears to be very strong. I can see why you are interested in him."

Pilar countered, "First you want me to have a relationship with the executive vice president of APS, and now you want me to have one with the boss's son. What's with you?"

"That's right, I forgot about the VP. What's happening with him? What's his name again?"

"His name is Carlos Mendocina and nothing personal is happening with him even though he still tries to take me to lunch every chance he gets."

Marcela's eyes widened. "Do you go?"

"Yes," responded Pilar, "about every third time he asks. I make sure we make it a working lunch and only talk business."

"Does Sr. Sandoval know that his executive vice president is pursuing you?" questioned Marcela.

"I think he does and may even be encouraging it. I'm often invited as Carlos' dinner partner when he's invited to the *Estancia*."

"So?"

"So, what?" responded Pilar.

"So why aren't you giving him a chance?"

"Marcela, first, he's not a member of the church. He couldn't take me to the temple if we got married. Second, we work together. I don't think it's healthy to date a coworker. Third, I'm not attracted to him."

"Oh," responded her sister, "but you are attracted to the boss's son."

Pilar protested, "Oh no, are you back to that again? I'm not attracted to him. He's just someone I work with."

Marcela noticed Pilar was blushing again as she had the last time they'd discussed Pablo Sandoval. Pilar had blushed again when she noticed Pablo at church. "I think he is interested in you, too."

"What are you talking about? He isn't interested in me or anyone else. For Heaven's sake, Marcela, the man just lost his wife a year ago. How could he possibly be interested in someone else?"

"Remember Brother Osorio. His wife died, and he was already married again less than a year later. It doesn't take long for a man to become interested again."

"Marcela, I am ashamed of you. Brother Osorio was in a

completely different situation. He had two young children he was trying to care for. Of course, it was important for him to find a new wife. Those children needed a mother."

Marcela grinned as she opined, "I've seen the way Brother Osorio looks at his new bride. I'm sure he is looking at her that way because she takes such good care of his children."

"You are impossible."

"Why be difficult when with a little effort one can be impossible?" Marcela joked. "Besides, I saw the way Pablo Sandoval looked at you. He was delighted to see you."

"He didn't know I was a member of the church. That surprised him," offered Pilar as Marcela again noticed how her sister's face was flushed.

"What is there about him the repulses you so?" Marcela loved the teasing game she'd played with her sister since the two girls were small.

"I said nothing about being repulsed. He just isn't what I want, even if he were available, which he isn't."

"What about him don't you want. He is very handsome, a member of the church and is very rich."

"Only one of those three characteristics is important to me," retorted Pilar.

"So, the fact that he is rich and a member of the church is not important to you," quipped Marcela.

"You know what I meant. Whether he's handsome or rich is of no consequence, only that he is an active member of the church and honors his priesthood. Besides, what I'm interested in is of no importance. It's more why he wouldn't be interested in me."

In all seriousness Marcela exclaimed, "I can't think of a single thing that would cause Pablo Sandoval to not be interested in you, Pilar. You are so loving to Alejandro and

Vanessa. It makes me sad that you don't have children of your own. You are very intelligent and very successful in business. You are attractive and vivacious. Why wouldn't he, or any other man be interested in you?"

Pilar paused for a moment in deep thought then added, "I think the only thing Pablo Sandoval is interested in is finding the killers of his wife."

Marcela considered carefully what Pilar had said. "Then help him."

Startled, Pilar couldn't believe what she was hearing, "What?"

"Help him find his wife's killers," suggested Marcela.

"How would I do that?" questioned Pilar.

"Oooh! Then you are interested in him."

Again, very thoughtfully Pilar offered, "Perhaps I could have been under different circumstances."

"What would those circumstances be?"

"Oh, if he were truly available and if he were Chilean."

"I thought you said he's the son of Alonzo Sandoval. Wouldn't that automatically make him Chilean?"

"I think he does have dual citizenship, but being born a Chilean and being raised a Chilean are two different things. He was raised in the United States."

"What else does he lack?" questioned Marcela.

"His deceased wife will always be first in his life. I always hoped that when I found the man of my dreams, I would be first."

"So, you could never be a second wife?"

"Definitely not to a divorcee."

"Oh, but possibly the second wife to a widower?"

"I didn't say that."

Marcela smiled as she replied, "No, you didn't."

They sat together for a long time without either of the

two sisters saying anything.

Marcela could see a hint of sadness in Pilar's eyes so she repeated, "So, help him."

"Help him do what?"

"Help him find his wife's killers."

Resigned now, Pilar questioned, "And how would I do that?"

"Pilar, you are the most resourceful person I know. You've never come across an obstacle that you couldn't overcome. You'll find a way."

***

Carlos Mendocina visited *La Clínica de Reposo de Las Amapolas de Los Andes* (The Poppies of the Andes Nursing Home) every Sunday and often two or three more times per week to visit with his mother, Maria Luiza Mendocina Pena. She resided in the one wing devoted to those suffering from senility of one form or another. It was located close to hospitals and her medical doctors in Providencia. With the excellent care provided by the staff, there was really no reason to leave for medical care. Her personal doctor often stopped by to visit with her in her room.

He would have preferred to have her stay in her own home. However, it seemed to be impossible to have her monitored twenty-four hours per day. Various full-time care takers had taken their turns caring for her until, even with their care, she'd wandered off. With the help of the police, they were able to find her in just two hours. Realizing she needed to be institutionalized, Carlos began a search for a proper nursing home.

One day at work, he happened to mention to his associate, Pilar Flores, that he was searching for a nursing home for his mother. Pilar had asked a few questions and a few days later, she handed him a brochure from *Las*

Amapolas. He'd not even considered this particular nursing home because of its reputation for being very expensive.

At Pilar's urging, he'd visited only to discover they were expecting him. The manager showed Carlos around the facilities and introduced him to many of the nurses and caretakers. He was very pleased and impressed.

When Carlos asked about the cost, the manager assured him that there would be no cost to him as the entire bill for his mother would be completely covered by APS. Carlos wondered if Pilar had made the arrangements. He didn't wonder who was paying the bill; that was obviously Alonzo Sandoval.

Maria Luiza Mendocina was still a beautiful woman, about five feet six inches, maybe a hundred and twenty pounds with thick, curly hair, which the nurses kept short because it was easier to manage. Physically, she was in excellent health, although her mind was only occasionally lucid. She had only one relative, besides Carlos, a brother who lived in North Chile. She'd always been a deep thinker, however, in the last few years, she often drifted into memories of the past.

Every Sunday, Carlos brought his mother fresh flowers and her favorite chocolate candy. At first, Maria Luiza greeted her son and let him know how pleased she was that he visited her. During the past year, however, she seemed to remember that he brought her flowers and candy, but she wasn't sure who he was. Occasionally, she called him by his own name. As often as not, she called him by the name of her brother. Sometimes she called him Joaquin. Carlos assumed that Joaquin was someone from his mother's past. He couldn't remember her mentioning that name as he was growing up.

When Carlos was young, and his friends all had fathers,

he'd often ask about his father. She had said his father had been a wonderful man, and he was dead. No matter how much he asked, she never answered any specific questions, and she always changed the subject. She'd never developed relationships with any other man. Carlos longed to have a father. He often daydreamed that his father would return from somewhere and surprise them.

When Carlos was old enough to understand adult relationships, he began to wonder who his father was. He'd been given the same surnames as his mother, so he wasn't carrying the name of his father. That must have meant that his mother and father were not married.

He suspected that perhaps his mother had had an affair, and he was the result. Perhaps his real father wasn't dead. Perhaps he couldn't marry Maria Luiza for some reason. The more he was tortured with the desire to know his father, the less she talked about it.

When Carlos discovered that the income that Maria Luiza received every month came from Alonzo Sandoval, he began to suspect that Sr. Sandoval was his father. He could find no actual proof, but he became convinced of that fact, especially when Alonzo Sandoval paid for Carlos' education, even the private schools of his youth. Perhaps Alonzo Sandoval felt a responsibility to provide for Maria Luiza and Carlos Mendocina. On each of his visits with his mother, Carlos tried to get her to talk about her past. Because she was often locked in the past, it wasn't difficult, and yet he still received no information that was truly useful. He thought he'd try again today.

As Carlos entered the front doors of *La Clínica,* he was greeted by the front desk clerk. "Señor Carlos, how pleasant to see you again. Your mother will be so happy you have come."

"Well, Osman, I'm sure she'll be happy, but will she be happy to see me or the flowers and candy?" he joked.

With and an exasperated expression, he replied, "I'm not sure, Señor Carlos. Oh, I'm sure it's you she is happy to see," he conceded. They both knew it was the flowers and candy.

"How is my mother today, Osman?"

"About the same," he replied. "Oh, here comes her nurse, let's ask her."

"Miriana," greeted Carlos. "You seem enthusiastic today. How is your family?" Carlo was very personable with the workers of the nursing home, both because it was his nature, and because he felt his mother would receive better care that way.

After exchanging personal greetings, Nurse Miriana responded, "She's about the same, Carlos. Right now, the movie she's been watching on the television is ending so you are arriving at exactly the right time." Then, almost wistfully she added, "I wish all of my patients had such diligent sons." Carlos smiled as he started down the hall towards his mother's room.

His mother suddenly smiled as she saw Carlos enter the room carrying flowers and candy. "Oh, Joaquin, I knew you'd come today."

He handed his mother the candy and replaced the old flowers in the vase with the new ones he brought. He tried to engage her in conversation that would give him more information on the identity of Joaquin, but she showed no recognition of that name when he repeated it. *Maybe she's using that name because it is my middle name. That doesn't make sense as she never called me that when she was coherent.*

Then he mentioned the name of Alonzo Sandoval to see if he could get any reaction from her. She gushed, "Oh Alonzo Sandoval, what a wonderful human being. He takes such good care of me." Then her mind seemed to suddenly go someplace else. Carlos knew this would be another visit in which he would get no helpful information. He stayed a little while longer, but she seemed to have lost interest in his presence. With more than a little sadness, he silently slipped out without her even noticing.

CHAPTER 19

Even though Miguel had assured them the pickup truck that crashed through the gate on Sunday had been an accident, Paul still wasn't convinced. Considering that breach of security and the information he was most eager to share with the FBI, he hadn't thought much about Janet, which allowed him to sleep.

He'd gone to sleep thinking he would immediately go to the FBI office and provide them with the names of those who had run him and Janet off the road in Idaho. Since awakening, Paul was haunted by the fear in Luiz Rossi's eyes. If he shared with the FBI the names of the Contreras brothers, special agent Riquelme would want to know where he obtained that information. That information would probably be shared with the *Carabineros.* They'd probably want to interrogate Rossi themselves. The more people who went to Rossi's establishment, the more danger he and his little girl would be in. Paul decided to try a different tack.

As he expected, when Paul left his apartment on Monday morning, the door across the hall immediately opened and Miguel Ortega appeared. "May I drive you somewhere this morning?" he offered.

"Possibly," Paul replied, "but first I want to ask for some

help."

"Certainly, how can I help you?"

"If I give you a telephone number, do you have any way to provide an address for that number?"

***

Riding to the APS offices, Paul decided he wanted more information. "Miguel, is there any reason to believe that the incident at the *Estancia* yesterday was also connected to the other incidents in the APS companies or the attacks on my father?"

"Paul, we don't even know if all the other incidents are connected."

"Until we have proof they're not, we need to treat them as if they are. That being said, I'd prefer that we treat the incident at the *Estancia* yesterday as if it were also connected."

"I don't see how it could be," replied Miguel. "The placement of that particular guard house is directly across Avenida Bosque from Avenida Mendoza. People who aren't familiar with Avenida Mendoza often travel too fast not realizing that it ends with a T at Avenida Bosque. We've had incidents before in which a vehicle traveling too fast can't make the turn onto Avenida Bosque and ends up going through the fence or the gate into the Estancia."

"So, it's happened before?" Paul questioned.

"A couple of times."

"Miguel, tell me about the connection between Red Security and the Sandoval businesses."

Miguel explained that previously not all APS businesses used the internal Red Security Service. Many of them had no security at all until recently. Those that had security often hired whatever local service was available, and most of those security people had no prior training. They were often men working a second job to support their family. They'd work a regular job during the day, get a few hours of sleep and then put on a security uniform and do another shift sitting in a guard house or taking walks through the business building at night."

"So, they're not trained security guards?"

"They weren't. Some were former police officers or off-duty police officers. However, for the most part, they were regular people trying to earn some additional income. They had no training whatsoever."

"Has that changed?"

"Yes, we've put all the security work for all APS businesses under the direction of our own Red Security. Red Security has made it a policy to hire only those with previous military or police experience."

Paul thought to himself, "*red*" in Spanish means net so Red Security means Security Net. He smiled at the pun. "Who's in charge of Red Security Services?"

"His name is Julio Batley. His office is located in the same building as yours."

Paul had a confused look on his face. "Batley?" he questioned. "That doesn't sound like a Chilean name."

"How should Chilean names sound?" Miguel sounded displeased.

Paul replaced his look of confusion with one of embarrassment. "Chile is a Latin country, and I guess I expected names of Spanish origin."

"Many of the early settlers of Chile came from countries other than Spain. Remember, one of the founding fathers of Chile was Bernardo O'Higgins. Batley is another non-Spanish name that goes way back."

"I apologize, I must be more open-minded. Could you

please introduce me to Sr. Batley when we get back to the office?"

Miguel didn't refuse but made it clear that he would be much more comfortable with the situation if Paul had Carlos Mendocina introduce them.

Paul's next stop was the Sandoval Building. He buzzed Pilar on the intercom and in less than a minute she entered his office.

"It was pleasant meeting your family yesterday," began Paul.

Pilar paused a moment before answering. "Thank you. How may I help you?" Pilar's response was terse and professional. Paul surmised she wanted to keep family talk out of the office.

Feeling somewhat chastened, Paul asked, "Can you tell me anything about Julio Batley?"

"Well, he's the director of Red Security. He came to us after retiring from the *Carabineros*. Other than that, I don't really know much about him," she politely replied.

"Do you know how long he's been the director?"

"He hasn't been here long, less than two years."

"I'm going to need information from him, do you know him well enough to introduce us?"

"I've been in meetings in which he was an attendee, but we really don't know each other. I suggest that you have Carlos introduce you. He's the one who brought Sr. Batley to APS."

"Thanks, can you see when Carlos would have time to talk to me."

Immediately, Pilar started from Paul's office. On the way out the door, she said over her shoulder, "I'll check on that immediately."

Paul didn't even have time to boot his computer before

Carlos entered his office.

"Good morning Pablo," began Carlos. "I wasn't expecting you in the office this morning. Pilar said you wanted to talk to me."

Paul was a little surprised that he wasn't expected. With an assignment from the president of APS, research was required. Paul wondered why Carlos wouldn't think he'd be in the office to do that. Perhaps Carlos thought it a token job to provide Paul with income without doing any work.

"If I am to make progress on the assignment given me by Sr. Sandoval, I'll probably need to spend a great deal of time here in the office."

There was just a twitch of apprehension in Carlos' face, however, he quickly recovered. "How can I help you?"

"I wondered if you could introduce me to Julio Batley of Security. I'm going to need information that he can probably supply."

Carlos frowned a bit as he asked, "How can Security provide information regarding the profitability issues with APS?"

Paul wondered if Carlos had forgotten their previous conversation. "The fact that many operations have been sabotaged and numerous people have been threatened could easily affect profitability."

Without acknowledging Paul's comment, Carlos asked, "When do you want to meet Sr. Batley?"

"Now would be great."

The command center for Red Security was on the bottom floor of the Sandoval building. The walls of Sr. Batley's large personal office were lined with large screen monitors allowing Julio Batley to peruse activities in many locations at the click of a switch. The outer office contained many additional monitors and was staffed with three uniformed men with work stations for three more. Red Security offices were filled with cutting-edge equipment and was built for work not show.

Julio Batley was a physically small man and the magnitude of his office made him appear smaller. Paul wondered if the *Carabineros* had a height and weight requirement. If it did, Julio Batley would have just barely qualified for either of them. There was no hint of a smile on his narrow face. He had dark hair with just a hint of grey. He didn't appear to be old enough to have retired, as Pilar had mentioned. His manner was "no nonsense" and full attention to detail. It was obvious in the way he responded to Carlos Mendocina that Sr. Batley considered him his file leader.

"Julio, I'd like to introduce Paul Merrick. He's here in Chile from the United States. Sr. Sandoval hired him to do an efficiency evaluation of APS. You've probably received the memo I sent to all heads of APS companies instructing them to provide Sr. Merrick with anything he needs to help us become more profitable."

Paul was startled to be introduced as Paul Merrick, having just been called Pablo a few minutes previously. He wondered if Alonzo Sandoval and Carlos Mendocina had made a decision to withhold the information that he was the son of the president and principal owner of APS. The next time he talked to his father, he'd ask. He'd already decided to be careful not to use his relationship with Alonzo Sandoval as a weapon to promote cooperation.

Paul also noticed that Carlos had given Julio instructions to provide him with any information that would increase profitability. It was definitely not carte blanche for all information Paul might want. Paul wondered who'd make the decision whether information given would increase profitability or not.

"Paul, this is Julio Batley, Director of Red Security. After completing a distinguished career with the *Carabineros*, Sr. Batley willingly took over command of Security. We were very lucky to find him."

Paul and Julio Batley shook hands and studied each other as Carlos excused himself and left the two men together.

"How can I best serve you?" questioned Director Batley with no hint of warmth.

"I've been informed that many of the APS companies have experienced incidents that could be construed as sabotage. Are you acquainted with those incidents?" asked Paul.

"Yes, Red Security has done a complete investigation," replied Director Batley curtly.

"I'd like to know the details of each of those incidents."

Julio Batley's eyes squinted just slightly as Paul made his request. He allowed just a small furrow in his brow as he asked, "And how do these incidents affect profitability, Sr. Merrick?"

Paul wasn't surprised at the question. Given the introduction Carlos had given and considering the memo Carlos had sent, it almost seemed that he was restricting the information Paul should receive to business practices rather than security questions.

"When consulting with businesses, I find it helpful to learn about any problems that affect it. Anything at all that could modify a leader's or an employee's confidence or attitude could very easily influence profitability."

Julio was still frowning almost imperceptibly. "Exactly which incidents do you want to hear about, Sr. Merrick?"

"To complete a thorough study, I'll need a complete

report on every incident that might be construed as sabotage."

"That may be very difficult, Sr. Merrick. Only lately have we begun to connect the incidents in all APS companies. When a tire goes flat on a truck owned by a Sandoval company, Red Security doesn't get a report unless that tire was purposely damaged. Unless an incident was deemed to have been caused by someone, we wouldn't necessarily have a report on it."

"You have begun to connect these incidents between the various companies?" asked Paul.

"Only lately," replied Director Batley. "Most of the companies were solving their problems internally. Even the elevator falling was, at first, considered to be faulty equipment not sabotage."

"What about employees receiving threats?" questioned Paul.

"Again, only lately was Red brought in to try to keep employees safe."

"Do you have a file on each case of an employee being threatened?"

"Yes, on those reported to us. There could be cases of an employee being threatened and not reporting it."

"I'd like to see every file of every act that could be construed as sabotage and every file where an employee or family member of an employee of an APS company has been threatened."

"I don't understand, Señor. Are you a security expert? Do you have police or investigative training? Do you think you are better equipped to look at acts of sabotage on this company than my security officers who have had years of training? I assure you, Señor, that my people are perfectly qualified to do what investigating needs to be done. It is my understanding that your contract calls for you to find ways to increase profitability, not solve crimes."

Paul hoped he could persuade Director Batley to be cooperative without having to call in the big guns. He realized that Julio Batley had an empire to protect, and no one wants his business scrutinized from outside, but Paul knew that there was a reason for these acts of sabotage and threats. He also suspected that even the death of his wife might well be connected. He wasn't going to let any empire builder keep him from the information he needed.

"I assure you, Sr. Batley, if we could suddenly put a stop to these acts of sabotage and to these threats to Sandoval leaders, employees and family members, the profitability of APS would decidedly increase. I need to see the report on every incident that could possibly be construed as sabotage. I need to see every report on every person who has been threatened."

Julio Batley wasn't happy, but he agreed to have the requested reports prepared for Paul promptly. Paul wondered what 'promptly' meant to Director Batley.

"Finally," Paul concluded, "I need a complete report on the incident that took place at security gate 4 at the Sandoval *Estancia* yesterday."

Paul realized that Director Julio Batley was close to the boiling point.

"You want what?" questioned Director Batley.

Paul reiterated his request for a report on the pickup truck running through security gate at the Sandoval *Estancia* the previous day.

"May I remind you that your contract is to improve profitability, not delve into that which is not your concern."

"Oh, it is definitely my concern. Can I expect a copy of these reports on my desk by the end of the day?"

"As I said," Julio Batley replied sullenly, "your reports will be provided promptly."

Then Julio Batley looked at Paul without the hint of a smile of friendship and asked, "How is getting you the address for this telephone number going to help the profitability of APS?" Without waiting for an answer, he handed Paul the paper which Paul had given to Miguel with the phone number on it, turned and walked away.

CHAPTER 20

"How much time do you think it will take Julio Batley to get me the reports I asked for?" wondered Paul out loud.

"What reports?" asked Pilar.

"I asked him for all the incidents in APS companies that could possibly be construed as acts of sabotage," replied Paul.

"Oh, is that all?"

"No, I also asked him for completed reports on any employee or family member of an APS employee who has been threatened."

"Wow! Is that all?"

Quizzically, Paul responded, "Yes, why do you ask?"

Pilar let out a deep breath as she answered. "I've received a copy of the memo Carlos sent to the directors and the chief executive officers of the APS companies. It explains that you've been hired to do an efficiency analysis of APS and its many companies. They're instructed to supply you with any information needed to improve the profitability within APS companies. The reports you have requested from Julio Batley relate only to security issues and not specifically to profitability."

Paul let Pilar's explanation sink into his head before

responding. "I think I see what you are getting at. In my mind, I'm here to track down the men who killed my wife. Carlos, and the leaders of APS see me in a completely different capacity. Because of the bombing of my father's car in Idaho, I quickly tied the sabotage issues with my wife's murder and forgot about everything else."

Pilar hesitated before taking the next step. "I've studied your work in revitalizing struggling companies in the United States. You're not using the methods here you've used in the past."

Chagrinned, Paul admitted that he'd not applied the same commitment to working with APS that he had taken previously with other companies.

"Do you plan to address the profitability issues in APS?" she asked.

"Yes," answered Paul pensively, "however, that commitment must not compromise the primary purpose for my being here."

When she asked, "How can I help?" she was reminded of the counsel her sister, Marcela, had given her.

"When I take on a huge company like APS, I usually bring with me a team from my own company. The problems in the APS companies require a team effort. It's too much for one person."

"I believe Sr. Sandoval would expect you to apply the same measures here that you have applied in similar situations in the past. Cost is not an issue."

"I haven't experienced similar situations in the past. I've never seen a company so blatantly targeted and sabotaged as I see here. Perhaps that is even more reason to assemble a team."

"Do you have a team available?"

"If we were in the United States, I know exactly which

people I would want with me. However, they're all busy on other projects, and very few of them are bilingual." Paul's mind raced toward assembling an effective team of cohorts. "We'll have to make do with whatever team we can assemble here."

Pilar was taking notes as she asked, "What do you need in a team?"

Paul pulled some folders out of his case and opened them on his desk. "We need an accountant who specializes in audits, maybe even two. We need someone with a management degree with a keen eye for efficiency, even better if this person has great leadership skills. We'll need an engineer, perhaps a mechanical engineer." Then he added in English, "And we could use an attorney and two or three gofers."

Pilar took the bait and asked, "What is a gofer?"

He grinned as he answered, "A person who will go for this and go for that."

She too grinned as she reverted to Spanish again. "Do you want these to be inside people or outside people?"

"I'm afraid that if we only use people from inside Sandoval, their loyalty could be tested as we dig deeply."

After adding to her notes, Pilar looked up and said, "One more question. Do you want me to contract these people from a local consulting firm or do you want to build a team from scratch?"

Paul had subcontracted work to other consulting firms in the past, some with great results, some with not so good. "I'm leaning toward subcontracting to a local consulting firm. What do you think?"

"I have some personal contacts with the skills you want. Some of them are out of work right now or are trying to upgrade. I know an accountant and an engineer, both of whom would love being on a team like this. The "gofers" will be easy to find," she kidded.

"What about a team leader?" Paul asked. She didn't answer, and finally he asked what both of them were thinking. "Do you suppose my father will let me have you full time for this project."

"I've already asked, and he approved. I'm all yours." Then she blushed and stammered, "I mean, he said I could devote full time to this project until it is complete."

"Well, then?"

He smiled as she suggested, "Well, then, let's get started."

"First, I need some background on Chilean history. Who would you recommend for that?"

Again, she blushed and then quickly replied, "My undergraduate minor was Chilean history, what do you want to know?"

"You'd be perfect, and it's time for lunch. Would you mind giving me my history lesson over lunch. I'm buying."

"Your father would never want you spending a penny of your own money while you are in Chile. If you mean you're paying with the credit card he supplied, I'm all for that."

Miguel drove the two of them to a well-known steak house near Plaza de Armas in the center of Santiago where they took an elevator to the third floor. When they discovered there would be a wait of forty-five minutes before they could be seated, Pilar suggested, "I know a small restaurant near here with excellent food where we probably won't have to wait."

"Good suggestion. Will we need to take the car?"

"No, it's just a couple blocks away."

Paul dismissed Miguel and told him he'd call when they

were ready to return to the office.

The restaurant was crowded but they were seated immediately. On the wall behind the counter, Paul noticed big pictures of each of the main courses available. The waiter handed each of them a menu. Paul noticed his was in English. He looked at it and then at Pilar. "Is it that obvious?"

She laughed as she suggested, "You don't look like a typical Chilean. Do you want a menu in Spanish?"

"Nah, this will do. If I have a question, I'll look at yours."

He looked at his menu carefully comparing it to the pictures on the wall. He noticed that one of the dishes looked like a steak with a fried egg on top. He tried comparing it to his menu and couldn't make any sense of it, so he asked Pilar.

She solved the mystery for him by instructing, "That's *bistec a lo pobre,* meaning a steak with a fried egg on top. You can order many dishes with an egg."

"That means 'to the poor' doesn't it?"

"Yes, but I'd probably write it 'the poor man's steak.'"

Paul looked at his menu, in English, found the comparable dish and began laughing.

"What's so funny?" she asked.

"On my menu, it is called a 'steak to the poor thing.'" They both started laughing as they found a number of dishes listed on the menu "to the poor thing."

Then they started comparing the Spanish and English versions of the menu. "The English menu must have been translated by a computer. No one knowing both languages would ever write some of this stuff." Paul laughed. "What does this mean, 'with attaché?'"

She compared it to her menu and again began laughing.

"That must mean it has a side dish." They spent the next twenty minutes comparing the menus and laughing at the terrible translations. When they noticed the waiters glaring at them, it only caused them to laugh harder.

"We better order something before they ask us to leave," he suggested.

"What are you going to have?"

"I think I'll have the steak 'to the poor thing.'" They both laughed as Paul signaled for the waiter to take their order.

As they waited for their food to arrive, Paul looked at Pilar and saw her in a light he hadn't seen before. "Pilar, you are good for me. I haven't laughed like this in over a year. In truth, I can't remember laughing once in that time."

"It makes me happy to see you laugh, Pablo. Spending all this time and energy trying to make sure the men who killed your wife receive justice has probably taken its toll on you."

"I'm sure that is a fact, but I am committed to making sure they receive their just rewards."

"Would you mind telling me about her, Pablo?"

"You want to hear about Janet?" He was surprised.

"If you don't mind."

"No, I don't mind." While they waited for the waiter to return with their meal Paul told Pilar about Janet and his life with her. They paused to laugh again when their meals arrived and his steak had a fried egg on top.

Pilar listened attentively while they ate as Paul talked about Janet. She thought, *I always dreamed that a man would love me as Pablo loved Janet.*

Her thoughts were interrupted by Paul stating, "We have talked about me long enough. It's been very therapeutic for me. Now it's time for me to learn more about you."

Pilar's face flushed a little as she responded, "What's to learn? I've already told you all there is to know."

"You have only told me about going to school and coming to work for APS. I really don't know anything about you personally."

Pilar didn't know how to respond. She was very skilled at getting people to tell about themselves. She made them comfortable, and she was a good listener, but talking about herself was difficult. "What do you want to know?"

"Pilar, I feel like I want to know everything. First, tell me about your family."

Pilar explained how she was raised with one sister and one brother. She told how her brother left home to serve a mission, attend school and then started his own family. Her eyes lit up as she told about her parents, Freya Donoso and Fernando Flores. He could see the worry she felt for her father, whose health was failing. She also worried that he seemed to always have a reason to stay home from church. She brightened again and became especially animated as she talked of her sister, Marcela, and her family. Paul could see the love in her eyes for her niece, Vanessa, and her nephew, Alejandro.

Paul really enjoyed the story of Pilar's family. He noticed then, even though he'd asked her to tell about herself, she talked about her family. "How did your family become members of the church?"

"That was my mother. She was walking towards the grocery store when she met a woman coming the other direction carrying too many bags of groceries. The woman had just passed when my mother heard her fall. She turned to find the woman on the sidewalk and her groceries spread all over. She was bleeding from her nose and seemed to be in much pain.

"My mother helped get her seated on the ground, propped up next to a fence. She was wondering how she would help this woman get to her feet and help her get home when two young men wearing white shirts and ties came running up. They knew the woman, as she was a member of their branch. The missionaries helped get the woman to her feet. They carried the groceries, and my mother supported the woman to get her to her home.

"After they arrived at the woman's home and got her settled, the missionaries introduced themselves to my mother. The rest, as they say, is history. She invited them to our home, where they taught my mother and father. My mother was converted immediately. My father took longer. She was baptized soon thereafter, and my father was baptized about two years later.

"That was before Sergio, Marcela and I were born. We were very blessed to be born and raised in the church."

"Have you always been in the same ward with Claudia and Vicente Troncoso?"

"Yes, the Troncosos befriended my parents when they first started attending church. *Hermano* Troncoso was instrumental in getting my father to join the church. He has had a great influence on our lives. Didn't you say he was also a good friend of your father?"

"Apparently, he was. They were baptized the same day."

"Your father is a Mormon?"

"He is or he was. I don't know now. I really don't know much about him. I didn't want to know until now. Now there seems to be a deep yearning to really get to know him."

The conversation continued as Paul looked at Pilar through new eyes. Very few people could put him at ease and make it comfortable enough to discuss intimate details of his life. He had shared those details with Pilar, and he was eager to learn about her. He was surprised that he still could carry on such a conversation. It had been so long. He looked at his watch and was surprised they had been visiting for more than two hours.

CHAPTER 21

Exiting the restaurant, they found Miguel leaning on the front fender of the SUV. Paul turned to Pilar and asked, "How far are we from the office?"

"Too far to walk. Why, do you feel like walking?"

"I do if you do. I still haven't had my history lesson."

"Miguel will be happy to wait for us."

He approached Miguel and told of their plans to walk for a while. He saw the faintest glimpse of a smile or a smirk. Miguel didn't say anything. He got in the SUV and drove away. Paul and Pilar both laughed, knowing he would return when they called him.

As they began, to walk Pilar asked, "Now, what do you want to know about Chilean history?"

"The other day, I guess it was yesterday, time is passing so quickly. Yesterday, in church, a woman said she knew my mother. She said she was sad to see her return to the United States, but it was dangerous for her here then. Do you know what that means?"

"You must have talked to Albina Jimenez. I don't know what she would have known about that time. She likes to think she knows everything about every subject. Let's see, when did your mother return to the United States?"

"That would have been a couple of months before I was born. That was early 1973."

"Yes, 1973 was a very difficult time in Chile. That was the year that Salvador Allende was removed from office. He was a Marxist physician who had been elected president in 1970. He won on a platform of nationalization of U.S. interests of many of the major copper mines as well as aggressive socialized government. The United States wasn't happy and tried to keep him out of office and later issued a number of financial sanctions against Chile. That caused many Chileans to be very unhappy with North Americans."

Paul asked, "Was it serious enough that an American woman living in Chile would have been at risk?"

"I don't know how dangerous it was for her personally. She was the wife of a very influential and wealthy Chilean. Many Chileans were angry with the rich and with the Americans. She was both."

"How bad did it get?"

"During his first year in office, the changes brought on by Allende improved the economy and the way of life for most Chileans. Inflation was lower and unemployment was low. Almost everyone was working. Then, in the second year of office, things began to deteriorate very rapidly. Production fell under his socialist programs and inflation skyrocketed. Because of high inflation and government induced price fixing, basic staples were no longer available on the supermarket shelves. Basic items like bread, milk and rice could only be found on the black market and then only after standing in long lines. It was not uncommon for a mother to stand in line for hours just to buy some bread for her family."

"That must have been horrible. Who did the people blame?" asked Paul.

"Some blamed Allende and his government while others blamed the Americans. By 1973, Chilean society was highly polarized. That polarization was so strong that violent, armed clashes began to take place."

"So, maybe that is what Albina Jimenez was talking about."

"Probably. I wouldn't have wanted to be known as a supporter of Allende or of the United States then. It was a dangerous period."

"How did Allende's programs affect APS?" asked Paul.

"When I was learning about this in school, I didn't relate it to Sandoval, but APS owns banks and mines, two of the industries that were nationalized by Allende."

"So, the Sandoval family lost some of their businesses then?"

"I'm not sure. Possibly."

"My father could easily have been involved with those who opposed Allende then?"

"He probably was."

"Another thing I remember *Hermana* Jimenez saying is that some thought my father had stolen businesses from others. Do you know anything about that?"

Thinking of *Hermana* Jimenez, Pilar rolled her eyes before answering. "No, I don't. Later in 1973, September 11 in fact … "

"September 11?" questioned Paul.

"Yes, Chileans have their special September 11 date too, two of them," replied Pilar.

"Two of them?"

"Yes, the first was back in the 1500s, when Ínez de Suarez led a defense against the indigenous people in the new community of Santiago.

"Where do you suppose that defense of Santiago took place?" queried Paul.

"I'm not sure, but it may have been right close to where we are, here in the Plaza de Armas."

Paul was wide-eyed as they circled around the plaza. Suddenly, he stopped and exclaimed, "Look," as he pointed to a glass-covered building. On the side of the of the modern building was reflected a large old church. He turned a little so he could gaze directly at the church. "What is that church?"

"It is the Metropolitan Cathedral, the church of the archbishop."

"I am amazed that a building that old could maintain its relevance in the midst of all these modern buildings. That is true tenacity."

"Do you want to walk through it?"

"Yes, I do, but let's hold that for our next history lesson. Now, what was your second September 11th historical event?" quizzed Paul.

"The second was in 1973, when a coup removed Allende from office."

"How did his removal affect Chile?" asked Paul.

"That depends on whom you ask. Even today, many socialists believe that Allende was on the right track. They think he didn't have enough time to prove socialism to be successful. The other side believes that Augusto Pinochet was the savior of the Chilean economy. He replaced the socialist, Allende, with a military dictatorship. Under that dictatorship, the economy of Chile improved and strengthened."

"Back to my question of my father stealing a business from others. Do you know anything about that?"

"Not specifically, no. There were complaints that those with big money, who supported Pinochet, ended up with more property and more businesses than they had before nationalization."

"*Hermana* Jimenez mentioned that my father may have taken a company from someone else. Carlos said he was warned that if Sandoval didn't return what was rightfully theirs, he would be next. Could that business *Hermana* Jimenez mentioned be the same thing mentioned in Carlos' warning?"

"I'm not exactly sure what you mean," suggested Pilar.

"Is it possible that my father took a company or a business that should have gone to someone else? Could this be what is causing the threats and sabotage today?"

Pilar responded, "I don't know but it reminds me of a conversation I had with Carlos. He said he has discovered a secret organization, I think he called it *Tierras Restauradas* (Restored Lands), whose purpose is to help people retrieve lands or property. They claim to not only help people who lost their property during the time of Pinochet but properties lost all the way back to the beginnings of Chile when land was taken from the Mapuche and given to Spaniards who helped in the conquest."

Paul looked quizzical, "The Mapuche?"

"They were indigenous tribes who inhabited southern Chile before the conquest."

Paul couldn't believe the Mapuche expected to get their lands back after almost five hundred years. "How is *Tierras Restauradas* planning to return lands to displaced people?"

Pilar answered, "According to Carlos, it uses terror tactics to force present-day owners to return the property."

"Like the sabotage being carried out on our companies?"

"Not just APS but, yes, that's a possibility."

"Why didn't Carlos tell me about it when we were discussing the sabotage?"

"I don't know for sure, Pablo. Perhaps he didn't yet know, or perhaps he feels displaced by you. Perhaps he is eager to solve this serious problem himself rather than have you do it," replied Pilar sheepishly.

***

Paul and Pilar found a guest waiting for him when they returned to the office. The receptionist had told him that she didn't know what time they would be back. He had chosen to wait. He was an unassuming man of about fifty with a paunch belly and short, greying hair even though there was very little of that. She didn't know whom he represented.

With a quizzical look, Paul shook his guest's hand asking, "How may I help you?"

The guest shook with a firm grip and replied, "I am Nelson Retamal, I'm hoping I can help you. Roland Williams called me from Los Angeles, California and asked that I look you up."

Recognizing the name, Roland Williams, as his case worker with Rodriguez Investigative Services, Paul pointed towards his office and suggested they visit there.

Nelson Retamal didn't object but with a nod of his head towards the elevator, suggested they visit elsewhere. Paul smiled as the two of them descended and walked out of the front doors.

When they were outside and out of earshot, Paul asked, "How can I be sure you're who you say you are?"

Nelson reviewed with Paul a few of the facts from his case and the reason that Rodriguez Investigative Services had been retained. When Paul had sufficient information to be assured of Retamal's legitimacy, he suggested they enter a coffee shop off the local hotel.

"What's this all about?" questioned Paul.

"Roland Williams was contacted by your partner, Jeff Harkin, who is worried about you. He thinks you may suspect that your cell phone and or your email is being monitored. Knowing that we have a presence here in Chile, he asked if we could contact you and offer you some solutions."

Paul smiled to learn about Jeff's concerns. He'd been worried about those exact possibilities when he had visited with Jeff on the phone Sunday, but he'd been careful not to mention those concerns because of the possibility of being monitored. He was pleased Jeff had picked up on his concerns. "So, what do you suggest?"

"It's up to you. We can either provide you with a separate cell phone to use when you want to make an unmonitored call, or we could supply you with a separate SIM card that you could insert in the phone you have."

"Which would be better?"

"Either could be better in different circumstances. Who do you think might be eavesdropping?"

"I don't really know, and they probably aren't, but I don't want to risk anyone's life just because I don't know. It could be an external group, it could be Red Security or it could be the Chilean government. I guess I'm probably paranoid."

"Having looked over your case and realizing what you are trying to do, it's probably best to be paranoid. You can't be too careful."

"Having two phones would be a little bulky and easy to get confused."

"You could get confused either way but there would be less chances of people knowing you had a second method of communicating with a separate SIM card. It is small and easy to conceal. It works on any cell phone." Nelson Retamal slid Paul a new SIM card.

"I've already put my personal cell phone number on that card so you can call me directly, any time day or night, if you need me."

"Thanks. What about the email?" Paul asked.

"Email is very easy to monitor if the people doing the monitoring know what they are doing." Nelson slid Paul another sheet of paper with a new email address and access code written on it. "After you memorize this information, get rid of the sheet of paper. There is no reason to be secretive with your email account, and then supply the information to the people monitoring you. Don't use this email account from any company computer, including the laptop they provided."

"How do I access the email account then?"

"If you've walked around town at all you should've noticed little internet shops. They have booths containing computers. You pay a few hundred pesos and use their computers to access your account. Spread your business around, just in case you're being followed. It won't take them long to figure out what you're doing if you use the same shop too often. Paul, I'm available anytime. If you get in a difficult situation, call me immediately or have someone you trust call me."

"I have a couple of people that I trust. Let me give you their names so you can help if they contact you."

"That will be great."

Since Director Batley wasn't going to help him get the address associated with the telephone number given him by Luiz Rossi, Paul decided to try the Rodriguez Investigative Services. "One last thing," suggested Paul. "I have a phone number which I believe connects to the two men who ran us off the road in Idaho and killed my wife. Can you trace that number and find out to whom it connects and the address?"

"How did you get that?"

"I'd rather not say. I don't want to put his life or the life of family members at risk."

Nelson thought for moment before answering. "I think we can do that."

"I suspect the two men who killed my wife may have also set the bomb that blew up my father's car. The Chilean government may not want to extradite on the first offense. Perhaps they would on the second, unless we can pin something more compulsive on them here in Chile. So, once we find these two men, we want any evidence that can connect them to either the bombing there or something similar here in Chile."

Nelson Retamal smiled because he knew he had just contracted himself a much bigger job and, therefore, a bigger paycheck than he had previously anticipated.

"Another thing," Paul corrected himself. "I'd like you to take down a list of people and check them out for me."

"I can do that," replied Nelson. "Is there anything I am looking for?"

"I want you to look for any grievance they may have with APS or with my father individually."

"Good. Let's meet again in a few days and see what we've uncovered."

"I hope we will have uncovered some rats," Paul replied.

CHAPTER 22

Pedro Velasquez parked his rented Honda on a side street near the *Restaurante Doña Inez* and walked the half block to the entrance. There was a ten-foot, metal fence around the exterior with a large, metal gate in front, which was open. The entrance was unlocked, even though the restaurant was closed. Pedro entered cautiously passing a bartender dressed in black who was preparing for the crowds that would arrive later.

"We are closed, Señor," exclaimed the bartender. "We'll open for dinner at 8:00 PM." Pedro looked at his watch and knew the restaurant was closed, but he'd been summoned, something which made him very uncomfortable. He'd been told to walk all the way to the back of the dining hall and take a seat at one of the tables and wait.

"I am here to meet Juan Opazo. He's expecting me."

The bartender raised his eyebrows slightly but said nothing as he continued to polish the glasses.

Pedro was nervous meeting Juan Opazo. He'd been associated with *Tierras Restauradas* for a couple of years, but he'd never met any of the leaders. He'd been instructed to never go by his own name nor to ask anyone else for theirs.

Each cell was assigned specific businesses or wealthy

families to terrorize.

According to *Tierras Restauradas*, businesses and properties had been stolen from the poor and given to the rich from the earliest days in Chile. Except for the rich and powerful, property could be in danger of confiscation. Law suits and redress from the government had also been unsuccessful. One needed money to gain property and to keep it. Pedro had been told that after centuries of trying law abiding tactics to get properties returned to their rightful owners, the leaders of *Tierras Restauradas* turned to more persuasive tactics.

Tierras Restauradas' stated objective was to restore properties to their rightful owners through any means. They always started simple with a few well-planned accidents. An automobile crash here or a cut brake line there were usually sufficient to get the attention of the current owners. Once *TR* had their attention, they contacted a key employee or owner and offered to make the incidents go away if the property in question was legally transferred back.

None of the companies responded to the first wave of terror. Step two was to increase its persuasion. Accidents then ensued in which employees were injured or even killed, after which other workers began to receive warnings that they could be next.

With an ever-increasing terror, employees began to look for work elsewhere. Insurance companies refused to cover certain risks. Soon it became impossible to operate profitably. The current owners of the properties in question were reluctant to have the police look too deeply into the acts of terror because they might discover that the property in question was acquired illegally.

In most cases, the purported rightful owners were invited to participate in the acts of sabotage and terror. They were usually reluctant at first. Soon they realized this to be the only way for them to retrieve their family property. Once they were heavily involved in acts of violence against the company they hoped to own, they learned there would be a fee paid back to *TR* for the work that had been done for them. The fee was based on the value of the company. They only had to pay once they had regained ownership of their property. Once the property had been retrieved, if they didn't pay what they owed, the acts of terrorism and sabotage, including threats of violence, continued against them. All paid.

Cell members within *TR* were paid well. Many had joined, well intentioned, to see justice served. Indoctrination quickly let them know they were working against the wealthy and powerful where justice couldn't be served but must be imposed. Cell team members were usually recruited in the universities where an ideologue could easily be identified. It took only a short time to discover which ideologue was also short of cash.

Team members found serving within *TR* an excellent way to fund schooling and the extracurricular activities associated with schooling. Recruited while in graduate school, Pedro was eager to help disadvantaged people retrieve their properties. The money from *TR* was very helpful.

Pedro found he enjoyed the process of intimidation. He quickly rose to be team leader. Through research on the internet, he'd been able to identify other properties that might have been confiscated illegally. He soon realized that after the overthrow of Allende, there were suspicions that nationalized properties were not always returned to their original owners. Through research, he was able to discover some in question. With that information, he'd alerted his *TR* contact. Soon, he received a hefty bonus and the notice of leadership.

Today would be his first to talk to anyone in *TR* outside his cell other than his previous contact. It was his contact who set up the meeting. "You'll be meeting with Juan Opazo," he began. "You will not drive your own car, and you will not go by taxi. Use a rented car and park at least one block from the entrance of the restaurant. It will be closed, but don't worry about that. Just walk to the back of the main dining hall and sit down at the farthest table."

"Why does he want to see me?" questioned Pedro.

"I wasn't given that information. Now, don't ask any more questions. Make sure you walk in the door at 6:55 PM, no later, no earlier. You will be summoned when Sr. Opazo is ready for you."

Pedro wanted to ask more questions but knew better. He'd been diligent in completing each assignment given him with exactness. He'd hoped to be noticed and to be able to move up the chain of command. He hoped this was his opportunity and not his execution.

He sat quietly, sometimes watching the bartender and sometimes watching other workers who came and went. The walls were covered with a dark burlap and were lined with paintings depicting scenes of early Chilean history. The most prevalent painting was that of Inez Suarez defending the village of Santiago. The restaurant was probably named after her. There was another painting depicting the Mapuche leader, Lautaro, holding a flag in front of a beautiful black horse.

Had he not been told to sit and wait, Pedro would have wandered around the restaurant looking more closely at the paintings and sculptures. He waited for twenty-three minutes during which time he was ignored by the bartender and the other restaurant workers. Finally, a huge man, dressed entirely in black, approached. He was well over six feet tall, very muscular, probably weighed over three hundred pounds and his head was shaved. He spoke with a deep, full voice. "Pedro Velasquez?"

"Yes," replied Pedro, nervously.

Without saying a word, the huge man motioned towards the swinging doors near the back of the dining room.

Fearfully, Pedro moved through the swinging doors with the huge, intimidating man in black following close behind. Inside the swinging doors, he was met by another man dressed in black, almost as large as the first, who signaled for Pedro to stretch out his arms for a pat down.

When it was determined that Pedro wasn't a threat, he was ushered through another door into a bare room with one table and a chair on each side. The chair on the opposite side of the table was occupied by a very expensively dressed man probably in his mid-fifties. He was wearing a dark suit, white shirt and silk tie. He appeared to be about five feet seven and weighed almost two hundred pounds. His black hair was cropped short, and he had a well-trimmed mustache. His complexion was so dark that Pedro wondered if he were indigenous.

The man, who Pedro surmised to be Juan Opazo, carefully examined Pedro without saying a word. *If he is trying to intimidate me,* thought Pedro, *it is certainly working.* Pedro waited quietly for Juan Opazo to do whatever it was he was going to do.

After what seemed to Pedro an eternity, the man sitting across from him said, "Tell me about the project on which you have been working."

Pedro worried about a trap. He knew he must never discuss projects with anyone outside his team. "Forgive me for hesitating, Sr. Opazo, but my instructions were to never discuss our projects outside our particular team. How can I know that you're someone with whom I should share that information?"

Instant anger flashed across the round, hard face of Juan Opazo, then his face relaxed followed by a slow smile. "Very good, Pedro Velasquez. You are obedient and cautious. We appreciate that. Do you remember the instructions they gave if you are approached by one claiming to be a leader in your organization?"

Carefully, Pedro attempted to recall the instructions he could remember only receiving once. Perspiration beaded on his forehead as he tried to recollect. Finally, he smiled as he asked, "Who was the hero of the Revolution?"

Juan Opazo also smiled as he answered with another question, "Was it Chief Lautaro?" Then he arose from his seat and circled the table. Pedro arose and Juan Opazo gave the secret *abrazo* clinching his identity.

Motioning to the seat on which Pedro had been sitting, Sr. Opazo spoke, "Please sit down, Pedro Velasquez, and let us continue our conversation." With great dignity, he returned to his own chair across the table. "Tell me about the project on which you and your team have been working."

"We have been working to return the *Esperanza* Mine to its rightful owner."

"Who is the rightful owner?" questioned Señor Opazo.

"The rightful owner was Rodrigo Contreras. He is one of those who disappeared in 1974, unfortunately. His two sons, Roberto and Esteban, are the current rightful owners."

"It was unfortunate. Many who disappeared during that time had their properties confiscated without justification. Their families justify our existence. Who is controlling the *Esperanza* now?" Juan Opazo knew better than anyone who owned and who controlled the *Esperanza* Mine. He asked anyway.

Pedro answered, "Alonzo Sandoval, through his holding company, APS." He noticed an immediate look of hatred flash across the eyes of Juan Opazo when he mentioned the name of Alonzo Sandoval.

With a look of bitter disgust, Sr. Opazo asked, "How did Alonzo Sandoval steal the *Esperanza* from the Contreras family?" Again, Juan Opazo knew the circumstances that existed between Alonzo Sandoval and Rodrigo Contreras without asking.

"When President Pinochet went through the process of returning companies that had been nationalized during the Allende regime, Alonzo Sandoval must have greased some palms because the *Esperanza* was returned to him instead of the Contreras family."

"Is there proof of that?"

Nervously, Pedro answered, "Documentation is very sketchy. We have only found one document that lists Rodrigo Contreras as the owner. As you know, the rich were able to use the services of the most expensive and best forgers available, and they were able to buy off any government official who questioned the documentation."

"Yes, Pedro, that is true. That is why our cause is so important. It was by illegal means, deception and bribery that many properties were confiscated. Therefore, we use extraordinary means to return them to their rightful owners. Tell me, Pedro, are the Contreras brothers completely enrolled in the project to return to them their rightful property?"

Pedro thought he understood what Sr. Opazo was asking. "Yes, they've been involved to the highest extent."

"That is excellent, my boy. Tell me exactly what they've

been doing."

Pedro felt uncomfortable discussing openly the actions he'd ordered. He was even more uncomfortable telling about the things the brothers had done on their own. He explained how they had only followed instructions when they were involved in sabotaging the Sandoval business. Only when they started attacking Alonzo Sandoval and his family personally did they take it upon themselves to make decisions. He finished by explaining how they had decided to blow up the car of Alonzo Sandoval while they were all in the United States.

A disgusted frown encompassed Sr. Opazo's face as he commented, "That would not have been good if Alonzo Sandoval had been killed. It is good that they got his attention, but we need him alive for the final transfer of property. After that …" He didn't finish.

"I think they understand that now. As they began to realize all they had lost, their anger turned them to revenge."

"Revenge without purpose is unprofitable," commented Sr. Opazo. "Pedro, you must carefully guide their revenge to accomplish our goals. Are they aware of the fees?"

"They've been told that *Tierras Restauradas* must receive a percentage of the *Esperanza* when it is transferred to them. I'm not sure they understand that *TR* continues to receive a share of the profits from that time on. They are so happy with the hope of restored property that they'll happily give up whatever percentage is asked."

"That may or may not be true. Sometimes, restored owners get resentful when they have to continue to pay. We'd hate to have to continue persuasion tactics after they receive their property. What about APS? Do they know what has to happen to make the persuasion stop?"

"We haven't communicated that yet. Our next big

project will set the stage to make our demands known." Pedro was beginning to enjoy telling Señor Opazo about team efforts. He explained what the next project was, and Sr. Opazo smiled.

"Let them stew about it for a while. Sometimes, if they don't know which property they have to give up, they reveal other stolen properties that should also be in play."

"What about the Sandoval family?"

"Keep them alive until the project is complete."

"And then?"

Juan Opazo said nothing more but smiled slightly. Pedro knew the interview was over.

CHAPTER 23

It only took Pilar a couple of weeks to assemble a qualified team to help in the analysis of APS. Paul discovered that she was a quick study. He'd taken time to describe the attributes and characteristics of the team he usually took with him from Segue Dynamics, and he'd given her a few project reports from recent operations. With that information and her suggestions, they began to assemble a team.

Pilar considered contacts she had from school, from church and even some who were currently working within the APS system. After interviewing a couple of people in the last category, they decided against hiring from within because of obvious biases already in place.

Pilar personally and carefully interviewed all prospects. When she felt she'd found the appropriate candidate, she scheduled an interview with Paul. Paul was pleased with her selections. Only once did he ask her to send in her second choice, and even then, he reverted to her original selection.

The first team member selected was an engineer. Considering the attempts to sabotage the various APS businesses, he felt a mechanical engineer would be the most help. Eduardo Nuñez had completed his schooling before serving a mission for the LDS Church. Eduardo was the only member of the church in his family. His parents didn't mind when he wanted to join, but they did object when he considered interrupting his education. After finishing his education, he took two years to serve as a missionary. As his parents had warned, it was difficult for him to find work when he returned from his mission. Companies were hiring new graduates, not those without experience with a two-year gap between graduation and securing a job.

Paul was impressed with Eduardo Nuñez. He was about five feet ten inches tall with a slender build. His dark hair was carefully groomed. He came highly recommended by his professors in the school of engineering as well as his mission president. He was not yet married even though he had a fiancé who had served a mission herself while Eduardo was gone. They were waiting for Eduardo to find employment before marrying. Eduardo was pleased to be contacted by Pilar, and the more he learned about the work they would be doing, the more excited he became.

The second and third members to be recruited for the team were hired together. They'd been best friends, even before entering college, and were the most mismatched best friends Paul could ever imagine. One, Florentino Orellana, was small and delicate looking while the other, Gustavo Toro, was big and powerful.

Because Florentino, called Tino by his friends, was very handsome and almost effeminate, he was often teased and called "baby face." His life was difficult in high school until he befriended Gus Toro, who also had difficulties in school but because of academics. Gus was intelligent but had difficulty focusing. Tino helped Gus with his school work and made sure that Gus knew his material and stayed focused. Without even thinking about it Gustavo Toro became the protector for Florentino Orellana.

They went on to enter the school of accounting because that was Tino's interest. Both graduated with honors. Gus didn't think he could have completed the work without Tino's help, but Tino knew that Gus was one of the best, even without his help. They both chose to specialize in auditing.

They hung out with the same group of friends and always double dated friends. Surprisingly, Gus was the first to get married to a gorgeous, vivacious, farm girl who was almost as tall as Gus himself though not nearly so big. Tino was still not married but seemed to always have plenty of prospects. Possibly, it was the number of prospects that made it difficult for him to choose. He decided he wasn't ready for marriage.

Yolanda Acevedo earned a law degree, however, had discovered she wasn't interested in the courtroom drama. Her forte was research. She loved digging out the details and had a knack for finding them. She had two offers on her desk when she was approached by Pilar. One was a lucrative option with a well-known law firm and the other was an offer to clerk for a federal judge. She'd delayed making a decision because she couldn't get excited about either. She'd already discussed all this with her dear friend, Pilar, when finally, Pilar suggested she look at another alternative. Even though the pay with Pilar's team was better than either of the other two opportunities, it wasn't guaranteed to be permanent but appeared to be much more interesting. She knew she'd enjoy working with Pilar. She was older and taller than Pilar by about two inches and had a hefty frame. She wore big, dark-rimmed glasses and pinned her thick, dark hair up like a librarian.

The last two hired were the gofers that Paul had requested. He knew the other four would need someone to run errands so they could remain focused on the tasks at hand. They could print copies and search out details that otherwise could waste the time of the four professionals. Adriana and Luis Medina were siblings, twins. They were nineteen years of age and were both studying business. Lack of funds had caused both to interrupt their education. After talking to their professors, Pilar became convinced that Paul would be getting a bargain if they hired the twins. She predicted they would be serving as much more than gofers. They were mature beyond their years and were very hard workers. A professor who had worked with Adriana said, "If you aren't completely pleased with her work, I'll be shocked."

As Paul looked over the team Pilar had assembled, he realized that he would have hired any of the six to work for him at Segue in the United States. The team was settling into the comfortable, leather chairs surrounding the massive, mahogany table in the executive conference room. Pilar was greeting the team members as Luis Medina connected her laptop computer and projector to be used in the presentation. She handed each of the team members a notebook which contained the mission statement of both Segue Dynamics and the assignment they would be undertaking.

Pilar, at Paul's instruction, conducted the meeting. "Welcome to Segue Dynamics and APS. You all know why you're here. Even though we're meeting in the Sandoval Building, you've been hired by Segue Dynamics, a consulting company in the United States. You've each met Paul, Pablo Sandoval Merrick. He's the director of this team and the president of Segue Dynamics. This is the first consulting assignment for Segue here in South America. You've been chosen with great care to represent and serve Segue Dynamics.

"The assignment we have is the holding company, APS. Sandoval has contracted Segue to help solve the profitability problem that exists here. We'll be investigating all companies held by APS. The project is expected to take about six months, but it could last longer. If you're all as sharp as I think you are, you will have already googled Segue, Sandoval and Mr. Paul Merrick. I'm sure what you have found has helped you make the decision to come to work here. At the end of this project, if you've made yourselves as valuable as I expect you will, you'll be offered a permanent position with either Segue Dynamics or APS. Of course, you'll also be free to seek other employment.

"You already know you're being paid much more than you would have received with other companies. There is a reason for that. We believe you are the best and deserve to be paid well. There are elements of risk in our assignment, which we discussed individually with you. If we complete our task faster than the six months we expect, your bonuses will more than make up for the shorter work period.

"I'd like to turn some time over to Mr. Merrick now."

"Thanks, Pilar. I commend you for the excellent team you have assembled in a miraculously short time. I commend each of you for your ability to make such an important decision on such short notice. Your ability to make decisions quickly will be a great asset to us here.

"The economy has been down for over ten years. However, we believe the profits are down at APS much more than they should be. We want to find those reasons, and we want to find them quickly. The reasons could be different in one APS company than they are in another.

We'll be making an individual report for each company to both the executives of that company and to the executives of the holding company, APS.

"We've assembled a team of professionals that will be able to discover the issues that are causing problems here at Sandoval." Paul continued by describing the specific assignments for each team member. He explained the different rolls they had as engineer, attorney and accountants.

"You have been informed that there have been numerous acts of sabotage perpetrated on the various APS companies. We'll be doing some detective work to try to determine how this sabotage is affecting profitability. We also want to discover who are the perpetrators of that sabotage and why they are attacking Sandoval companies.

"Pilar informs me that you've already been shown your personal office space here in the Sandoval Building. You'll also be provided work space at each APS company that you visit. Even though we're hoping for the highest level of cooperation in all companies, by sad experience I've discovered that consultants are often resented. It isn't uncommon for our work to be hampered by well-meaning people. Try to solve those problems yourselves but if not solved immediately, contact Pilar or me.

"Finally, there are some questions with some of the leaders at APS that our mission be restricted to efficiency and profitability. Some may try to direct you away from security. We believe those acts of sabotage mentioned earlier may well have been a contributing factor in the decline in profitability. As there have been some serious threats against Sandoval employees as well as sabotage of equipment and buildings, we want to take extra care in detailing any of these incidents.

"Please don't put yourselves at risk. If anything happens that could be construed as a threat against any of you, please let Pilar or me know immediately. These risks were explained to you by Pilar and by me in our interviews with you. You chose to join us in spite of those risks. If you have any question whatsoever about whether you want to be involved in this endeavor, this is the time to get out." He waited a minute before going on. Some looked a little nervous, however, none made the move to quit the team. "We appreciate you. Please be careful. Always keep your teammates and Pilar aware of where you are and what you are doing."

The rest of the meeting was spent with Pilar giving each team member their specific assignments. As Paul watched on, he hoped he had not brought bright young people into an assignment where they would be threatened or even worse, killed.

CHAPTER 24

Tino Orellana and Gus Toro were riding the *Transantiago* rapid transit as they returned from their second visit with the folks at *Almacenes Pacífico*. They still had nothing to show for their efforts after two visits to the head offices of the largest department store chain in Chile. Since they'd been hired by the holding company that owned *Pacífico*, they'd expected more cooperation.

As directed by Pilar, they'd set up an appointment with the President of *Pacífico* and requested that he meet with them and bring an officer of the company that would act as liaison between *Pacífico* and Segue. When they arrived at the first meeting, they were met by an assistant to the president who informed them that he'd represent the president in their meeting. He explained that he hadn't been assigned as the liaison. As far as he knew, no one had that assignment. He'd deliver the packet they brought to the president. Tino and Gus had informed him that they'd return the next day to pick up the first packet of paperwork requested and meet with the liaison officer. The next day, they were met by the same assistant who told them that so far, a liaison officer hadn't been appointed and the paperwork hadn't been prepared for them, but he was sure it would be prepared soon.

"I wonder if the others are having as much difficulty gathering information as we are," mused Tino.

"Maybe we don't look like we have much authority," retorted Gus.

"With your humungous size and commanding voice, I would have thought that the assistant to the assistant to the something or other would have marched right into the president's office and demanded the reports we need."

"I would have thought with your handsome baby face and warm, endearing charm that he would have personally taken the last twenty-four hours to accumulate the data requested."

"Maybe my handsome face and endearing charm would've helped if he'd been a she."

"Instead, he asked, 'And what is Segue?'" retorted Gus.

Tino added, "He must not have read one single page from the packet we left him yesterday."

"In all likelihood, he didn't even open it. Chances are, he dropped the packet intact on the desk of the secretary to the assistant of the president."

Since they'd not been successful in their endeavors, they realized they were going to need help. Tino suggested, "We're probably going to need a phone call from someone higher than our pay grade to get these people to be helpful."

"With the amount they are paying us, we should be able to get results. We are at the higher pay grade."

"We aren't supposed to talk to anyone about how much we are getting paid," Tino reminded.

"I'm not talking specifics here, but I'm getting far more than I ever expected," countered Gus.

"I am too, much more than any of the other offers

coming out of accounting school. I wonder why. I would have worked for much less."

Gus continued, "Me too, but I'm not complaining. Yeah, it makes a guy wonder why."

"Perhaps because it's temporary. We could be back on the streets looking for another job in six months or less."

"However, they did tell us that if we're successful, jobs will be available to us with either Segue Dynamics or APS. I wonder if we're getting paid this much because of the danger. Paul thinks we may be dealing with the same people who killed his wife." Gus became very serious and they both wondered what they had gotten themselves into.

Tino thought about the danger for a few minutes before he continued, "And Pilar said there have been incidents of sabotage in which Sandoval employees could have been severely injured."

They stood up from their seats and exited the rapid transit car. With the rest of the crowd, they climbed the stairs to the street to begin the last few blocks on foot.

"I think we can take care of ourselves," Gus started up again confidently.

"Maybe we can, but I'm not so sure I can." Tino was not nearly so confident.

"I'll take care of you, my little friend." Then trying to change the mood he added, "Maybe we'll even find a wife for you in this adventure."

"Not on this team," responded Tino.

"You're not impressed with the ladies on our team?"

"I'm very impressed with their capabilities. I just don't see any of them as marriage prospects. Besides, I'm not yet ready for holy wedlock."

"Is it the holy you're not ready for or the wedlock?"

Tino gave Gus a look of distaste before answering. Gus

had been trying to get Tino to settle down with one girl and get married ever since his own marriage. "I'm not ready for marriage," Tino said, but he wasn't very convincing.

"I'm sure you aren't." Gus questioned, "Why don't you see the ladies on our team as marriage prospects?'

"They seem to be very intelligent and well qualified for our team work," Tino answered uncomfortably.

Gus understood that Tino was very selective of his women friends. He was very meticulous about his own appearance and the appearance of any woman he dated even though he wasn't nearly as selective regarding her intelligence. "So, what is it about our team members that causes them to fail your selection process?"

He knew that once Gus got going on a topic, it wouldn't conclude until he was good and ready. Finally, Tino sighed and finally answered, "Gus, you know I might weigh fifty-five kilos if I'm dressed and all my clothes are wet. Except for our team leader, the other female team members probably best me by ten kilos each."

Gus chided, "So, you think they are fat? Is that what you think? Do you know what my wife would say to you, Tino? You realize she, too, would best you by ten kilos?"

Tino decided not to answer because they'd accessed the Sandoval Building and the elevator was nearing their floor. As they entered their team work area, they found Adriana Medina and Yolanda Acevedo both in their cubicles studiously perusing the piles of papers stacked up on their desks.

Pilar had successfully commandeered a work space that could accommodate the team of six and still allow each a private cubicle. Each cubicle had been equipped with a new desktop computer, a smart phone, a small printer, a desk, a small file cabinet and book shelves. Adriana and Eduardo had quickly and naturally taken over the IT responsibilities of setting up each computer in a network which connected all the computers of the group as well as a large, laser jet, colored printer.

The work space Pilar had appropriated was situated right next to her own office and just down the hall from that of Paul. The cubicles lined both sides of the work space with a large conference table in the middle. It had been placed there to accommodate the frequent meetings they expected but, in reality, was a place for team members to lay out the papers that were being examined. At the front of the room was a large, flat screen monitor on which any of the team members could display a document for the others to examine. Next to the monitor was a large whiteboard.

There was a connecting door which led to a storage room full of supplies, the laser printer, a table for lunches, a refrigerator and file cabinets for storage.

All the team members were impressed with the ultra-modern equipment provided and how quickly it had been acquired and assembled. As they stood back and looked, it would be difficult for anyone to believe the whole setup had not been here for years.

Their first job was to prepare the packets necessary explaining what the APS companies would need to provide to the Segue team. Through contact with Jeff Harkin, back in the States, they were able to accumulate similar packets that had been used by Segue in the past. It wasn't difficult to translate the forms and the requests as well as the background the Sandoval employees would need. Yolanda made sure the proper legalese was included so some legal beagle at one of the APS companies wouldn't be tempted to hold up the process while Tino made sure it could be easily understood by any employee.

Because of the sabotage issues, requests had been made to each company to report any unusual incident which had stalled production, caused bodily harm or just seemed out of place. They also asked for reports of any threats to top employees or family members of employees. Instructions were given so the reports could be emailed to the Segue team, but it included an offer that a team member would drop by and personally pick up anything provided.

Each company director or president had already received Carlos' memo. Most had not yet assigned a liaison officer when they first met with a team member. Most were put off that the team member would return the next day at the same time to review the packet with the liaison officer. They couldn't understand the urgency that the Segue team was putting on the whole consulting process.

One president had informed the team member that it would not be necessary for him to return the next day as he would brief the liaison officer he chose of his duties and what was expected of him. Within a few minutes, that president received a phone call from Pilar explaining the urgency of the team's work. She had to remind him that he was one of the people who had received a threat, and it was imperative to solve the conspiracy. In a subsequent call to Carlos Mendocina, Carlos also informed him there were no other options, he must comply with the Segue requests.

Because he and Gus hadn't received cooperation from *Almacenes Pacífico,* Tino was surprised to see Yolanda and Adriana studiously perusing reports from *Banco República.* "You already have something to work on?" he asked in disbelief.

Yolanda replied, "Yes, we received the preliminaries requested."

"I think we are being stonewalled by *Pacífico,*"

complained Gus.

Tino added, "Either that or they don't think our project is urgent. They're taking their own sweet time. Maybe they think if they stall long enough, we'll forget to follow-up."

Adriana questioned, "Can they do that?"

"They think they can," responded Yolanda. "They're not in the habit of receiving directives like ours from outside their particular company. They're used to doing their jobs running their company and occasionally reporting to the board of directors."

"What board of directors?" Adrianna wasn't acquainted with the workings of companies owned by a holding company.

Yolanda explained, "APS is a holding company which, in turn, owns a number of other companies. APS has a board of directors which, not only oversees APS but all the other Sandoval companies. Alonzo Sandoval is the chairman of the board of directors, and Carlos Mendocina is the executive to whom the presidents of the various companies report. The board of directors chooses a president or director for each APS entity. That president or director appears before the board on a regular basis to report about his company. He probably reports much more often to Sr. Mendocina."

As Yolanda was completing her explanation, Eduardo Nuñez and Luis Medina returned empty handed from their visit with APJ Engineering.

Adriana and Yolanda raised their eyes and looked at each other when they realized that two teams of men struck out while the all-female team had returned with the requested preliminary reports. It was Tino who gave voice for the men that the ladies had been more successful.

Pilar soon joined them. She was pleased to see Adriana

and Yolanda scrutinizing the preliminaries from *Banco República*. "Do you have much hope that we're soon going to receive the preliminaries from the other companies?"

Tino replied, "We were told it will be provided soon with absolutely no specifics.'

Eduardo added, "That's the same wording we received. I'm not expecting anything in the next few days."

"Do they understand the urgency?" questioned Pilar.

"I don't think they do," continued Eduardo. "They're looking at this as an efficiency study not an emergency solution to a very dangerous situation."

"How can I help?" asked Pilar in desperation.

"Has it helped when you personally called," questioned Yolanda.

"Not really. I think the instructions have to come from others above me. Paul and Alonzo are meeting right this minute. I'm sure they are addressing this very issue."

She stopped to pull her cell phone, which was vibrating, from her pocket and held it up to her ear. "Hello." She listened for a few short seconds during which all the blood drained from her face. She excused herself from the rest of the team and rushed from the room.

CHAPTER 25

Paul answered the intercom to hear his father say, "Pablo, could you spare me a few minutes. If you have time, I could come to your office."

Paul chuckled to himself. *Here he is, the principal owner, chairman of the board and CEO of one of the largest holding companies in South America, and he's willing to come to my office if I can spare him some time?*

"Of course, I'll spare you a few minutes, however, I'll come to your office."

As Paul entered, Alonzo looked up and smiled motioning to one of the leather chairs situated near the fireplace. Alonzo gave him a familial *abrazo* and took a seat in the adjacent, matching chair. The elegant office had two oversized windows in the corner both of which had breathtaking views of the majestic Andes Mountains. "Thank you for coming. It is so good to see you, My Son."

"Good morning, Father," he responded. "It is good to see you again, too."

"Have you made any progress in discovering the identity of Janet's killers?"

Paul was pleasantly surprised that the first question was about Janet's killers rather than about his consulting assignment with APS. Paul answered, "I think I have their names," describing the setting and the conversation he had with Luiz Rossi. He also explained how he had received their phone number. Paul wondered if he saw a flicker of recognition when he mentioned the Contreras name, but he wasn't sure.

"Red Security has many contacts," suggested Alonzo Sandoval. "You might give Miguel that phone number, and he might be able to trace an address for you."

"I tried that," Paul responded, explaining how Julio Batley had returned the number to him when he wasn't willing to share with Sr. Batley how that number affected APS profitability.

"He wouldn't help you?" asked Sr. Sandoval incredulously.

"No. I don't think he likes what I'm doing."

"Does he know who you are?" asked Sr. Sandoval.

"He received the same memo that the other APS heads received."

"What memo was that?"

Paul was taken aback. *Is he so far out of the loop that he doesn't receive copies of memos between Carlos Mendocina and the heads of Sandoval companies?* Paul pulled a copy of the memo from his folder and handed it to the CEO of APS.

Alonzo Sandoval examined the memo with great care. He gave Paul a questioning glance as he said, "This memo seems to limit what the APS companies should give you, and it doesn't acknowledge who you are."

"My team is having difficulty collecting any data that doesn't show up on the ledger or management records. We are informed that is beyond our purview."

"Of course, that is within your purview. I'll have Carlos send out another memo and make it clear what I have authorized you to do and who you are."

"Who am I?" questioned Paul, knowing what the answer would be.

"You are my son."

"With due respect, I'm not sure that is the best thing to do at this juncture."

"Pablo, why don't you want the leaders of APS to know who you are?"

"Whether I'm a long-lost son or a consultant brought in from outside, I'm still the interloper, a threat to the status quo, especially to Carlos. If you give orders from on high commanding all below to obey my every word, I'll still be viewed as the enemy, and you'll be viewed as naive or compliant. Right now, you are honored and respected throughout APS. We don't want to jeopardize that. One of our jobs, as consultants, is to gain respect and win trust."

Genuinely concerned, Alonzo asked, "What should we do?"

"Let's let the Segue team do their jobs. If they're worth their salt, they'll soon prove not to be a menace but an asset."

"I like that. Pablo, you are a threat to Carlos' expectations to become the CEO of APS. You know what my dreams are for you."

"Father, my first priority in Chile is to make sure those responsible for Janet's death are required to face justice, and I'll do everything I can to help put APS on firm ground.

Other than that, I can't make any promises."

"I'm pleased with that commitment. Knowing why you're here, I wondered about your willingness to revitalize our business interests. At least you're not dismissing the possibility completely."

"No, I'm not ready to do that either, even though I

consider the possibility very remote," retorted Paul.

"I believe the solution to both problems requires the same course of action. If I'm to be successful in revitalizing the holding company, my team and I must show the leaders of the various companies that we have their best interests at heart. Similarly, if I ever do take over leadership in APS it is equally important that the leaders of the various companies come to trust me and the direction I'm taking them."

"I like the way you think, Pablo. It may take a little longer, but the leaders will come to trust you, whether you are their boss or their consultant."

"We'll have to reserve judgement on that. Now, if you still have more time for me, I'd like to discuss with you why someone or some organization would want to destroy your business."

Alonzo Sandoval looked into space as if trying to recall something for a few seconds before responding. "I'll be honest with you. I've had many enemies over the years."

"Have you ever received personal threats?"

"Ever is a long time. Yes, during my life I have received many threats, even though none have been recent enough to be part of the problem we are discussing."

"Can you be sure of that?"

"What do you mean?"

"Have you ever taken property that rightfully belonged to someone else?"

"Are you asking about me personally or about the Sandoval family?"

"I guess both."

"The original Sandoval received land grants from the King of Spain shortly after the conquest. For years, the Mapuche have been trying to get the government of Chile to help them retrieve land they thought belonged to them. I'm sure Sandoval land is included."

"Have you received any specific requests to return land to the Mapuche?"

"In general, yes, specifically, no. Do you think these problems can be traced to land grants in the 1500s?"

"I don't know, but we have to consider everything. Were any of the Sandoval companies nationalized during Allende's time in power?"

At first, Alonzo frowned, and then he smiled realizing that Paul was digging much deeper than he'd ever expected, possibly too deep. "*Banco República* was nationalized for a time. We thought the *Mina Esperanza* was also going to be nationalized, however, that ended up not happening."

"Why was that?"

"The *Esperanza* was small potatoes in comparison with the immense copper mines like Kennecott and Anaconda which had American ownership and management. Therefore, the Allende government wanted to take them over and control them. The *Esperanza* was wholly owned by the Sandoval family, and even though the Allende government didn't like it, the mine was never nationalized."

"How was the *Banco República* returned to APS?"

"Most of the businesses nationalized by the Allende government were returned to their previous owners during the regime of General Pinochet."

"While Pinochet's government was privatizing property which had been nationalized, were there some properties that weren't returned to the proper individuals."

Alonzo was pensive as he responded, "I heard rumors. I think there may have been situations in which more than one entity was requesting the return of the same property."

"Was APS ever one of those entities pressing to have property returned in which another entity was also pressing for the same properties?"

"Yes, of course."

"Of course?"

"Pablo, as always, there are unsavory characters in business. When the government began the process of privatization, some of those dishonorable characters started looking for situations to steal property. Some of them tried to get the *Banco República*. Others tried to get the *Mina Esperanza*. Others tried to get the government to give them trucks that had been confiscated from Sandoval companies."

"Is there a possibility that someone or some group believes APS received property that really belonged to them?"

"I doubt it. I think those who were trying to get the government to give them property knew beforehand that they had no legitimate rights. They were just looking for opportunities to steal property. Why do you want to know about APS so many years ago?"

"The saboteurs aren't giving us any information, they're probably letting us stew for a while trying to figure it out. I'm afraid that if we don't figure out what property they want returned soon, someone else could be hurt badly or killed."

"Well, I think we should let Security know that your team is taking the lead on this. What if we assigned Miguel to your team as the representative from Red Security? He could be your liaison and bring you the information you need."

"Does he have the authority to bring us the information if Sr. Batley doesn't want him to?"

"He does if we give it to him," replied Alonzo.

"Are you the one that usually calls him with directives?"

"No, not really. They usually come from Carlos." He

leaned across his desk and punched a button on his telephone.

Carlos' voice responded over the intercom. "Yes, Sr. Sandoval. May I help you?"

"Do you have a minute to come in to see us?"

"Us?" questioned Carlos Mendocina.

"Yes," replied Alonzo. "Pablo and I are talking about the investigation he is doing. I want to make sure we're all on the same page."

There was a brief silence on the line, and then Carlos answered, "Absolutely. I will be right there."

Alonzo and Paul didn't need to wait very long before Carlos arrived. Alonzo pointed to another empty chair near the fireplace. Carlos gave a friendly greeting to both Alonzo and Paul as he took his seat.

Looking directly at Alonzo, Carlos asked, "How can I help you?"

"Pablo's team isn't getting the immediate cooperation from the various APS companies that I'd hoped. More pointedly, Red Security isn't providing the information the team needs to further their investigation."

"Investigation?" questioned Carlos. "I thought Segue Dynamics was consulting with APS on efficiency and profitability. What investigation are we talking about?"

Carlos looked uneasy as Alonzo explained how the killing of Paul's wife, the sabotage of various companies and the threats to various employees seemed connected and at the root of the profitability issues within APS.

Carlos' face turned almost white as Alonzo mentioned the threats to Sandoval employees. "You mean the people who killed Pablo's wife are the same ones who threatened my life?" he asked incredulously.

"That is a distinct possibility," replied Paul.

"So, they aren't kidding when they say I could be next!" Carlos had terror in his voice. "Shouldn't Red be doing the investigation on this?"

Alonzo thought for a moment before answering. "Red Security doesn't have the manpower to do this investigation and provide the security necessary for all the Sandoval companies. The people at Security should put every effort into protecting our holdings and the employees. I want Segue Dynamics to lead the investigation into what has happened, and I want one of Security's best men assigned to Pablo's team to be the liaison between Segue and Security."

"I'm not sure that Julio Batley will be happy with that instruction."

Alonzo reached over, smiled and gave Carlos a friendly tap on the shoulder. "That is the job of our fearless Executive Vice President, to convince him."

As Alonzo arose, so did Paul and Carlos, and everyone knew the meeting was over. Before anyone could leave the room, Pilar, white faced, appeared in the doorway.

"What is it?" quizzed Alonzo.

"There has been a terrible automobile accident. President Gallardo of *Banco República* is in intensive care at the *Las Condes Hospital*. He's not expected to live."

"What happened?" Alonzo quizzed.

"His car was run off the road by a large SUV. The SUV sped off. It doesn't appear to be an accident."

CHAPTER 26

Paul and Pilar rushed to the elevator and headed down to the parking garage where Miguel was waiting for them. They noticed Alonzo and Carlos getting into another SUV and leaving the parking garage ahead of them. Both SUV's hastened towards the hospital.

Paul looked at Pilar, who obviously was still shaken by the news. "Do you know any of the details?" he asked.

"All I know is I received a message from Security that President Gallardo had been in a terrible automobile crash and was being rushed to the hospital. I don't know who called me, but he said it was a hit and run and didn't appear to be an accident."

"That sounds way too close to home."

"I have an idea how it must sound to you. I'm so sorry, Pablo."

Alonzo and Carlos were already standing in the waiting room with Julio Batley when Paul and Pilar arrived. Paul hoped there would be a possibility to talk to President Gallardo and yet realized he would have to wait his turn. There were uniformed *Carabineros* also waiting. They would be the first to talk to Gallardo.

A small woman of about fifty entered the waiting room,

and immediately, Alonzo and Carlos went to her side. Pilar identified her as the wife of the bank president. She was crying, and Alonzo was obviously trying to console and reassure her.

There were more than three hours of awkward waiting and idle conversation before a doctor came out and visited with the Señora de Gallardo. Paul and Pilar couldn't hear the conversation, but they could see the relief on her face as they conversed. She would be allowed to visit with her husband for just a brief time and then the police would need to ask him some questions. She glared at them but cooperated fully.

Just a few minutes later the police were advised that they could talk to the bank president. They nodded to Julio Batley, who immediately joined the police as they entered the patient's room.

There continued to be light conversation in the waiting room between the leaders of APS. When Julio Batley returned from the patient's room, he, Alonzo and Carlos stepped into another room just off the waiting room. Paul and Pilar couldn't hear their conversation, but they could see the gestures through the window in the door. During the conversation, Julio Batley looked in the direction of Paul and Pilar with an unfriendly glance. When Alonzo came out of that brief meeting, he signaled for Paul to join Carlos and Julio.

"Paul," Carlos began, "I have informed Sr. Batley that your analysis of the APS companies is to include the incidents of sabotage and the threats to Sandoval employees. I've also instructed him that he is to use all the resources available in Red Security to safeguard the companies and its employees. I've also asked him to supply a member of his staff to assist your team." Looking now at Julio he continued, "I know you have staff members who are well equipped to do this investigation, but you don't have enough staff to both investigate and protect Sandoval companies. So, your charge is protection, and Paul's is to investigate. Do you both understand?"

When they both nodded that they understood, Carlos left them together as he returned to the side of Alonzo Sandoval and the wife of President Gallardo.

Julio began, "So, Sr. Mendocina informs me that you and your team will take the lead in the inter-company investigation of President Gallardo's misfortune. I don't agree, but that is the call of Carlos Mendocina and Alonzo Sandoval."

"With all the calamities that have already transpired, I'm sure that Red Security, under your able direction, will have its hands full protecting Sandoval employees and helping them feel safe."

"But many of my people are experienced in this kind of investigation, and we have many contacts within the police," protested Julio.

"Sr. Batley, I'm sure some of your people are very capable, but the decision has been made. Segue Dynamics will try to discover who are perpetrating these malicious acts."

Paul was blown away by Julio Batley's next question. "Sr. Merrick, is it true that you are the son of Alonzo Sandoval?"

Paul stalled, "Why do you ask?"

"We were under the impression that you are part of a United States company which helps companies, whose profits are lagging, get back on their feet again. Then I heard a rumor that you are the son of Alonzo Sandoval. Which is true?"

After careful consideration, Paul answered, "Both. Alonzo Sandoval is my father, and I'm the president of Segue Dynamics, a company which helps companies get back on their feet."

"Why didn't you tell me?"

"We were concerned that if everyone knew I'm the son of Alonzo Sandoval, we would be treated as though I own the company. I don't."

"But you will someday," protested Julio Batley.

"Sr. Batley," Paul responded politely, "I really don't want to discuss my personal life nor the personal affairs of Alonzo Sandoval. I've been asked to solve some serious problems existing within the APS companies. There have been numerous acts of sabotage. Employees and some members of their families have been threatened. Sr. Sandoval's car was blown up while he was in the United States. His car was attacked near the *Mina Esperanza*. Finally, my wife was killed in the United States. We believe all these acts of violence and threatened violence are being executed by the same people. We want these people stopped and punished."

Julio thought for a while before asking, "Isn't it a big leap to think all of these incidents are connected?"

"We don't think it is. I've been investigating the people who killed my wife for more than a year. The more we uncover, the more we believe all these incidents are connected. Now, can I count on your cooperation and that of Red Security?"

"We will do what we can. How can we best serve you?"

"Carlos mentioned that he'd asked you to assign someone from your staff to my team to help us make sense of these investigations. Is Miguel one of those with investigative experience?"

"Carlos suggested that Miguel be assigned to your team. He's already assigned to protect you so I don't see a problem, and yes, he was a very successful investigator before he left the armed forces."

Paul wanted to ask him why Miguel left the military, but for the time being, he was satisfied with all they'd accomplished. "Now, may I ask you what you found out from President Gallardo. Perhaps I won't need to visit with him after I hear from you."

"He was on his way to visit with one of the branch managers in *Viña del Mar*. He didn't notice until the last minute that a large SUV was right beside them. As the highway curved to the left, the SUV banged into them pushing them off the edge. As he glanced up, there was a man in the passenger seat waving at him and grinning."

The hairs on the back of Paul's neck stood on end. If he hadn't been sure that the acts of violence in Chile were connected to Janet's death before, he certainly knew it now. He debated whether to share that information with Julio Batley. Because he was going to need Batley's support, he told him how Janet had been killed and the fiendish look on the face of the passenger in the pickup as they were forced off the road and into the river. Batley agreed that it sounded as though the same men were involved in both crashes.

"I'll keep Miguel informed on what is happening within Red Security," offered Julio Batley, "and I expect to hear what you are discovering on your side from him. Only then will we be able to readily protect Sandoval assets."

Paul agreed, and they both returned to the main waiting room. Señora de Gallardo had returned to the side of her husband who was expected to recover. Paul already knew what he needed, so he and Pilar decided to leave the clinic and return to their offices.

Wanting privacy to call Nelson Retamal, Paul slipped out of the Sandoval Building and walked to the park a block away where he found a secluded spot surrounded by bushes. When he was sure he couldn't be seen or heard, he slipped his cell phone open and removed the SIM card and replaced it with the one that Nelson had supplied.

He dialed the number and connected the Bluetooth to his ear. He talked as he walked.

"Were you able to trace that number I gave you?"

"We were. The name listed for the number is not the one you gave me, however, that doesn't mean anything. The billing address is the office of a small construction company in *La Granja* just off the *Autopista Vespucio Sur*. I drove by, inconspicuously and checked the place out. It's an office connected to a residence. The home is owned by an older woman. Her two sons run the construction business." He gave Paul the exact address but suggested that Paul not go there alone.

Paul thought about it and wondered who would be best to take with him. He didn't want to confront the Contreras brothers, but he did want to see them and verify that they were the same ones who forced him off the road in Idaho. He voiced his concerns to Retamal.

Nelson suggested, "They might become suspicious if you start hanging around. Why don't I spend some time in that neighborhood and see if I can discreetly take some photos of those who come and go."

When he finished the phone call to Retamal and while he still had the private SIM card in his phone, he dialed another number. Jeff Harkin answered on the third ring.

"How's it going in Chile, buddy?"

"I don't know if we are being stonewalled or whether leaders are just protecting their empires."

"Why? What are you discovering?"

"The typical or worse," Paul responded. "There seems to be the mindset that if you're the ruler, you should control everything and if you aren't, you don't do anything until given orders."

"Well, I've seen that in companies we have analyzed here."

"Yes, so have I. Perhaps I'm too caught up in this one emotionally, but it seems much more severe here," complained Paul.

"Do you have any idea why?"

"It may go back to the earliest days when the conquistadors came to this land. They were explorers and adventurers seeking fame, power and gold. The conquistadors were given huge land grants, and they victimized the indigenous people to become very rich and very powerful. Those original leaders passed down their riches and power for many generations. From the slaves came the laborers, who for generations were taught to follow orders and do only what they were told."

"Wouldn't that begin to change over the centuries?"

"It has, but it's taken an interesting turn. If a person who's been raised to follow is suddenly thrust into a position of leadership, he leads as he's seen others lead, by control and making all the decisions."

"That's going to make your analysis of Sandoval companies more difficult," offered Jeff.

"That's one of the reasons I wanted to assemble my team with Chileans. I wanted them to have a clear understanding of local leadership dynamics."

"Considering the team members with whom I have contact, they all seem astute. I'm especially impressed with Pilar. How does having a female team leader fit into the macho dynamics?" Jeff wanted to know.

"Honestly, I hadn't even considered that when I chose her. Maybe that is one of the reasons we are being stonewalled by some of the leadership in some of the companies."

"I don't know," responded Jeff. "I'm not there, but no one, whether here or in Chile, wants his empire threatened, whether the person doing the threatening is male or female."

"I'm sure that's true and the females on our team are getting quicker results than the males. One of the problems here is we have to get to the bottom of the terrorist attacks on APS holdings quickly before anything worse happens."

"What's happened now?"

"We just had the president of our bank run off the road. He was almost killed."

"Similar to you and Janet being run off the road?"

"Too similar, including the fiendish grin and waving as the car was forced off the freeway."

"Wow! They must be the same thugs then," suggested Jeff.

"I think so."

"That explains your time constraints."

"The opposition is obviously increasing their persuasive pressure."

"Do you know what they want yet?"

"Not yet, but I think we're getting close. It may even be that property given to my ancestors at the time of the conquest. Like Pilar said, 'if they want something, don't you think they will eventually let you know what they want?'"

"Smart girl. She sounds like a keeper. Paul, I don't need to tell you that you need to be careful. They already tried to kill you once."

"I'm worried about my team. I'm not sure they all know

what a dangerous game we're playing."

"I wish I were there with you. What can I do to help?" pleaded Jeff.

"You've already been a big help supplying the team with the paperwork they need. I'm a bit more confident knowing I have the help of Nelson Retamal of Rodriguez Investigative Services."

"OK, just be careful."

Having finished both his phone calls to Nelson Retamal and Jeff Harkin, Paul replaced the SIM card in his cell phone. He exited the park and waited for the light to change to cross the street. A large, grey sedan pulled up in front of him, blocking his way. He turned to his left to walk around the back of the car. When he was directly behind the sedan, both back doors of the car swung open, and a man jumped out of each door. They converged on Paul, and before he could react, they took hold of him. Paul noticed the trunk of the car suddenly pop open. The two men forced Paul into the trunk. Furtively, Paul looked around seeking help. There was no one in sight. The door of the trunk slammed shut entombing him, and the grey sedan sped off.

CHAPTER 27

His first reaction was panic. He screamed for help and banged on the trunk lid. Soon he realized that wouldn't help. He endeavored fighting off claustrophobia by imagining himself on the warm sand of a peaceful beach, something that proved impossible cramped in the confined space of a car trunk.

Paul quickly began to assess his alternatives. He assumed they had kidnapped him to take him to a remote place to complete his murder. He didn't have much time.

He realized he still had his cell phone. With difficulty, he was able to maneuver to a position to pull his phone from his pocket. He would have chosen the other SIM card because it had the phone number of Nelson Retamal stored in it. He tried to remember that number but couldn't. He tried to reach for his wallet but knew that was an impossibility. He had Pilar's number on his speed dial, so he called her.

Paul was grateful she answered on the first ring. "Where did you go?" she asked.

"Pilar!" Paul screamed. "I've been kidnapped by three men in a large, grey sedan. I'm in their trunk. I don't know where they are taking me, but I'm afraid they plan to kill me."

"Oh no, Paul! What can I do to help?"

"Call Miguel and let him know what happened."

"Where did they kidnap you?"

"As I was coming out of the park down the street."

"Do you know which direction they took you?"

"The car was facing east when we left the park. Within just a block or so, we turned right. Since then, I have been thinking of other things. I think we are still going south, but I really don't know."

"Do you know who kidnapped you?"

"I didn't recognize them."

"Could you tell what kind of car it was?"

"No, I didn't have time to look. I think it is grey sedan, fairly late model."

"I'll call Miguel immediately. Don't disconnect your phone. Most new cell phones are equipped with GPS. Maybe he can trace you."

Paul hoped she was right. He worried that he didn't have much time. He caught himself starting to panic again. He concentrated on breathing slowly and calming his thoughts. He realized there was enough oxygen in the trunk to last him a few hours.

They will probably pull me out and kill me before that, he thought.

The easiest way of escaping would be through the back seat. He knew he couldn't do that because the thugs were seated there. *Unless they leave the car parked somewhere with me in the trunk, that's not an alternative.*

Paul wondered whether Chilean cars were equipped with emergency release handles like cars manufactured in the U.S. He couldn't see anything that glowed in the dark, and he couldn't feel a handle.

Perhaps I can pry the latch open, he thought. He could feel the latch with his fingers but didn't have enough strength to pry it open. He fumbled about the interior of the trunk with his hand trying to find anything that could be used as a tool. Nothing!

Some cars have the jack over to one side or the other. As difficult as it was to move in such tight quarters, Paul couldn't find a jack. *It must be underneath the trunk.* He felt below himself again and found a small hole that led to the spare tire. *The jack must be under the tire.* There was no way to get his weight off of the tire cover so he could get down to any tools underneath.

Frustrated and puzzled, Paul remembered his Grandpa Merrick. Paul's dog had gotten lost when the two of them were camping. After hours of searching, Paul had begun to cry. Grandpa Merrick suggested they pray. The two of them knelt under a tall pine tree and took turns praying. Paul had hoped they'd immediately find Toby. That didn't happen for another two hours of searching and calling. What did happen immediately was a feeling of peace.

Being angry with God, Paul had quit praying soon after Janet's death, but now he needed help again. He decided that continuing to be angry with God had not served him well, so he prayed. As he did so, he began to feel hope.

He wondered if Miguel had been able to initiate any kind of a trace using his cell phone. He checked his phone and remembered he was still connected. "Pilar," he whispered, "are you still there?"

She replied, "Yes, I am. Are you OK, Paul? I heard you praying."

"Really? Sorry, I forgot our phones were still connected. So far, I'm fine. Were you able to contact Miguel?"

"Yes, they're attempting to trace your phone as we

speak. Keep connected to me if you can."

"I will. I've been trying to locate a release lever, but I can't find one," complained Paul.

"Do you remember how they opened the trunk when they put you in it?" she questioned.

"The two from the back seat held me and the trunk popped open."

"The driver probably opened it. There must be a cable from that lever to the latch."

"Where would it be?"

She wasn't sure, however, she wanted to sound confident to help Paul stay calm. "It could be over the top, or it could be along the side of the trunk on the driver's side."

Paul groped over the top and along the side. "I can't find anything," he called out.

Pilar was also praying in her heart that she would be able to help. "Maybe it's under the carpet."

Paul grabbed hold of the rug near the edge and jerked up. Sure enough, he found a cable underneath. He tried to pull it, but nothing happened. Then he tried to pull it towards the front of the car, but he couldn't hold on to the small cable tight enough. "It's here, but I can't pull it."

"Are there any tools in the trunk?"

"If there are, they're probably under the tire. I can't get under there."

"Sometimes people throw their tools on top of the tire. Have you checked?" Pilar was trying to give him ideas without causing him to panic.

"I checked once, but I'll check again." Paul found the small hole over the top of the tire. With great effort, he was able to force his hand through the hole. Even though the sharp edge was scraping his wrist, he reached in as far as he could. He felt something at the very tip of his fingers. After stretching them as far as they could go, he was able to retrieve a tool with the tips of two fingers. He gradually worked it towards the hole and finally pulled it out. "OK, I have some pliers."

"Great. Now pull the cable toward the front of the car."

Paul tried to get a good grip on the cable with the pliers and pulled. The pliers slipped off the cable. He twisted his body into a position in which he had better leverage and tried again. This time the pliers held, and he felt the latch release. The lid of the trunk started to open, but Paul quickly grabbed it. He hoped the driver hadn't seen it move. He didn't want the trunk door to open until the car was either stopped or going slowly. He pulled the trunk shut but not far enough for it to latch again.

He waited for the car to slow or stop. He had been in such a cramped position for so long, he wondered if he'd be able to run.

Finally, the car slowed, perhaps for traffic. Paul held the trunk door open just an inch so he could see. They were on a narrow street in an industrial part of town. There were cars parked on both sides and barely room for two cars to pass on the street. When the car was almost stopped, Paul threw open the trunk and scrambled out. He was a big man in a small trunk so he couldn't move quickly.

He barely had his feet on the cobblestone street when he heard the driver yell. Paul began to run as fast as he could, however, the two thugs from the back seat didn't have stiff legs, and they were quickly in pursuit. He ran into the nearest shop hoping for assistance.

It was full of all kinds of wheelchairs, some motorized, some not. A man in a manual wheelchair was seated at a desk. *He won't be much help,* thought Paul. "Call the police," he yelled as he continued running through the store. He ran past an office where a woman was seated at a desk. He ran into the shop in the back where a worker was assembling a new motorized wheelchair. Paul heard the door of the store slam and heard a woman's voice screaming for someone to get out.

Paul quickly looked for something he could use as a weapon. He spotted a two-inch, metal pipe about a meter long which he grabbed just as the first of the two thugs rushed in, brandishing a handgun. Paul swung the pipe at the pistol with all his might and heard the clang as the pistol and the pipe collided. Screaming in pain, the goon grabbed his hand as Paul swung again connecting with the side of his head.

As he fell, he held onto Paul, dragging him to the floor. Paul got to his knees just as the second thug rushed around the corner into the shop. From his knees Paul swung the pipe again at the man's legs with all the force he could muster. The villain went down screaming as his weapon skidded across the floor.

Paul raced out the back door, turning right into the alley. He ran up the alley to the end of the block. He heard a car honk and looked to see if it was the grey sedan, but it was Miguel in his SUV. Paul ran across the busy street through the heavy traffic and jumped into the car.

"How did you find me?"

"Security has been following you by tracking the GPS on your phone. They've been guiding me on my cell phone. In another few minutes, I would have caught up with you."

The two of them headed back toward the Sandoval Building. Paul was still shaking, and it took a few minutes for the adrenalin high to subside. As he began to calm down, he again thought about Miguel being at the end of the block when Paul ran out of the wheelchair store. He thought, *I'm sure glad I changed the SIM card back or they wouldn't have been able to trace my phone.* Paul wondered how long it had taken Pilar to contact Security, and how long it had taken them to start the trace. The car Paul had been in had stopped at stop signs and had driven slowly in traffic but, for the most part, had been traveling the whole time since Paul had been thrown into the trunk. *How did Miguel get there the same time I did? Have I made a mistake to put him on my team?*

When it was ascertained that Paul was safe and not injured, Miguel drove him directly to the Sandoval Building. He made sure that Paul was ensconced in his own office, and then he retreated to the Security room.

Paul barely had time to enter his office when Pilar and Alonzo rushed in. First Pilar and then Alonzo pressed forward to give him a hug. Realizing what she had done, Pilar backed away embarrassed. They both wanted to talk to Paul, but Pilar hesitated and then acquiesced and began to leave so Alonzo could be alone with his son.

Alonzo saw her start to depart and sensed she wanted the details of Paul's abduction as much as he did. "Don't go, My Dear. Unless Paul has some objection, you have as much need to be here as I do. They both looked to Paul for his decision."

"No, no," Paul quickly began. "We all need to talk."

As the three of them sat in Paul's office, he rehearsed to them the details of the kidnapping, leaving out only the real reason he was walking alone in the park. At times, while Paul was talking, he got up from his chair and walked, compelled by his need to have the freedom to move about.

Both Pilar and Alonzo kept their eyes glued on Paul every second, almost as though a blink of their eyes could cause him to disappear again. Sometimes, they asked questions for more detailed information. Mostly, they allowed Paul to talk through every detail of his abduction and escape.

All three agreed that his abduction, so quickly on the heels of the attack on Guillermo Gallardo, meant the terrorists had exponentially advanced their agenda. All three realized that no one was safe.

Alonzo voiced the uncertainty they all had, "What do we do now?"

"Well, for one," chirped in Pilar, "there will be no more solo walks in the park." She then flushed, surprised that she had vocalized what she had been thinking. Pilar continued, "We have to take every precaution to make sure you are both safe."

"I believe we have already made sure I'm safe," observed Alonzo. "I don't go anywhere without my contingency of Security guards. I'm well protected both here and at the *Estancia*."

Paul inquired, "What about en route?"

"I'll talk to Julio and see if there is something we can do to make the trip safer," promised Alonzo.

Paul suggested, "How about just staying at the *Estancia* until we win this war?"

"It is a war, isn't it," acknowledged Alonzo, "but who are we fighting, and what do they want?"

Paul thought he knew the answer to the former but not the latter.

Pilar looked directly at Alonzo. "Couldn't you stay at the *Estancia* until this is over? You can work from your office there. Except for personal contact, is there anything you have to do here that you can't do from home?"

"No, I suppose not. I'll consider that. I just hate to have those hoodlums dictate where I can be."

"I can understand that," sympathized Paul.

Still looking at Alonzo and talking about Paul as if he weren't there, Pilar said, "What about Paul? Maybe he would be safer at the *Estancia,* too, or maybe back in the United States."

Paul shook his head. "I can't do what I need to from Idaho or from the *Estancia*."

Pilar's voice came out very tense and high pitched. "You can't go out there alone again. You can't!"

Both Paul and Alonzo turned to stare at her. They were surprised at her intense outburst but shared her sentiment. Alonzo responded, "You are right, Pilar, I agree."

Turning to Paul, "You must make sure to have Miguel with you whenever you are outside of this building or your apartment."

Paul thought for a moment before voicing his concern. "How reliable is Miguel? How far can we trust him?"

Alonzo submitted, "Why do you ask?"

Paul responded, "I don't know for sure. There is a question in my mind. He arrived at the location precisely at the time of my escape. How could he do that?"

Pilar answered, "They were tracing your movements by the GPS in your phone."

"It took me a few minutes to call you. Then, you had to contact Security. They had to set up the trace. Only after setting up the trace could Miguel have started in my direction. By that time, we'd already travelled many miles."

Shocked and unnerved, Pilar replied, "You're right. Miguel could have only been in that location if he were already in the area when he received the call from Security."

"Or, if he were part of the abduction," offered Paul.

"Perhaps there is one other possibility," proposed Alonzo.

"What would that be?"

"Perhaps they were tracing you before you called. Perhaps your call only allowed Security to know how you were moving, in the trunk of a car."

Paul looked incredulously at Alonzo. "You're tracing me everywhere I go?"

"Not me, but perhaps Julio Batley is. I suspect he traces me one hundred percent of the time so he can react quickly if I'm attacked. I charged Security with keeping you safe. When you chose not to have Miguel with you all the time, maybe this is the way they do it."

CHAPTER 28

Saturday morning Pilar looked around the house for something to do even though she felt she wanted to be at work. She knew Paul and the other members of the team wouldn't be at the office. She wondered what she could do if she were there. The attacks on President Gallardo and the kidnapping of Paul were just more than she could grasp. She felt she should be doing something, yet she didn't know what to do.

Her sister, Marcela, entered the living room and noticed Pilar sitting in the overstuffed chair looking out the window. "Something must be bothering you, Little Sister."

"Oh, that is an understatement. There is a lot bothering me."

With a twinkle in her eye, Marcela spoke, "Is it that new boyfriend of yours?"

Pilar looked her sister directly in the eye and didn't crack a smile. "Not today, Dear Sister, not today. I'm not in the mood to be teased. He isn't my boyfriend, but it is concern for him that is bothering me."

"What is it, Pilar?"

"I'm not sure how much I'm allowed to tell you, but I have to talk to someone. He was kidnapped yesterday."

Marcela's eyes opened wide. "He was kidnapped? Pablo Sandoval was kidnapped? I didn't hear anything on the news."

"We didn't report it to the police."

"He was kidnapped, and you didn't report it? Why on earth not?"

"He escaped from his kidnappers within an hour, but that was the scariest hour of my life."

"So, he is safe now?" questioned Marcela. "Pilar, for heaven's sake, tell me what happened."

"Marcela, it wasn't the only evil thing that happened yesterday, it was just the last and the worst, at least for me."

"Speak, Pilar. Tell me what happened."

Pilar explained how President Gallardo of Banco República had been injured and his driver killed by a hit-and-run vehicle.

"Is he going to be OK?"

"He was badly injured, but he is expected to recover."

"Will he be coming back to work?" quizzed Marcela.

"Right now, we aren't sure he'll want to come back. He had received a warning that if he didn't resign his post with *Banco República,* his life would be forfeited. He and his wife are frightened. We all are."

"Pilar, you have to quit working for Sandoval immediately," warned Marcela.

"Abandon Pab–, APS? I can't quit. I have to help Pablo."

"Oh, Pilar, you do care about him, don't you? And I am not teasing you."

"I know you're not, Marcela, and yes, I do. I didn't want to. Then I didn't want to admit it to myself. We almost lost him yesterday, and I felt like I would die if we had. I don't know what to do."

"What happened?" queried Marcela.

"We'd just returned to the office from the hospital. He said he needed to take a walk to clear his head. Perhaps the disaster of President Gallardo reminded him of the tragedy that killed his wife. Maybe he just needed to get some fresh air. I don't know.

Anyway, the next thing I knew, my cell phone was ringing. It was Pablo calling from the trunk of a car."

"He must have been scared to death. What did he do?"

"He tried everything he could think of, and then he thought of his cell phone."

"So, he called you?"

"Yes, isn't that interesting that he would call me when he has a Security officer assigned to him as a bodyguard."

"Maybe you were the first person he thought of."

"It's probably because I set up his phone for him and stored my number."

"Maybe you are the only one he truly trusts."

"I don't know, but he called me."

"What did you do?"

"The first thing I did was pray. Even though I was frightened out of my mind, I tried not to let on. I encouraged him to be calm. I also told him to keep his phone on. I'd heard that the newer phones are equipped with GPS. I thought maybe they could trace him if he left his phone on. I didn't disconnect mine either but went to my office phone and called Security. I told them what had happened, and I told them about his phone."

"Were they able to trace him on his phone?" asked Marcela.

"Yes, but I don't know how that works. They encouraged me to keep talking to him. I went back to my cell phone, but I couldn't get his attention. I could hear the road noise, and I could hear him moving around, but he didn't talk to me for a long time."

"What did you think?"

"I thought they were going to kill him. They tried once in Idaho. They'd shown earlier in the day that they are capable of killing here in Chile."

"Oh, Pilar, it must have been terrible. How did you stay coolheaded?"

"I don't know, maybe it was the prayer. I just thought of him cramped in that car trunk. I thought of how I would feel. Frankly, Marcela, I just longed to hear his voice again to reassure myself that he was all right."

"How did he get out?"

Pilar explained to her sister the process they went through of opening the trunk lid and allowing Pablo to escape.

"Did you get a chance to see him, to talk to him?"

"I did. Oh, Marcela, I'm so embarrassed. I was so horrified before and so elated to see him alive and healthy that I ran up to him, and gave him a hug."

Marcela laughed as she quipped, "You didn't!"

"Yes, I did. Luckily, Sr. Alonzo also gave him a hug so hopefully he will just think it was the natural thing to do."

Still laughing, Marcella chuckled, "Maybe you're not as subtle as I thought you were. Wow!"

"Marcela, I don't know what to do. Here I am the team leader, and all I'm worried about is what Pablo must think of me."

***

"Miguel," Paul began, "I have a question about yesterday. How did you arrive at the scene so quickly when I escaped from my abductors?"

"Oh, that wasn't difficult. I was receiving directions on my Bluetooth from Red Security."

"How did Red know where I was?"

Miguel paused. He was reluctant to supply the information he was afraid Paul was seeking. "Red was following your GPS signal on your cell phone."

"I thought that was probably the case. When did they begin tracing me?"

"I don't understand the question," Miguel stalled.

"I think you do. When did Red Security begin telling you where I was? Was it before Pilar called to tell you I had been kidnapped or after?"

Miguel knew he had to answer truthfully if he wanted to maintain any degree of trust with Paul. "Before."

"How did they know to be tracing my movements today?"

"Paul, they're always tracing you. At first, it wasn't necessary because I was with you. When you decided you wanted to be out on your own, Red Security began tracing you any time you were without protection. We couldn't be right by your side; however, we could be nearby if something happened. I'm sorry. We'd been charged with keeping you safe. We didn't know how else to do it."

"You didn't think of telling me?" Paul was half pleased and half angry. He definitely felt safer knowing that Security was always near, but he felt like a little child being watched by a nursemaid.

"Would you have given your permission if we'd asked? We also always know where Sr. Sandoval is. I think he knows that."

"He suspects and appreciates it. He didn't know I was being traced but also suspected it."

"We have a responsibility to keep both you and Sr. Sandoval safe," Miguel began.

"I know, Miguel. You don't need to apologize, but I do

want to be kept in the loop in my regard in the future. I'll cooperate. I've learned today that my enemies, the enemies of my father, will stop at nothing."

Miguel really didn't know what else to say. As they were entering the lobby of the apartment building he was relieved to see Paul stop to visit with Vicente. He kept his distance but stayed close by.

"Sr. Pablo," invited Vicente. "Come on in and visit for a while."

Paul smiled as he entered Vicente's office. He noticed Miguel standing in the foyer talking into his Bluetooth.

"Did I hear correctly," asked Vicente, "that you have had a very exciting day."

"How did you hear that?"

"Oh, I have my ways." He grinned and then continued, "I called Pilar regarding a church matter. She told me."

"That's interesting. What is your assignment at church?" He'd been so involved in accomplishing his personal goals that he'd not even shown enough interest in those who had befriended him to ask what they did.

"At my age and with my years of experience in the church, I've done almost everything. Right now, I'm the ward Sunday School President. Even though she hasn't been sustained yet, Pilar has been called to teach the Gospel Doctrine class. I was checking to see if she is ready to start this tomorrow."

"Is she?"

"She said she can't stop thinking about what happened to you yesterday, but she'll be ready. She thinks preparing a lesson will help her forget."

Paul smiled, "She is truly amazing. We put her in charge of our team at APS."

"She told me. She really enjoys working with you when

you're not frightening the daylights out of her."

"I'll have to make sure I attend the Gospel Doctrine class tomorrow."

Vicente chuckled, "That may frighten her more than having you locked up in a trunk. So, do you want to ride with Claudia and me to church tomorrow?"

Paul thought to himself, *Miguel is not going to be far off whether I ride to church with him or with the Troncosos.* "That would be great, Vicente. I'd love to get a ride with you."

"Claudia asked me to invite you to dinner after church, if you don't have other plans."

"I'd like that."

***

The same day Eduardo started to work with Pilar, Alicia set the date for their marriage ceremony. Now that date was in jeopardy.

"So, let me get this straight. One employee of APS was killed, another severely injured in an attempted murder and another was kidnapped all on the same day?"

"Essentially, you're correct, and yes, it all happened yesterday," replied Eduardo.

"And you are seriously considering continuing to work for them? I love you dearly. I want to marry you soon, but I want a live husband."

"I want to marry you, too. We both felt this job offer from Segue was an answer to our prayers. Didn't we both feel that way?"

"We did, but I didn't know your work was so dangerous," protested Alicia.

"We don't know that it is. If I understand correctly, the president of *Banco República* was warned, and he didn't heed the warning. None of my task force has been threatened that I know of."

"Did you know of the threat to the bank president?"

"No."

"Did anyone else know he had been threatened?"

"No."

Alicia was almost crying from frustration. "Then how do you know that other members of the team haven't been threatened?"

Eduardo looked around the restaurant to see if anyone was looking. "Alicia, we were told from the beginning there were dangerous aspects to our job. We're being paid way more than I could ever have expected precisely because there is some element of danger."

"Some element?" cried Alicia. "A man died yesterday because of an element of danger. Another is seriously wounded. Another was kidnapped. Some element of danger?"

"I know. I was naive and didn't expect things to turn out the way they have, but I could get killed crossing the street."

"Yes, you could, especially if the bad guys you are up against happen to see you crossing the street."

In frustration, Eduardo asked, "What do you want me to do, Alicia?"

"I want you to quit. I'd rather have you stocking shelves at a grocery store than working where I have to worry about you every day. You didn't train to be an investigator, you are an engineer. Engineers' jobs are not dangerous."

CHAPTER 29

"How terrible it must have been for you yesterday," began Maria Isabella. "First, the president of *Banco República* and second, your own son."

"It was terrible, M*i Amor*. How can I subject my family and my employees to such risk?"

"What alternatives do you have?"

"We can keep you and Jorge safe here on the *Estancia*."

She interrupted, "How long can we be kept here, Alonzo? Your son needs a life. He can't be cooped up in the *Estancia* forever."

"It won't be forever. We hope to have this problem solved soon."

"How soon?"

"I really don't know, but we hope to reach the conclusion of this disaster in a few days."

"How many people will be hurt or even killed in a few days? We almost lost Pablo yesterday."

"I tremble when I think of that," said Alonzo as he visibly shuddered.

"Why can't we keep him safe here at the *Estancia* as well?"

Pilar and I both encouraged him to do that, but he felt he

couldn't do his job there."

"What job is that?"

"The same task he's had from the beginning, to track down his wife's killers. The mission has expanded now that he is sure the other threats to our employees are being perpetrated by the same people. When he tracks them down and turns them over to the *Carabineros,* our lives will return to normal."

"What would motivate people to try to do so much damage to our companies, our employees and our family? What are they trying to accomplish?"

"We don't know yet, but we think we will find out soon."

"Let's just give them what they want and be done with it."

"I would seriously consider that if I had any idea what they wanted."

"I hope you're correct, Alonzo. I don't think I can take much more of this."

***

Carlos was getting closer and closer to his goal, and he wanted his mother to know about it. Even if she wasn't coherent, she was really the only person with whom he could talk. Perhaps it was better that she wasn't lucid and couldn't repeat it to anyone else.

"Oh, Joaquin," she giggled as he entered. "I knew you'd come today. Oh, what beautiful flowers. I can see you have my favorite candy."

Oh well, thought Carlos, *at least she recognizes the candy.*

"Mother," he began. "I have some good news for you today."

A small furrow of a frown crossed her brow when he

called her Mother. Then that muddled look replaced it. *I shouldn't have called her Mother. She gets confused when I do that.*

Starting over as though he'd never made the opening statement he began again. "Maria Luiza, I have good news for you today."

This time her eyes brightened like a small child just before opening a wrapped gift.

"What is it, my dear?"

"You remember Alonzo Sandoval?" Carlos questioned.

"Oh, yes, of course I do. What a wonderful man. He always takes such good care of me and my baby." Then the confused look returned. "I wonder why he doesn't come by anymore."

"Of course, he's always taken good care of you. You are the mother of his son."

Maria Luiza Mendocina didn't respond to what he'd said. She was busy lightly fingering the petals of the flowers as she chewed another piece of chocolate candy.

Disappointed, Carlos continued. "Sr. Sandoval has given me a copy of his most recent will and testament. It names you as the mother of his son and provides for your care here at *Las Amapolas* for the rest of your life."

Carlos might as well not have been in the room as she was completely oblivious to having a visitor.

"He has named your son as a joint heir with the other two sons. He's finally acknowledged him for what he is, a blood heir who will soon be the chief executive officer of the Sandoval businesses, which is his legal right."

How sad, he thought, *I'm giving her the most important information she will ever receive, and she doesn't even hear it.* Carlos quietly moved to his mother's side, kissed her on the forehead before quickly exiting her room.

***

Paul rode to church with Vicente and Claudia Troncoso realizing that Miguel was nearby. *Perhaps I should have invited him to attend church with us.* Paul smiled at the thought. It felt comfortable being back in church. He'd missed most of the Sunday's since Janet's death. He just didn't want to be there without her, but somehow, he didn't feel that way in Chile.

There were only a few introductions at church as Paul had met many of the congregation the previous week. He noticed *Hermana* Jimenez staring as they entered the chapel. Pilar was already seated with her family. There was space enough for the three of them, so Paul approached Pilar. "Mind if we sit here?"

She blushed and Marcela grinned as Paul sat down next to her. Marcela and Orlando reached over and shook his hand. During the meeting, Pilar was asked to stand while the bishop read her name as the new Gospel Doctrine teacher. The congregation voted to sustain her. Paul smiled at her, and she pretended not to notice.

Pilar gave an excellent lesson about Ruth and Naomi during Sunday School. Only she knew that she was shaking from nerves on the inside.

When the meetings were over, Marcela quickly approached Paul and invited him to join their family for Sunday dinner. He asked for a rain check as he already had a dinner date scheduled with the Troncosos.

She frowned as she asked, "What is a rain check?"

Paul started to explain when Pilar interrupted, "Never mind, I'll explain it to her later."

"Then can we invite you for next Sunday?" gushed Marcela as Pilar, with her back to Paul, glared at her.

"That would be wonderful," responded Paul. Pilar noticed Vicente wink at Marcela.

The Troncosos and Paul made small talk as they returned to their home and Vicente and Paul continued to visit as Claudia put the final touches on a meal she had prepared in advance.

Vicente invited Paul to give a blessing on the food. Paul realized he hadn't prayed in Spanish since his mission years ago. In his mind, he vowed he would pray every day in Spanish, as long as he was in Chile. He found the language of prayer came back to him quickly.

Claudia opened the conversation, "I miss our Sunday afternoons with our dear friends, Alonzo and Kathleen, so many years ago. What a pleasure to now have their son with us."

Quizzically, Paul asked, "How close were you two with my parents?"

"Then, very close. Claudia and your mother were the dearest of friends."

"Yes, my heart was broken when she didn't come back to Chile after your birth."

"Did the two of you continue to correspond after I was born?"

"Oh, yes, at first we wrote each other every week. I read all about what a good baby you were. Over time, we began to write less often, and finally, when she discovered she wouldn't be returning to Chile, our communications dwindled to birthdays and Christmas."

Paul wondered how much Claudia knew about why his mother had not returned to Chile. "Did she say why she wasn't coming back?"

"She was quiet about that. Her stated reason was, 'Alonzo and I aren't together anymore.'"

Vicente exclaimed, "That didn't make any sense at all."

"Why not? Marriages fall apart all the time," Paul

wondered.

"Not those two, not with people so much in love."

"They adored each other, and they were so compatible."

"It's hard to maintain a marriage when one of the two is having an affair."

Vicente shook his head as he frowned. "That seems highly unlikely."

"When I was older, I asked why my mother didn't return to live with my father. My grandparents explained that my father had taken a mistress." Paul wondered if the Troncosos could sense the bitterness in his voice.

"You know, Pablo, your father and I maintained our relationship. For a while, he continued to come to church. I knew him well enough to know he had a testimony.

When our country was in such an uproar and people were disappearing, he quit coming. I assumed because it was too dangerous."

"Did you still do things together?"

"Our association had always been related to the church. So, when he quit coming to church, we didn't see each other very often. We came from two different worlds. He was rich and powerful while I barely earned enough to feed my family, however, we still saw each other occasionally. Even so, I find it doubtful that he was with someone else."

"He said he had a mistress. He wrote it in a letter."

"Hmm, that is very curious."

"Wasn't there a rumor that he had another child?" asked Paul.

"I heard that but never believed it."

"I didn't either," added Claudia.

"How did you come to work for him?"

Claudia and Vicente smiled at each other knowingly. "I'd been laid off. Work was really hard to come by. We were late with our rent and had very little food.

"We worried that the children wouldn't have enough to eat. We tried to think of any place that Vicente could find work."

"Claudia and I spent a lot of time on our knees praying that I would find work, any work. One day, out of nowhere, your father called me. He said he was having problems and wondered if I could do him the favor of managing the apartment building for him. He offered me a very generous salary, more than I'd been earning. He also wondered if we'd mind living in an apartment in the building so I would be available twenty-four hours a day. I began earning more than I had, and we didn't have to pay rent. I went to work immediately, and I've been here ever since."

"Imagine, he had problems and wondered if Vicente would do him a favor. He was a godsend for us. We've been eternally grateful."

Paul wondered how his father had known that Vicente needed help just as he had always wondered how his father always seemed to know when tuition was due or cash was needed for books and fees. He was curious if his father was anything like he'd always imagined.

CHAPTER 30

Paul chose not to attend the team meeting Monday morning. He didn't want to waste time answering questions regarding his abduction and didn't want his presence to put undue pressures on team members who might be inclined to find work elsewhere.

Pilar began, "I'm sure all of you have considered the danger we are all in by working on this team considering Paul's kidnapping on Friday. You've probably received pressure from family members to quit your jobs before you get hurt. I know I have. Paul and I decided that I should have this discussion with you first thing, before we start on our projects. Do any of you think you ought to discontinue your employment here?"

Gus joked, "I didn't know that was an option. I thought the only way we could get off this team was through death."

Yolanda continued the joke, "So, our options are die for sure if we leave the team or take the chance of dying by staying on?"

Tino added, "I was afraid that if I quit, Paul might use a pipe on my legs." Everyone laughed.

"So, you heard that too?" asked Pilar.

"What we're hearing has given us a completely different

image of our boss than we had before," continued Tino.

"Is this how Segue does business in the United States, or is Paul learning how we do business in Chile?" quipped Luis.

Pilar allowed them to wisecrack as long as they wanted. She knew how much pressure she'd received from her own family to quit. She assumed they'd all had like experiences in the past forty-eight hours. The joking eased the tension and probably strengthened the team for those who chose to remain. Still, the joking was frustrating for Pilar: first, because there was so much to do and second, because the abduction of Paul had been so serious.

It was Eduardo who broke up the joking by asking, "How are you dealing with the pressures of others to have us quit? Alicia is acting as though there are no other alternatives."

Pilar allowed the others to answer.

Tino started. "I really didn't tell my family enough about it for them to say anything."

Yolanda continued, "I didn't either, even though I think my dad figured it out. He knows I'm a big girl and will do what I think is right."

"Adriana and I aren't getting that kind of confidence in our judgement. Maybe our parents don't have the trust in us that your dad has in you, Yolanda," offered Luis.

"That's because you're so much younger," chuckled Yolanda. They all laughed again.

"Cecilia and I talked about it. She's not happy that Sandoval employees are being threatened, but she explained it like this: 'If your team doesn't find the culprits, who will? If you don't help your team correct this terrible wrong, who will?' She doesn't like what is happening, however, she gives me full support to continue if I desire, and I do desire."

Even Pilar smiled at that. "Maybe I should've hired Cecilia."

Tino quickly responded, "She would've done a great job. She won't be intimidated, even by big Gus. Maybe we need to have her talk to Alicia."

Again, everyone laughed. The conversation continued as they talked about the potential risks they faced. They talked about how urgent their mission was. In the end, the team remained intact, although Eduardo wasn't sure what he'd tell Alicia.

Pilar passed out additional preliminary information that had arrived from Red Security which seemed to be on board providing reports on all known and suspected acts of sabotage. She assigned Eduardo to begin looking into anything that might have disrupted the normal flow of business. She assigned Tino to inspect the threats that had been received by any employee or their family members. The others were instructed to return to the companies which had yet to provide information.

"Perhaps the attack on President Gallardo and the abduction of Paul will help persuade the various institutions to cooperate. We had already suggested that none of you work alone in the field. Now it's imperative that you follow that strict decree. Keep your eyes open and watch out for each other. We certainly don't want another kidnapping or worse to happen to any of you. The work we are doing is so important. I can't tell you how proud I am of each of you for being willing to stick it out.

"Paul promised Sr. Sandoval that he could meet the team members the next time we have a meeting, but at Paul's direction, Sr. Sandoval is doing his work from home until the risk here has abated."

"So, it's safe enough for us to continue working but not Sr. Sandoval?" kidded Gus.

"I'm not going to tell him you suggested that," replied Pilar. "Just remember that his convoy of cars was attacked by gunfire near *Mina Esperanza,* and his car was blown up in Idaho. Let's be careful so similar things don't happen to us. Yolanda, would you stay after the meeting for a moment?"

A somber but dedicated team returned to the mission at hand and their specific assignments. Yolanda stayed behind.

"Yolanda, Paul has a specific investigation he wants you to pursue. He wants you to look into the APS companies that were nationalized during Allende's term of office. Then he wants you to trace all of those companies and see if all of them were privatized and returned to the Sandoval fold. Especially watch for any companies or properties that were returned to APS or Alonzo Sandoval individually which were not part of Sandoval before. When you get that information, report back to either Paul or me immediately."

***

Paul and Miguel were meeting with Nelson Retamal when the call came from Pilar that the team was intact. Paul had expected some to drop out after the scares of Friday. He thanked her, and asked her to thank the team members.

Nelson explained that he'd been surveilling the address linked to the phone number provided by Luiz Rossi and taking photos of anyone who entered or exited the construction office or the attached home.

Looking through the photos, Paul exclaimed, "This is the one who waved as Janet and I went over the edge into the river." He felt his blood boil and knew it was a good thing he hadn't been the one watching that address. For one, he might have been spotted, and for another, he wasn't sure he could've constrained himself to walk away without a confrontation. Three photos later, he found another face that matched that of the other man in the store in Horseshoe Bend, Idaho. Pulling the two photos together on the desk he asked, "Who are they?"

"They are Esteban and Roberto Contreras."

"Let's get this information to Victor Riquelme and see if the FBI can put together a case which will compel the Chileans to extradite them to the United States."

"We can do that," replied Nelson "but may I suggest something else?"

"In addition to or instead of?" questioned Paul.

"I would say in addition to."

"OK, what's your suggestion?"

"Didn't you say that the passenger in the SUV, which ran your bank president off the road, also waved and sneered?"

"Yes, he did."

"Why don't you show these photos to your bank president and see if he recognizes anyone? If he does, we have these guys for murder here as well as Idaho. Does it matter to you where they're tried?"

"No, not as long as they're convicted and put away so I won't feel the compulsion to take justice into my own hands."

"I understand. Do you want me to go with you when you meet with Riquelme?"

"Yes, but let's show these photos to President Gallardo first."

"Good," replied Retamal.

Miguel hadn't made any comments while they were meeting with Nelson, however, he gave Paul a valuable suggestion on the way to the hospital. "When you show the photos to the bank president, give him the whole packet of photos and let him pick out the person he saw. We don't want you to plant the idea before he looks. We want a really good case to take to the *Carabineros*."

"Thanks, I wouldn't have thought of that."

President Gallardo was hesitant but very pleased to help. There was no doubt in his mind when he came to the photo of Esteban Contreras. "This is the demon who grinned at us and waved as we were pushed off the freeway."

Paul called Victor Riquelme from the hospital room to tell him what they'd discovered. He offered to meet them, but Paul told him they would drive straight to the FBI office from the hospital. Then he placed a call to Nelson Retamal, who agreed to meet them there.

Riquelme was very pleased with the file that Nelson presented. "This will be very helpful. I'm sure this will make the *Carabineros* very happy. They should be able to put together a strong case for the arrest of the Contreras brothers."

***

Pedro was disappointed that his cell hadn't been able to contain Pablo Sandoval. Both men who had chased Pablo into the wheelchair store had been injured. One had a broken leg and the other a concussion. At first, they'd been taken into custody by the *Carabineros* but were later released. They claimed to be the victims of a vicious attack.

They couldn't give a believable reason for chasing their attacker into the store.

Three people in the wheelchair store testified that a first man had run through their store screaming for them to call the police. The second two men, brandishing firearms, chased him into the shop in the back of the store. Unarmed, the first man defended himself, disabling the two. He yelled again for them to call the police as he ran out the back door.

Since the *Carabineros* couldn't charge the two disabled men with any crime, they'd been released. The police had no idea who the first man was and nothing else had been reported.

Pedro told the injured men to stay home until their wounds were healed. He'd been surprised when two events that he had scheduled for some time had happened on the same day. Roberto and Esteban Contreras had been watching the bank president for days waiting for the opportunity to cause an accident. It was due to luck that they were able to run him off the road in a place that was dangerous. It hadn't been important to kill or not to kill him. He had been warned, and he hadn't heeded their warning.

When Roberto discovered that Pedro was also scheduling the kidnapping of Pablo Sandoval, he asked to be transferred to that assignment, but Pedro hadn't allowed it. He told them they had their chance with Sandoval in the United States, and they'd failed. Pedro complained that Pablo had seen their faces. He didn't want him spooked before he was kidnapped.

What Pedro hadn't anticipated was Pablo Sandoval finding a way out of the trunk of the car.

"We'll just have to try again," he suggested.

"This time, let us do it," pleaded Roberto. "He won't escape from us."

"We can't let you do that. He knows your faces. We can't let him see you until he is completely in our control."

"When he is, Alonzo Sandoval will be forced to give us back the *Mina Esperanza*."

"Yes, he will. You boys are going to be rich men."

"How soon?" asked Esteban.

"Very soon," answered their benefactor.

CHAPTER 31

Paul was in the midst of going through the reports gathered by his team from the various APS companies when his phone rang. He was somewhat startled because the call was from Jorge, who'd never called him before.

"Pablo, when are you going to come out to the *Estancia* so I can show you around on horseback?" Jorge asked.

Even though being shown around by Jorge had been mentioned when he first visited the *Estancia,* he thought being shown around had already happened when they drove around in the Land Rover.

"When would you like to do that, Jorge?" replied Paul.

"How about this afternoon?"

Paul would have preferred a later date because he was finally receiving some information from Julio Batley, Director of Security, and from the other APS companies, but Jorge wasn't someone Paul felt comfortable postponing. He also wanted to look around security gate 4. "This afternoon will be fine, Jorge. I'll have Miguel drive me out there."

There was a brief pause, and Paul could hear Jorge talking to someone in the background. "Wait a minute, Pablo. My mother wants to speak to you."

Paul wondered why Maria Isabella would want to talk

to him. He simply replied, "OK."

After cordial greetings, Maria Isabella asserted, "I'm so pleased you're willing to take time from your busy schedule to be with Jorge. He's talked of nothing else for days. Thank you for coming."

"Think nothing of it. I enjoy being with Jorge."

"Since you are coming out here anyway, why don't you join us for lunch before your ride with Jorge." Paul could think of no reason why he shouldn't, so he agreed.

He was greeted at the front doors of *El Castillo* by Maria Isabella. "Please come in, Pablo. Jorge is completing a project upstairs. He will be down in a few minutes. Why don't you and I visit while the cook is putting the finishing touches on lunch?"

Paul wondered if he'd been manipulated into coming out to the *Estancia* so she could talk to him. In a sense, she was his stepmother, just about the age of his own mother, but he felt no kinship to her. He wondered, *Does this woman want to become my mother? What's going on here?*

"Pablo, I've wanted to talk to you ever since you first visited the *Estancia*. I realize I can't be your mother, but you are Alonzo's son and Jorge's brother. They both need you in their lives. I personally invite you to be a member of our family."

Paul stammered, "I really don't know what to say."

"I'm so grateful that you are now part of Alonzo's life. I've seen a light come on in his eyes that had been extinguished long ago. Alonzo has suffered greatly because he couldn't be close to his son."

Paul surmised that Maria Isabella was sincere, however, he didn't really want to be part of Alonzo's life. He came to Chile to find Janet's killers not to join his estranged father's family. His hesitancy was obvious to Maria Isabella. "I can see from the look in your eyes that what I suggest is uncomfortable to you. Pablo, may we speak frankly?"

Even though Paul didn't care for the direction of this conversation, he didn't know how to head it off. He wondered, *Perhaps talking with Maria Isabella can help me get some answers.* "Yes, I would like that," he responded hesitantly.

Maria Isabella came right to the point. "Pablo, why have you avoided becoming close to your father?"

Paul was stunned by the abruptness. There were thousands of times, when he was a boy, that he wanted nothing more than to have a father. He loved Grandpa Merrick, however, Grandpa Merrick wasn't his father. Paul didn't feel it was his fault that his father and he weren't close. "I never looked at Alonzo Sandoval as anything other than my biological father."

She was taken up short. "Pablo, didn't your father provide for you and your mother, Kathleen?"

"Do you mean provide money? Yes, he provided plenty of money. I'm very grateful that we never needed to worry about finances," admitted Paul.

"Wasn't your father there for you at the important crossroads in your life such as your graduations?" asked Maria Isabella.

"Oh, he showed up for all my graduations, but he wasn't there to play catch. He wasn't there to teach me how to ride a bike. He wasn't there to watch me play football. He wasn't there to hear me sing in the high school musical. Maria Isabella, I'm sorry. He just wasn't there," protested Paul.

"How could he do those things when he lived in Chile, and you lived in the United States?"

Paul replied, "Exactly my point! He was my biological father. He provided for all of our financial needs, but he wasn't part of our lives. My mother loved him. She wanted to come back to Chile, so we could be a family. He wouldn't allow it. I was too young to know anything about this, however, my grandparents let me know. Often, I would ask them why I couldn't go live with my father. They explained that he didn't want us." Paul could feel the anger and resentment building up inside him. He didn't want anyone to see him when he felt this way. He lost his mother at age five. His father didn't want him, and recently he lost Janet. He fought back the tears that were beginning to well up in his eyes.

"Pablo," her tones were soft and motherly. "I'm so sorry. He did want you, and he wanted your mother. Do you know why he wouldn't allow you to come to Chile?"

Paul blurted out in anger, "Yes, I know. It's because he had a mistress." Seeing the shock and hurt in her eyes, Paul apologized, "I'm sorry Maria Isabella. I don't know who …"

Softly and slowly, Maria Isabella responded, "It wasn't me. I doubt very much that it was anyone. I don't think Alonzo Sandoval ever had a mistress. That's not in his nature."

Paul thought, *That is what Vicente and Claudia said.* He shook his head as he answered, "That doesn't make any sense. My grandparents saw the letter. It was very explicit. After months of stalling my mother's desire to return to Chile, he finally said that she shouldn't come back because he had a mistress. Everyone knew about his mistress, and it would be very uncomfortable for everyone."

Maria Isabella exclaimed, "If your father had a mistress, no one knew about it. Everyone I knew expected her to return. We couldn't understand why she stayed in the

United States unless she was afraid."

Paul questioned, "You weren't his mistress, and yet, you knew my father then?"

She replied, "I knew both of your parents. I considered your mother, Kathleen, one of my dear friends. I believe she felt the same about me. She and I exchanged letters until a few months after your birth when she quit writing to me."

"How did you and my father, uh …?"

"As I said, I was friends with both of your parents. Your father was very much in love with your mother. Without his beloved wife and child, he threw himself into his work. He worked eighty hours per week almost every week. All his friends tried to get him to take it easy, but he wouldn't. He knew your mother was ill and tried to contact her, but her parents would not allow it. When she died, he became very sad and depressed. I tried to console him; we all did. Over time, he and I came to love each other. One day he said, 'I don't know what I would do without you.' I replied, 'You don't need to be without me.' We saw each other for many years before we married."

Paul stammered, "I'm very confused. I thought …"

She responded, "I know what you thought. I suspect that is what your father wanted you to think."

Perplexed, Paul asked, "Why?"

"Those were dangerous times, Pablo. Your father's life was in danger. He, other members of the family and key employees were threatened. Some were even killed."

Paul exclaimed, "Killed?"

"Yes, Pablo. Your life and the life of your mother would have been in grave danger had you been here. I think your father was trying to protect you."

Devastated, Paul asked, "So it was all a lie?"

Maria Isabella sighed, "I don't know for sure, but I

suspect it was."

***

Paul, Jorge and Maria Isabella completed a very pleasant lunch. Paul was pleased there was no more talk about Alonzo Sandoval. Because of feelings elicited from his earlier conversation with Maria Isabella, Paul realized the resentment he carried for his father was much deeper than he thought.

Jorge was eager to begin showing Paul around the *Estancia* by horseback. As he led Paul out to the stables he asked, "Are you an experienced rider, Pablo?"

Paul responded, "I've never been trained to ride properly, but I've been riding horses most of my life."

With a huge grin on his face Jorge suggested, "If you grew up on horses, you will probably want to ride *Terremoto.*"

Paul quickly replied, "*Terremoto* means Earthquake. I don't think I am ready for *Terremoto,* I think I am more prepared for *Tremblor* (Tremor) or *Tranquilidad* (Tranquility)."

Jorge laughed as he led Paul into the tack room. Paul was pleased to see some Western saddles from which to choose. He noticed that Jorge also grabbed a Western saddle.

"So now, where is *Tranquilidad*?" questioned Paul.

Jorge laughed again as he led Paul to a beautiful, tall, bay gelding with a glistening, black tail and mane. Then Jorge took his own saddle to an equally tall, strawberry roan. They both took time to saddle their mounts and then took them to the arena for Paul and his gelding to become acquainted.

As they exited the arena, Jorge led them on a completely different horse path than the ones that paralleled the paved road they had taken in the Land Rover.

They first passed a herd of mother cows with their newborn calves. Jorge explained that these were all registered, polled Herefords. Jorge pointed out various cows in the herd, reciting their pedigrees and their characteristic traits. He could also identify the sire of many of the newborn calves. He explained how their father shopped around each year for the best registered sires to be brought into the herd. Often, they were shipped in from the United States or Australia.

Paul was impressed with the knowledge that Jorge had of the cattle business down to the pedigrees of many of the animals. Jorge explained that he'd been showing cattle since he was twelve.

Jorge next took Paul past a corral of registered bulls, explaining that they wouldn't be turned in with the cows until early summer, so the next birthing of calves would be in early spring. He pointed out one old bull which was smaller than many of the others. Jorge explained that this bull would be used to breed heifers so their first calf would be smaller and not a difficult birth.

They also went by pastures which contained last year's calves. Only the very best males remained bulls. The lesser bulls were neutered to be raised as beef. Very seldom were the registered bulls kept at the *Estancia*. Most were raised and sold to other ranchers for a profit.

Jorge next took Paul by another operation, very similar to the polled Herefords, but this time the animals were all Santa Gertrudis. He seemed to know almost as much about the Santa Gertrudis as he knew about the Herefords.

Paul asked, "Do you also breed and raise your own horses here on the Estancia?"

"I wish we did," responded Jorge, "but we buy most of our horses already trained."

As they were passing the last of the Santa Gertrudis yearlings, they noticed a black Mercedes security van rushing in their direction.

Hector, one of the security guards, motioned for Paul and Jorge to rush over to the van. Almost out of breath, he exclaimed with great excitement, "We've had another break through at security gate number 4. This time it's not an accident. This time three vehicles broke through the gate. All the passengers of the vehicles are armed. The guard in the guard house called before the intruders realized he was sending out a message. There was shooting. You two need to get off your horses and get in the van where we can protect you and drive you back to the *Castillo,* where you will have better protection."

At first, Paul and Jorge thought they would just as soon ride their horses back to the *Castillo,* but Hector insisted that they couldn't be protected if they were on their horses. As Paul and Jorge dismounted, Hector held the back door of the van open so they could crawl in. He told them to sit on the floor so they couldn't be seen. When Paul and Jorge were on the floor, the van lurched forward.

There were three Security guards in the van, one in the driver's seat, one in the passenger seat and one on a jump-seat in the back with them. Hector stayed with the horses. They expected the van to continue in the direction it was facing towards the *Castillo,* however, it immediately made a rapid U-turn, and made a beeline in the other direction. Paul and Jorge looked at each other with questions of doubt on their faces.

Jorge looked at Paul with fear in his eyes and said, "They're driving away from the Castillo. They're headed directly towards security gate number 4."

Immediately, Paul jumped up and looked out the windshield. He demanded to know where they were going and why they weren't going in the direction of the *Castillo*.

The guard, in the back with them, shouted, "Relax, the driver knows what he's doing. We're just trying to get you to safety quickly."

The van passed two other vehicles inside the *Estancia* fence as they rushed past and through security gate number 4. They continued right across Avenida Bosque up Avenida Mendoza away from the *Estancia*. Looking out the back window, Paul noticed they were being followed by a caravan of the vehicles he'd seen which had crashed through the gate. *Not again. I just went through this Friday.*

Again, Paul started towards the front of the van demanding that they change their course and return to the *Castillo*. The guard pushed him aside. Paul swung around to the left and caught the guard on the chin, knocking him to the floor. Paul again started towards the driver with Jorge following when the guard in the passenger seat turned and pointed an automatic rifle at Paul. The guard had fire in his eyes. "Lay down, and don't move."

CHAPTER 32

"This is a new model Mercedes van, just like the ones Red uses, but I don't think it is one of theirs," whispered Jorge.

"What about the guards, do you recognize any of them?"

"The one rubbing his sore chin looks familiar, but I don't recognize the other two."

Paul searched for any way to escape, facing two automatic rifles trained in their direction.

"Those are FAMAE SAFs," said Jorge pointing at the submachine guns. "That's what the military and police use."

"How do you know that?" asked Paul in amazement.

"Every boy my age knows the weapons used by the *Carabineros*. Where are they taking us?"

Not wanting Jorge to know as he worried they were being taken someplace to kill them, he said, "They are probably planning to hold us until their demands are met?"

"You mean a ransom?"

"Probably."

"Do you think they'll hurt us?"

"Don't think about that. Think of what we can do to escape."

Jorge's eyes brightened as he suggested, "Why don't you punch this one again while I rush the one in the passenger seat?"

"Don't you think they might shoot us before we can do that?"

"That would be stupid of them. How would they get their ransom?"

"Let's not chance their being very bright. Remember, they did kidnap us right from the middle of the *Estancia*. Let's concentrate on where they're taking us in case we get a chance to escape later."

"We can't see much from down here on the floor."

"Maybe one of us could concentrate on what we can see through the windshield and the other on what can be seen through those two small windows on the back doors?"

"Shut up," screamed the guard on the jump seat.

Paul and Jorge looked at the guard and then at each other. "Do you think the back doors are locked?" continued Jorge.

"I told you to shut up." This time the guard pointed his SAF in their direction. "Give me your cell phones."

Blasting the guard with looks of defiance, both Paul and Jorge handed him their phones. He handed the phones to the guard in the passenger seat who pulled out the batteries and the SIM cards before throwing all the pieces out the window.

Paul thought about the SIM card he still had within the folds of his temple recommend. *I don't know what good it is going to do me without a phone.*

Finally, Paul answered Jorge's question in defiance. "I think they're locked. I think the side door is locked, too."

Paul and Jorge watched carefully from the floor of the

van as they traveled mostly west and then north. They traveled in the same direction for almost a half hour. Then the van turned north on what seemed to be a well-used but not busy highway.

"I think we must be on E-89," whispered Jorge.

"Where does that go?"

"It goes north to San Felipe. At that point, they'll either have to continue north, which really goes nowhere, or turn southwest again on 60."

They both continued to watch the hills through the windshield and through the back windows. About twenty minutes later, the van made a couple of turns and entered a busier highway where they seemed to travel in a northwest direction for about ten minutes. Then they turned left and began traveling in a southwest direction.

After they had traveled about an hour, Jorge commented, "It shouldn't be too long until we reach Route 5, I think you'd call it a freeway."

"Where does it go?"

"It goes the full length of Chile from Arica in the North to Puerto Montt and farther in the South."

Just like Interstate 5 goes from Canada in the North through Washington, Oregon, and California to Mexico in the South, thought Paul.

Sure enough, just a few minutes later the driver turned onto the on ramp and entered Route 5 heading west and then north.

Paul continued to watch for opportunities to overpower the armed guards. Even though they kept the radio blaring neither of them took their eyes off Paul and Jorge for more than a few seconds.

It was a little over an hour later that the driver turned off Route 5. He made numerous turns in a short distance on rough roads before he stopped next to an older, two-story house, badly in need of paint. The guard in the jump seat trained his weapon on Paul and Jorge while the one in the passenger seat got out and opened the sliding door of the van. He, too, had his firearm at the ready.

Walking from the van to the house, Paul tried to picture where they were. The area was covered with jagged boulders in every direction. He couldn't see any other structure no matter which way he looked. The house overlooked the Pacific Ocean on the west side and hills on the east. The freeway had to be close, because he could hear the trucks passing by.

They were ordered into a sparsely furnished house and down the stairs into a basement room with a high ceiling which had a door, a high, small window overlooking the Pacific Ocean and two mattresses. "Don't get the idea you can escape through that window. You are too large to get through it. If you did, the drop onto the rocks at the edge of the ocean would kill you. If you want to live, you will cooperate." The guard closed the door, and Paul heard a padlock being attached and locked.

***

When the alarm sounded on his radio that security gate 4 had been breached again, Miguel bolted into action. He'd made the mistake of assuming Pablo was safe within the confines of the *Estancia*. Immediately, he swung the SUV around and headed in the direction that Pablo and Jorge were last seen. He soon found Hector with the two horses, but the Sandoval boys were nowhere to be seen.

Screeching to a stop near the horses, he shouted, "Where are Pablo and Jorge?"

Hector, with his face contorted in confusion, stood holding the reins of both horses. He didn't seem to know what he should do next. "A Red Security van picked them up to take them to safety."

"Did it take them back to the *Castillo*?"

"I thought that is where they would go, but the van spun around and headed in the other direction."

"Towards the guard house?" Miguel questioned in alarm. "That doesn't make any sense. That was the gate that was breached." Miguel didn't wait for a comment but rushed off in the same direction.

When he reached the gate, he found it open. One of the guards was bent over the other who was lying on the ground. "Where did they go?" he shouted.

The upright guard pointed across Avenida Bosque up Avenida Mendoza and continued caring for his fallen partner.

"Do you need any help?"

"No, I've radioed for help. It is on the way. Go after them?"

Miguel sped through the gate and onto Avenida Mendoza while simultaneously calling Red on his cell phone. "Do you have a current signal on Pablo?" he asked.

"Yes, it has them moving west."

"Where are they right now?"

"They're about thirteen kilometers from E-89, about five kilometers ahead of you."

Miguel accelerated, but he knew there was a good possibility the van was traveling just as fast. As he drove, he asked why a Red Security van had been used to whisk Pablo and Jorge away from the Estancia.

"It's not one of ours," replied the dispatcher.

"Hector said they were picked up by a Red Security van with Security guards inside."

"It's not one of ours. All the guards working today are

accounted for. None of them are in that van."

We just went through this two days ago. Has he been kidnapped again, this time with Jorge? I should never have left the armed services. I'm terrible at this, Miguel judged himself.

"Am I getting any closer?"

"The distance between you is about the same, but you are headed in the right direction." Miguel thought of increasing his speed, but knew he couldn't do so safely.

Miguel wondered which direction the van would turn when it arrived at Route 57. It could either turn south and head towards Santiago or it could turn north towards San Felipe.

"We need to anticipate which direction the van is headed and try to get some help. Have the police been notified?"

"No, they haven't."

"Why not?"

"The guard at the security gate was told not to notify the police if they wanted the Sandoval sons back alive."

"Why wasn't I told this earlier?"

"We've been so busy trying to get Red Security people in place that I haven't had time to tell you."

"Do we have anyone ahead of them?"

"Not yet."

"Do you have anyone closer?"

"You are the closest, and you're still about four kilometers behind them. Wait a minute. I've lost their signal."

"You what!"

"Wait a minute."

Miguel unconsciously pressed a little harder on the accelerator. *What is going on here?* "What have you got?"

"Nothing, I'm not getting any signal at all from Pablo's

cell phone?"

"Try Jorge's cell."

"I am, nothing there either."

After following the trail of the fake Red Security van to E-89 and not finding anything, Miguel returned to the *Estancia,* deeply frustrated.

Locating Hector, he asked, "Why did you have Pablo and Jorge get into a van that wasn't secure?"

"I thought it was secure. I thought it was one of ours. It looked just like our vans and had the insignia."

"It had a Red Security insignia?"

"Yes, and the guards in the van were all wearing Security uniforms."

"Why didn't Pablo and Jorge return to the *Castillo* on horseback?"

"It wasn't my idea. Sr. Pablo insisted."

"He insisted on dismounting and entering the van?"

"Yes, sir. It was his idea. He said they'd be safer. He asked me to bring the horses so that's what I did."

"So, he wasn't reluctant to get in the van."

"No sir, he seemed to recognize the guards in the van. I heard him order them to turn around. It seemed to me that he was in charge."

Miguel was truly confused. Hector was intimating that Pablo was in control. *What is going on?*

CHAPTER 33

It was bad enough that Miguel had allowed his charge to be kidnapped on Friday, but to have it happen again three days later was unforgivable. He'd called Julio Batley to report his failure, hoping that Julio would then divulge it to Sr. Sandoval. Instead, his boss ordered him to return to the office immediately to give a personal account. Having to report the kidnapping to Alonzo Sandoval is what he most dreaded.

Upon arrival at the Sandoval Building, Miguel scurried to the Red Security offices on the main floor and reported to Sr. Batley.

"Do you know any more than you did when you called me earlier?" prodded Sr. Batley.

"No, sir, I don't."

"OK, let's head upstairs. This isn't going to be pleasant." He signaled for his secretary to let Sr. Sandoval know they were on their way.

"Does he know anything?"

"I've already told him that Pablo and Jorge were both abducted this time and were driven off by a counterfeit Red Security van. Other than that, I don't think he knows anything."

When they arrived at Sr. Sandoval's office, they found Carlos Mendocina and Pilar Flores already there. Alonzo Sandoval appeared to be shaken and pallid, ten years older than the last time they'd seen him just days earlier.

"What word do you have?" Sr. Sandoval quickly asked.

Miguel took the next few minutes to explain how Paul and Jorge had been abducted. He told how he'd followed the van and was attempting to catch it when the GPS signal from their cell phones went dead.

"I have no idea where they went after they reached E-89. They could've gone north or south at that point."

"What about the police?" questioned Carlos. "Have they been any help?"

"No, we haven't contacted them."

"Why not?" questioned Carlos, obviously surprised.

Julio Batley answered. "The kidnappers told our guard at the security gate that if the police were notified, the Sandoval heirs would be killed. He said their demands would be made known soon enough."

Alonzo Sandoval remained tight lipped and quiet while being debriefed. Carlos verbalized the questions.

"What about you, Julio, do you think we should notify the *Carabineros*?"

"That's not a decision I should be making."

"No, but you are our resident expert."

Julio Batley retorted, "The kidnappers warned that contacting the police would trigger Pablo and Jorge being killed, and yet the police may be our only hope of getting them back."

Turning to Miguel in anger, Carlos questioned, "How did Security allow this abduction to happen?"

"We thought they'd be safe within the walls of the *Estancia*."

"Why weren't they?"

"A convoy of three vehicles crashed through the gate again. According to Hector, two vehicles stayed at the gate. The other drove directly to the location where Pablo and Jorge were riding their horses."

"I don't understand. How could they know?"

"Hector seemed to think that Pablo had signaled them."

"Pablo?" cried out Alonzo and Pilar simultaneously.

"How could that be?" asked Carlos.

"I don't have any explanation. Hector said the van drove right to Pablo and Jorge.

Pablo insisted they get off their horses and get in the van to rush them to safety."

Looking directly at Miguel, Alonzo Sandoval asked, "Do you believe that Pablo was involved in the abduction?"

"I have no reason to believe that Pablo was involved. However, I also have no reason to conclude that Hector was lying or was mistaken."

Pilar had a questioning frown on her face. She finally asked, "How did Hector get to the exact spot where Pablo and Jorge were riding at the exact time that the van to abduct them arrived?"

Julio confirmed, "That's a really good question. On my part, perhaps I need to relieve Hector of any additional duties until this is resolved. I also need to consider the possibility that Pablo was somehow involved. That being said, we still have to make the decision whether to involve the *Carabineros*."

Everyone looked toward Sr. Sandoval for a decision. He had his head in his hands for the longest time and then looked up slowly and said, "Not yet. At least one attempt has been made on Pablo's life which took the life of his wife. This is the second time he has been kidnapped. I would assume both kidnappings were by the same people. He injured two of the men who kidnapped him on Friday. It doesn't make any sense to me that he would then work with the same people to arrange another kidnapping."

Julio asked, "So, you'd choose to not involve the police?"

Carlos suggested, "Perhaps we should involve them because we need all the resources we have available to rescue them."

"Even though the kidnappers may well kill my two boys anyway, I don't want to give them any reason to take action soon. Didn't the guard say we would be receiving a demand for a ransom soon?"

"Yes, he did."

"Then we will wait."

***

"Can you see anything?" Paul asked Jorge as he hoisted him high enough to peer out the basement window.

"Not really, this house seems to be built on the edge of a cliff. It seems to drop immediately down to the sea."

"Is there anything to stand on if we could get out the window?"

"Nothing that I can see; but I can't tell for sure."

The window was small, so small Paul was positive he couldn't get through it. It also had metal, ornamental bars outside the glass. To escape, they'd have to break the glass and then kick out the ornamental bars. If the metal bars were anchored in wood, they should be able to kick them free. If there was a place for sure footing, his thought was to help Jorge get through the window and to safety. There were many "ifs" to consider.

Not knowing how much time they had or the objectives of the kidnappers, Paul and Jorge considered their alternatives.

"Jorge, we need to be ready at any opportunity to break free. If we get that opportunity, you must run away, even if it means leaving me here."

"Pablo, I couldn't do that. I would never leave you here alone!"

"We'll try to escape together, but if that isn't possible, you must make every effort to free yourself. When you get help, come back and get me."

"I don't think I could do that."

"Prepare yourself so you can. Can you hear the trucks on the freeway?"

"Yes," answered Jorge, not sure what Pablo was getting at.

"You must sprint to the freeway quickly and hitch a ride south before the kidnappers have time to come after you. The kidnappers will expect you to run there so that is the first place they'll look. You must catch a ride before they have time to intercept you."

They continued to plan what Jorge would do without any idea how he would escape. Paul still feared the objective of the abductors. Since they'd tried to kill him before, he didn't doubt their capacity to kill Jorge and him now. He decided to do everything in his capacity to make sure that Jorge was no more a victim than he already was.

"Jorge, do you pray?"

"I did when I was little."

"I didn't for almost a year after Janet's death. When I was in the trunk of that car the other day, I realized I needed God's help more than I needed to be angry with Him. I prayed that I wouldn't panic. Then I prayed that I would find a way to escape. I believe that is how I was able to maintain my composure and escape. I believe God helped me."

"Do you think we should pray now?"

"Yes, I do."

Paul dropped to his knees and Jorge followed. Paul voiced his concerns to their Heavenly Father, pleading for assistance. He prayed that God would soften the hearts of the kidnappers so he and his brother wouldn't be harmed. He explained their plan to get free and asked for help. After he said, "Amen," he looked up to find Jorge staring at him. No words were spoken.

The silence of the moment was broken when their door opened and two of the kidnappers entered the door with weapons in hand. They signaled for Paul and Jorge to climb the stairs. They were met at the top of the stairs with the third thug also holding an SAF.

They were ushered into a room which had a video camera mounted on a tripod aimed at a table with two empty chairs. On the table was a small stack of papers. "Sit down in those two chairs," ordered the guard who'd been sitting in the passenger seat of the van. "You will address me as José," he commanded.

Paul and Jorge took the seats, never taking their eyes off the three ruffians brandishing firearms. "What do you want with us?" questioned Paul.

"I want you to look over this document," ordered José.

Paul picked up the document and held it so both he and Jorge could examine it. It appeared to be a deed for the *Esperanza* Mine. Paul studied it carefully and was surprised to see the name of Rodrigo Contreras as the owner. The date the deed was filed was April 15, 1971. Paul tried to remember how long his father had owned the *Esperanza,* but he couldn't recall any reports covering that subject. He thought the Sandoval family had owned it before 1970 because his father had mentioned the attempt by the Allende government to nationalize the mine. For all practical purposes, the deed appeared to be valid.

"Is that a bona fide deed?" asked José.

"It appears to be valid but I'm not an attorney."

"The *Mina Esperanza* was stolen from Rodrigo Contreras by the Sandoval family when Pinochet came into power. If that mine is returned to the Contreras family without recrimination, you two boys will be freed. If it's not returned, we'll begin sending body parts to your father until he is persuaded to part with it. You boys need to hope your father loves you more than he loves this mine."

"Is this even possible?" asked Jorge in English.

"Speak only in Spanish," screamed José.

Paul shrugged because he truly didn't know.

"Now, read the prepared statement that you will read for the camera."

Paul read, *I have examined the deed to the Mina Esperanza, dated April 15, 1971.*

It reveals the true owner to be Rodrigo Julio Contreras Mora. My father, Alonzo Sandoval, made sure that Rodrigo Contreras was among those who disappeared when his friend, Augusto Pinochet, came to power in 1973. Rodrigo Contreras was never seen again and is assumed to have been assassinated. If my father ever wants to see me or my brother, Jorge, again, he must transfer ownership of the Mina Esperanza to the Contreras family without recrimination. He must convince the government that he is transferring it without coercion because he has discovered the mine truly belongs to the Rodrigo Contreras family. When the mine has been officially transferred to the Contreras family, my brother, Jorge, and I will be released. If the police are notified of our disappearance, we will immediately be killed. If the transfer has not been accomplished in seventy-two hours from this very minute, one of Jorge's fingers will be sent to Sr. Sandoval to convince him these men are serious. An additional finger will be sent, alternating between the two of us, every hour until the transfer is complete. Do not try to find us. If anyone comes snooping around, we will be killed immediately.

Paul shuddered as he finished reading the dialogue. He looked at Jorge, whose face was drained of color.

CHAPTER 34

Carlos rushed into Pilar's office. "Come, Pilar, you must see this."

"What is it?"

"I just received a video from the kidnappers."

Pilar's countenance turned pale. "Are they all right? Are Pablo and Jorge okay?"

"They seem to be. Come and see for yourself."

Pilar followed Carlos as he led the way to the lavish conference room. A large screen monitor was prepared for them.

The video opened with Paul and Jorge seated at a wooden table with a blue sheet hung up behind them as a backdrop.

The first to speak was Jorge. He was nervous but brave as he read from a prepared script. "Pablo and I are safe. We haven't been mistreated. We were promised that we would not be harmed if you do exactly what Pablo tells you to do." He stopped and turned to look at Paul.

Paul looked directly into the camera without so much as a blink. He read the script directly from the sheet of paper in his hand. When he finished the screen went blank.

Pilar turned to Carlos, "Has Sr. Sandoval seen this?"

"Not yet, I wanted you to see it first. Has your team discovered anything which would refute or collaborate what Paul is claiming."

"Is he claiming it to be true or is he reading something written by the kidnapper?" questioned a peeved Pilar.

"How can we know? There is nothing in this video to prove or disprove that Paul is behind all of this."

Incredulously, she asked, "Do you even remotely believe that Pablo is the instigator of this abduction and demand for the *Esperanza* Mine?"

"You heard what Hector said. Pablo was giving the orders."

"Well, I don't believe it. I don't have confidence in what Hector said. It makes no sense. Sr. Sandoval needs to see this. We don't have much time."

"Before we invite him in, has your team discovered anything which confirms what Pablo said."

"No, they haven't. Let's let Sr. Sandoval watch this and then I'll go over it with my team."

Immediately, Alonzo Sandoval hobbled in, looking even more haggard then he had the day before.

Carlos began, "We just received a video from the kidnappers. It shows both Pablo and Jorge. It makes the kidnappers' demands known."

Showing great apprehension, Sr. Sandoval signaled with his hands to run the video. He remained standing, looking at the large screen until Pilar took his elbow and gently guided him to his large, black, leather chair. Once seated, he again motioned to Carlos to begin the viewing. He was greatly relieved to see that both of his sons appeared to be unharmed. He watched the video carefully to the end. When it finished, he sat looking down at his hands for a full minute without saying a word. Then he said, "Carlos, would you please start that video again from the beginning?" The three of them watched the video thoroughly three more times before anyone made any comments.

Alonzo Sandoval looked at Carlos and then at Pilar before asking, "Who has seen this?"

"Just the three of us," answered Carlos.

"Good, have the police been notified?"

"No, you heard what Pablo said. He warned us ..."

Alonzo curtly interrupted, "Pablo is warning nothing. He's reading a prepared script provided by their abductors."

Pilar glared at Carlos as if to say, "I told you so."

Carlos shrugged in acquiescence before asking, "Do you want us to notify the police?"

Pilar added in warning, "According to what Pablo read, we don't have much time."

"Do either of you have recommendations?" Sr. Sandoval wanted to know.

Carlos was the first to respond. "It is my opinion that we should never negotiate with terrorists. These people are acting like terrorists."

"Perhaps we should call the police," suggested Pilar.

Alonzo Sandoval paused for two or three minutes considering the alternatives. Finally, "Carlos, have the APS attorneys prepare the paperwork necessary to make the transfer of the *Esperanza* to whomever the kidnappers are demanding."

Carlos sputtered, "But what if . . ."

Very determined, Sr. Sandoval interrupted. "That mine would mean nothing to me if I lost my two sons."

Carlos winced as he thought to himself, *You would still have one son.*

With a questioning look, Pilar stated, "I don't want to think of it, but kidnappers often kill their victims after receiving the ransom so they cannot be identified."

"I thought of that," responded Alonzo "and it could happen, however, I don't think they would in this case. We already know who the kidnappers are. Their objective is to facilitate the transfer of the *Esperanza*. The only way they can be sure we don't alert the *Carabineros* is to return my sons safely."

"Do you know the Contreras family?" questioned Carlos.

"There was a Rodrigo Contreras who served as the general manager of the *Esperanza* in the early seventies. His only connection to the mine was as an employee. He never owned the mine."

"Do you think this is the same Contreras family?" asked Pilar.

"I'm convinced it is. When nationalized companies were being privatized during the early years of Pinochet, there was a petition brought forward by the Contreras family to have the mine turned over to them. I believe Rodrigo Contreras had disappeared by that time. An attorney represented the family. Because the mine had never been nationalized, privatization wasn't necessary. Nothing came of their petition."

***

Pilar introduced her team to the ransom video. "This is the video of Paul and Jorge reading the demands of their abductors."

Pilar waited for the team members to assimilate what they had seen and heard before continuing. "Our charge has changed. Now we must uncover any piece of information that will help us find and rescue Pablo and Jorge."

The fact that Pilar began by mentioning the kidnapping of Paul and finished by emotionally calling him Pablo was not lost on the team.

"What can we do to help?" questioned Adriana. "We aren't trained for this kind of investigation."

"That's true," continued Yolanda. "Shouldn't Red Security be doing the investigation?"

"They already are," replied a frustrated Pilar. "They're doing everything humanly possible to locate and rescue the Sandoval Brothers, but they're limited in personnel. They still need to protect the Sandoval companies and their personnel. We need to help by going through all the files we've received to see if anything pops up which would help us identify the people holding Pablo and Jorge. If we find anything, that information will be given to Red so it can implement the rescue."

"Doesn't the video already let us know who the perpetrators are?" asked Tino. "If the Contreras family wants the *Esperanza* transferred to it, isn't that family behind the kidnapping?"

"Tino, why don't you and Gus see what you can discover regarding members of that family. Find out who they are, where they live and where they might hide Pablo and Jorge if they're involved. Adriana and Luis, go through all the files we have. See if the Contreras name comes up in any of the investigations. Yolanda, see if you can find a copy of that deed to which Pablo referred. See if you can find a gap in ownership in which the Contreras name surfaces."

"Do I need to begin preparing paperwork to transfer the mine to the Contreras family if that becomes necessary?" asked Yolanda.

"The APS legal team is already doing that. You just try to discover if a Rodrigo Contreras ever owned the *Esperanza*."

The team quickly dispersed to begin the assignments

they'd been given realizing that at best, a piece of the Sandoval estate was at risk, and at worst, it could lose both of the Sandoval sons.

***

Paul and Jorge had quickly been removed from the room in which the video had been recorded. The windows of the recording room had been covered, so they weren't able to see how close to the edge of the cliff the house was located. They were able to glance at windows as they were led to the stairway leading back to their cell in the basement. As far as they could tell, the house was built some thirty to fifty feet above the ocean. The house was built upon rocks and the drop-off seemed to be severe.

"Is that deed legal?"

"I don't know," replied Paul. "It seemed to be, but we can't tell for sure."

"Do you think that family is the rightful owner of the *Esperanza*?"

"Again, I don't know, perhaps it doesn't make much difference."

"Why wouldn't it make a difference?"

"Because, if it did, they want it back. If it didn't, they still want it and have gone to great extremes to get it."

"Yeah, they're threatening to cut off fingers and stuff." Jorge was visibly frightened.

"They said they would kill us if they don't get their way."

At first thought, Paul didn't think it would be all that bad to be killed. *I would soon be with Janet again, but what has been driving me since her death is finding the perpetrators and getting them punished. I haven't been able to think of anything else. Now I have a younger brother to think of, and I've put him in harm's way. I can't let the same men kill him too.* "Jorge, we've got to make sure that doesn't happen."

"How?"

Paul didn't want to frighten his younger brother unduly, so he didn't tell him he really didn't know, but he was persuaded he needed to make sure that Jorge escaped.

Paul thought to himself, *I should care what happens to me, but I don't. I do care what happens to Jorge. He must not suffer or die because of my drive. Let's see if we can put that tenacity to better use.*

He walked over to the door and studied it. The hinges were on the other side so removing it wasn't a possibility. He thought the door could be broken but not without a racket. Their captors were armed and appeared to be strong. They'd arrive quickly if they heard a loud noise. The same thing would happen if they tried to break through the walls. At least two of the walls were made of concrete so that wasn't viable either. He kept coming back to the window. *Perhaps they want us to crawl through that window knowing we will fall to our deaths.*

"Pablo, look here." Jorge pointed at a loose board in the floor molding.

"What are we going to do with it when we get it loose?"

"I could hit them over the head. You could grab their guns."

They both looked at the scrawny piece of wood and then they looked at each other. They both shook their heads and vocalized, "Nah," at the same time.

CHAPTER 35

Roberto and Esteban Contreras were both staring at the screen of their laptop when the face of their benefactor appeared.

Pedro Velasquez smiled into the webcam saying, "Congratulations, boys. We have Alonzo Sandoval right where we want him. He has no choice but to transfer the *Esperanza* mine to you."

Roberto conversed with their benefactor while Esteban watched from behind. "When will that happen?"

"It will happen immediately, perhaps as early as tomorrow morning."

"What will keep them from throwing us in jail and taking the mine back?"

"They don't dare. Alonzo Sandoval knows he stole that mine from your father. If the government checks into it too carefully, that will be discovered, and Sr. Sandoval will go to jail. He doesn't want that."

"His sons could still have all of us arrested for kidnapping," Roberto protested.

Pedro Velasquez frowned into the webcam. "Have they seen you?"

"No, just those you assigned to do the kidnapping and

to guard them."

"They're expendable. If they're arrested for kidnapping, they have no connection to you."

"Won't they be able to trace it to us through the video?"

"No, *Tierras Restauradas* will take credit for the video and the kidnapping. There is no way to connect you to the kidnapping."

"What about the motorcycle accident and the car bombing in the United States?"

"Now, there we have a problem because Pablo Sandoval can identify you, however that problem is solvable."

"How?"

"He, too, is expendable."

Esteban smiled. Ever since Pablo Sandoval had survived the motorcycle crash into the river, he'd yearned for the opportunity to finish the chore.

"What about the younger brother?"

"Unfortunately, for him," began their benefactor, "it will be much cleaner for you if he is eliminated too."

Esteban offered his only part of the conversation. "OK, when we know the mine has been transferred, we'll take care of that."

"I think it would be better all the way around if that were accomplished immediately."

"What if we need to show them again before Sr. Sandoval makes the transfer?" questioned Roberto.

"That won't be necessary."

"What if we need to send a finger or an ear?" asked Esteban.

"Won't you still be able to do that?"

Esteban frowned. He'd hoped to cut off a finger or two while they were still living.

Roberto knew better than to argue more with their

benefactor. Pedro Velasquez had always delivered on his promises and had financed the brothers all the way through this ordeal. He would let Esteban finish the Sandoval brothers off, but he wondered if they ought to wait until the transfer of property was complete.

As if he were reading their minds, Pedro continued, "Don't wait too long. Every minute you wait gives them opportunity to escape."

"There's no way to escape from that basement room. The window is way too small for a person to climb through. If they did, they'd fall to their deaths on the rocks below."

Seeing their benefactor frowning again and seeing the look of anticipation on the face of his brother, Esteban, Roberto conceded, "We'll complete the job tonight."

***

Adriana appeared to be deep in thought as she entered Pilar's office. "Pilar, could I have a word with you?"

Pointing to the chair across from her desk, Pilar replied, "Of course, Adriana, sit down. Are you still worried that we might be in danger?"

"I am, but that isn't what I want to talk about."

"Have you found something?"

"Not yet, but I do have a question." Adriana was twirling her pen around her fingers absentmindedly. "How did we get that video?"

"I don't know. Why do you ask?"

"There may be a way to trace the original feed back to the computer and location from where it was sent."

"Do you mean the place where Pablo and Jorge are being held?"

"If they sent it from that location."

"That would really be helpful. Let's check with Carlos."

The two women quickly hurried down the hall to

Carlos' office. As they both entered, Pilar spoke. "Carlos, Adriana has a question about the video."

A slight crease of concern crossed his brow as he asked, "What about the video?"

"How did we get it?" began Adriana. "Did it come attached to an email? Was it hand delivered on a DVD? How did it show up on the big screen in the conference room?"

Carlos considered the question carefully before answering. "No, there was no email or DVD. A popup occurred on the screen on my laptop. I don't remember exactly what it said. It was something about my needing to accept an incoming video feed. When I accepted it, the video downloaded and then started. I saved the download on my laptop and then showed you the video."

Adriana continued, "Did the message come in on any other computer or just yours?"

Slightly nervous and concerned, Carlos responded. "That is curious, isn't it? It only arrived on my laptop."

Pilar asked, "Have you had any other contact with the kidnappers?"

Frowning pensively, Carlos answered. "Not that I know of. I wonder how they got my IP address. Perhaps they are connected with someone else with whom I've been communicating."

"The computer we've been using to reshow the video, is it the same laptop?"

"Yes, of course."

"Could you get us a list of people with whom you have communicated using that computer during the last couple of weeks?" asked Adriana.

"That would be nearly impossible. I've been in contact with all the APS heads of companies as well as numerous other people within those companies. I've communicated with vendors and government officials. Any of them could have had contact with the kidnappers."

"How are we supposed to contact the kidnappers to let them know the deed has been transferred?"

"You know everything I do. The only communication we have is on that video."

Pilar and Adriana paused, thinking about what Carlos had said, thanked him and then returned to Pilar's office.

Pilar looked at Adriana quizzically and suggested, "You have something on your mind, don't you?"

"Yes, the video was probably routed from their computer to a remote network. Maybe I can track back to the kidnappers' computer, if I can find that network. In the meantime, I'll have Luis search through all the messages sent out on that computer to see if anything makes a connection."

As Adriana returned to her cubicle, Pilar moved across the room to the cubicle of Yolanda who was perusing a large file of documents. "Have you been able to discover the deed that Pablo mentions on the video?"

"I've not been able to find a thing. The *Esperanza* Mine had already been in the Sandoval family for many decades before the 1971 deed that Pau. . . Pablo mentioned."

She noticed Pilar staring at her, but neither of them mentioned it.

"How could Pablo be holding a copy of a 1971 deed if the property has always been owned by the Sandoval family?"

"I've been racking my brain and can only think of two possibilities. Sr. Sandoval was either in the process of transferring the property to Sr. Contreras or the deed is a forgery."

"Why would he be transferring the property to Sr.

Contreras?"

"Perhaps arrangements were being made to sell the mine to him. The deed would have been prepared, but if the deal fell through, the deed wouldn't have been signed or filed with the state. When Allende was nationalizing the copper mines, there may have been an attempt to hide the ownership of the company in the name of another person.

What better person than the general manager of the mine?"

"You're positive that didn't happen with the *Esperanza*?"

"It didn't need to be. The *Esperanza* was never nationalized because it was wholly owned by Chileans, namely the Sandoval family. The mines that were nationalized were owned by foreigners, mostly North Americans or Europeans." She thought for a moment and then added, "I'd really like to see the document that Pablo had. It probably is a forgery."

"Since we don't have a copy of the deed, we have no way to know for sure."

Suddenly, Pilar realized that she hadn't contacted Jeff Harkin or Nelson Retamal to inform them of the kidnapping. Her faced emptied of blood when she thought of what she had to tell them. She returned to her own office so she could make the calls in private.

She made the first call to Nelson Retamal of Rodriguez Investigative Services, knowing it would be the easiest. After hearing her story, he promised he would immediately come to her office to be of whatever help he could.

She remembered that Jeff liked to get right to the point immediately so she blurted, "Pab … Paul and his brother, Jorge, have been kidnapped."

"Yeah, I know. Paul told me about it when he called me

on Sunday." He paused before stating, "But, he didn't mention that his brother was with him."

Almost crying, Pilar continued, "No, Sr. Harkin, this is another abduction. Pab … Paul escaped from the kidnappers last Friday, but he and his brother were abducted again yesterday."

"Again! What on earth is going on down there, Pilar?"

By this time, Pilar could no longer control her emotions. She tried to talk but couldn't. Her throat seemed constricted. When she did talk, it came out in squeaks. "It was bad enough the first time, but at least he was talking to me from the trunk of the car on his cell phone. This time the only contact we have is a video of him and Jorge with P … Paul reading the demands of the kidnappers."

"Pilar, this will go much easier if you just call him Pablo."

She sobbed again, this time Jeff could hear her over the phone. He gave her time to regain her composure before continuing. "Pilar, are you okay?"

"I'm so sorry, Sr. Harkin. This has shaken me so."

"I don't blame you, Pilar. It would be difficult for anyone in your situation. What are the kidnappers demanding?"

"A mine," she replied.

"A mine, that's crazy. How can they escape with a mine? Millions of dollars, or whatever mintage you have down there, would make sense, but a mine?"

"They claim the mine was stolen from the Contreras family in the early years of Pinochet. They want it back with no recriminations."

"Can you email me a copy of that video?"

"I'll do that when we complete this call. Sr. Harkin, what should I do? I usually know exactly what needs to be done, but I feel like I'm paralyzed."

"What have you done so far," asked Jeff.

Pilar explained everything that had happened since the kidnapping and especially since they received the video. She included the assignments she'd given to each member of the team.

"Pilar," Jeff interrupted, "you don't seem paralyzed at all. You're doing everything you could possibly do."

After disconnecting, Pilar burst into tears again. In the privacy of her own office, with the door closed, she sobbed and sobbed.

CHAPTER 36

Roberto and Esteban Contreras drove to the same old cliff house they'd visited many times as children.

"How are our prisoners doing?" asked Roberto as the brothers entered the house.

José looked up and responded sullenly, "Pedro Velasquez said we were being replaced, but he didn't say when you were coming. We'll be glad to get out of this hell hole."

"Don't you have everything you need here?"

"Yeah, but we can't leave, even to go get something to eat." José and his two accomplices began gathering their things.

The house was very much as Roberto remembered, but without furniture or friends, it felt empty. He had no idea how Pedro had acquired access. Perhaps he'd rented it or maybe even bought it. In any case, Pedro had jumped at the chance to secure this house once Roberto described it.

The house was separated from other houses by more than a mile. It was not visible from any other building in the area. Their comings and goings were unnoticed. They were close to the freeway and there was easy access to either drive north or south from this location.

Again, he asked, "How are our prisoners?"

"They're locked in the room in the basement as we were instructed. The only way out is the door and it's locked. We take them down something to eat from that box over there." He pointed to a box that had snack bars and bottles of water.

"Do they have a bucket or do you let them out to go to the bathroom?"

"There's a bathroom in the basement, but we have to unlock the door and then stand guard while they use it."

"Is there another way out of the bathroom?"

"A window, just like the one they have in their room. There's no way they could get through the window; it's too small. If somehow they squeezed through, they'd fall to the rocks below. They aren't going anywhere."

The three that Roberto and Esteban were replacing couldn't get away fast enough and Roberto and Esteban were glad to have them leave.

Once they watched the car pull away from the premises, Esteban looked at Robert with an evil glint in his eye. "Are we ready to finish them off?" he asked.

"How do you want to do this?" questioned Roberto. He knew that his brother had been itching to kill Pablo Sandoval ever since they had failed in their first two attempts in the United States.

"I think we need to finish it the way we started." Esteban answered gleefully. "This time we have an ocean instead of a river."

Roberto Contreras couldn't help but smile at the childish anticipation of his brother. He just hoped that Pedro was right, that it was better to kill them now rather than wait until after the mine was legally transferred.

***

After considering all other alternatives, they returned to the window. They couldn't see well enough to see whether the drop off was into the water or onto the rocks, but it seemed to be far enough to kill them either way.

"Do you want to see out, Pablo?" Jorge asked noticing Paul staring.

"I would."

Jorge got on his hands and knees on the floor underneath the window.

Paul frowned, realizing he had no other alternative. He stepped up onto Jorge's back so he could see better. He still couldn't get high enough to look straight down, so he still didn't know exactly what was below them. He could see how the cliff looked to the left. In that direction he could see the cliff dropped off just ten or fifteen feet to a narrow ledge. That ledge continued to wind along underneath the cliff until it was out of sight.

"Jorge, if that ledge continues back this direction until it is right underneath this window, the initial drop off may only be ten to fifteen feet."

Jorge laughed, "So instead of killing myself, I'll only break my legs."

They were both trying to avoid thinking the unavoidable. So, they laughed when they could, even though it was nervous laughter.

Paul's eyes filled with fear as he looked above his head and saw a vent. "Be very quiet, Jorge." Up close to the vent, he could just barely hear conversation in the room above. At first, he worried that he and Jorge may have been overheard discussing their plans to escape, but as he listened carefully, he realized the guards weren't talking about overhearing the boys, they were talking about killing them.

"What are they saying?" grunted Jorge. It was obvious that Paul's weight on his back was making it difficult for him.

Paul wasn't sure he wanted to tell Jorge what he was hearing. Jorge was already struggling with the fact that he'd been kidnapped. Now the kidnappers were talking about killing rather than freeing them at the receipt of the ransom property.

Jorge was impatient. "Tell me or let me get up there and listen."

"That would probably be better anyway because you are much lighter than I am."

As they were exchanging places, Jorge was exasperated as he almost shouted, "What did they say?"

"They said they're going to kill us. They want to finish the way they started, but now they have an ocean instead of a river."

"The guys who kidnapped us aren't the same ones who ran you into the river, are they?"

"No, but it sounds like the ones who are upstairs are."

Paul got on his hands and knees as Jorge climbed on his back. Jorge put his ear as close as possible to the vent. Jorge began to reiterate in whispers what the men upstairs were discussing.

"They are going to get the property back that is rightfully theirs. Alonzo Sandoval stole the mine from their father. They've lived in poverty all their lives because our father is so evil. They tried to get it back through petition, but our father has so much money, he bought off the judges. Now that they've found the deed with the correct signatures, there is no way our father can deny their request. To make sure it happens, they have kidnapped us. They worry that our father is so selfish, he would rather have the mine than his sons. They're going to kill us right away to finish the job they started earlier. They are laughing about how much fun it will be to throw us off the cliff into the ocean."

Jorge stepped down off Paul's back. His face was ashen and lacked animation. He was almost in tears as he asked, "What can we do?"

"We've got to escape before they have time to kill us."

"How? We've considered every alternative. We can't find one that is even possible."

"Maybe there is. I think we can get through that window." Paul knew that he couldn't but possibly Jorge could. If he told Jorge that fact, Jorge might refuse to go without him. He thought maybe Jorge could crawl out the window and drop to the ledge below.

Paul reviewed with Jorge what he must do if they became separated.

"Are you saying you aren't coming with me?"

"We're going to make every effort to get out of this together. If something happens and we're separated, remember what I told you to do."

"I don't want to leave you here."

"I hope you don't have to."

"What if you get away and I don't?"

"The same rules apply." Paul said it, but he knew it was a lie. He wouldn't leave Jorge alone knowing the Contreras brothers were planning to kill them.

CHAPTER 37

Pilar had just begun briefing Nelson Retamal when Adriana rushed into her office. "I think I might know where they are being held."

"Where, where?" questioned Pilar.

She listened as Adriana explained how she had done a back-door track that led her to the computer from which the ransom video had been sent and an approximation of the physical location. "It appears to be somewhere on the coast about fifty miles north of Viña del Mar. Should we call Red Security?"

"I've been thinking about that, but I'm worried that Red Security has been in on the kidnapping from the beginning. I've never believed what Miguel said. I don't think he is involved, but possibly Hector is. Since we don't know for sure, I worry about making things worse by telling them."

"I don't think Paul had full confidence in your security company," added Nelson.

"Who can help then?"

They looked up to see Gus and Tino walking by. Adriana and Pilar looked at each other and smiled. "Tino, Gus, could you come in for a moment?"

After explaining the situation and what they had

discovered, two-hundred-and-forty-pound Gus volunteered immediately for the task. Tino, who was probably more than a hundred pounds lighter, complained. "Gus, you're married. You have a family. You shouldn't risk your life like that. I'll go."

They all looked at Tino and then at Gus and broke out in laughter. Then Tino shrugged and said, "OK, we'll both go."

Pilar added, "All three of us will go with Nelson Retamal, if he is willing." She introduced the private investigator to the team. Then she turned to Adriana, "You continue fine tuning your search and call us if you get any additional information."

The four of them rushed out of the building and jumped into the SUV. Pilar started to get in the driver's seat until Retamal suggested she sit with him and complete her briefing. They had to hurry. They knew it would take approximately two hours to get to the location Adriana had mentioned. As Gus drove, Tino loaded the location they had into the GPS. Immediately, the voice on the GPS advised them to turn left at the next intersection. Knowing that was a one-way street going only to their right, Gus continued in the direction they were headed. They looked nervously at each other when the voice on the GPS said, "Recalculating."

***

Paul reached up and unlatched the window. He knew why the kidnappers were not concerned because the window appeared impenetrable. First, it opened on a hinge from the top and swung in just a few inches, less than six. Second, there were ornate metal bars on the outside. He cocked his head to the side and stared at the window.

"You think there is a way to get through that window, don't you?" asked Jorge.

"I believe God will provide us with an opportunity.

Perhaps the window is that option."

"You really believe in God?"

"I always have, but I've been doubting Him lately."

"Why?"

"I blamed Him for letting Janet die. Before we left on our adventure that day, she insisted we pray. We knelt down, and she prayed that we would have an enjoyable day and that we would be protected from harm and evil. We weren't protected from either. She was harmed and evil men prevailed."

"If He exists, why didn't He help you? Why did He let your wife die?"

"I don't know the answer to that one, Jorge. I just know He loves us and wants what is best for us. I'm starting to remember that again."

"I don't understand how He could let your wife drown. How could a loving God allow terrible men to do what they did to you?"

"That is the question I've been asking every day since she died. Oh, He exists all right. He just didn't do what I wanted Him to do."

"If He didn't help you then, why would you think He would help us now?"

"Part of having faith is determining what God wants and then believing it will happen. Sometimes we know what we want, but God may have a different idea. He knows what is best for us, but sometimes we want something different. I think I knew immediately that Janet wasn't going to come out of that river alive, however, I still kept asking God for it anyway. I wouldn't allow myself to think that God may have needed Janet on the other side."

"The other side of what?"

Paul didn't know how to respond to that question. In his

mind, he was thinking of the other side of the veil, but he didn't want to get into a protracted conversation when there was so much to do, so he answered in the vernacular that he thought Jorge would understand, "In Heaven."

"So, you think God wants us to escape from these men?"

"I do."

"So do I."

"Then let's do everything that we can and pray that God will do the rest."

"You were looking at that window like you had an idea. What is it?"

"Well, they didn't leave anything in this room that we could use as a tool to open the window, so we are going to have to use brute force."

"You are much stronger than I so I guess I'm down on my hands and knees again." Jorge immediately got down on all fours, while Paul stepped up onto his back. He opened the window and used all of his force to try to pull it open further. It didn't budge. He reached through the window and took hold of the ornate iron bars. He shook them to see how much give there was. There was a little but not much. He stepped down to the floor again, and Jorge stood up. They both studied the window trying to come up with some plan to open it.

Again, they heard voices through the vent. That reminded them that their time was limited. As Paul looked at the vent, he had another idea. "Jorge, may I get on your back again?"

With Jorge on hands and knees and Paul standing on his back, Paul could barely reach the vent. He moved it carefully, trying not to make any noise. It moved a little, and Paul could see it was held in place by two screws. He tried to remove the screws with his fingernails, but they weren't strong enough.

Stepping down from his perch on top of Jorge's back, he began looking for a tool that could be used as a screwdriver. He couldn't see anything. Jorge went to where he had been working on loosening the floor molding and returned with a nail. Paul grinned and took the nail.

Again, Jorge got on his hands and knees, and Paul stepped up. After several tries, he was able to use the head of the nail as a screwdriver and the nail itself as a handle. In a few minutes he had removed the cover to the vent. He stepped down to take a more careful look.

"Are you going to use the vent cover as a tool to open the window?" asked Jorge.

"That might be a possibility, however, that isn't what I have in mind. I hope to be able to grab hold of something, inside the vent, that will allow me hold myself up in the air. Then I hope to swing up with my force and kick out the window. If I'm successful, I'll drop down and hoist you so you can climb through the window."

"Why don't we have you go through the window first."

"You're smaller so I want you to go through first. I'll follow. In any case, remember what you are supposed to do."

"I remember. What if I fall off this cliff and get killed?"

Paul worried about that too. "When we knock out the window, we'll look to see whether it is even possible, but we'll have to work fast in case our captors hear the window crashing and come running."

"Maybe we better have you say one of your prayers before we start."

After kneeling and praying, the two brothers shook hands, and Jorge returned to his position on his hands and knees. Paul stepped up onto his back again and reached for the vent. "I'm going to have to jump; prepare yourself."

Jorge braced himself as much as he could.

Paul jumped up shoving both hands inside the vent. As he suspected, he was able to grasp the floor joist with his hands. Jorge braced himself for Paul to fall back down onto his back. It didn't happen. He got up and looked as Paul swung back and forth, gaining momentum. "Get ready," Paul instructed.

The first time Paul swung his feet up to hit the wood around the edge of the window, he almost fell but he hung on. He kicked hard against the wood and felt it give a little, but he worried their captors would hear. He swung again into the window with his feet, and the window gave a little more. Finally, he put everything he had into a final kick which caused the window and the ornate bars to break loose and crash to the rocks below.

Immediately, Paul dropped down and hoisted Jorge to the window. "Look around first and see how you can escape once you are out of the window."

Jorge first looked down, expecting a drop of thirty-five or forty feet to the rocks below. Instead he saw the same ledge that he and Paul had noticed farther out. It was narrow and tilted towards the ocean. He still had to drop about ten to twelve feet. He worried that if he didn't catch hold of something on the ledge, his momentum would carry him off to his death. Bravely, he said, "OK, Pablo, I'm going."

The window was a tight fit, but by tugging and pulling, he was able to squeeze through. By reaching up, he could get a hold of part of the decking above the window. With that, he was able to pull himself upright. Looking down, he could see that if he held onto the window sill and hung down, he would only have to drop about eight or ten feet. He looked carefully to make sure he dropped onto something solid. Then he let go.

Paul wanted to call out to make sure that Jorge was fine, but he worried about being overheard. He hoped the crashing of the waves covered up the sound of the window breaking and falling.

He jumped up and grabbed hold of the window sill and pulled himself up. When he tried to crawl through, he knew he was in trouble. His body was much thicker than that of Jorge. He didn't know whether he could get the leverage necessary to squeeze through. He pulled his head through the opening and began the contortions necessary to work his broad shoulders through the window.

Paul began to panic. He didn't know for sure whether he was panicking because of claustrophobia or because it was taking such a long time. Finally, he was able to get one arm and shoulder through and then the other.

Looking down he could see that Jorge had landed safely on the narrow ledge below. Jorge was watching him. Frustrated that Jorge hadn't run away immediately, but not wanting to scream and alert his captors, he frowned and pointed in the direction he wanted Jorge to flee. Jorge hesitated and then looked both directions. He looked back up, and again, Paul urgently pointed and motioned for Jorge to run. Jorge looked up one more time. Then he ran off in the direction Paul had pointed.

With his shoulders already through the window, Paul felt sure he could eventually get his hips through. Just as he was maneuvering his body into a position which would allow him to extricate his hips he heard one of the Contreras brothers screaming at him from behind.

"Stop right now, or I'll shoot you where you are!"

CHAPTER 38

Maria Isabella sat on a chair near the bedside of her stricken husband. She was sure the anxiety caused by the kidnapping of his sons had caused the flare-up. They'd known he was terminal for over a year. The doctor didn't want to give a life prognosis, but he finally divulged that Alonzo could live a couple of years or he could be gone in six months. They'd been able to deal with that knowledge, especially with the possibility that Pablo could take over the business, but with Pablo and Jorge kidnapped, all hope had seeped away.

"How long have you been here?"

"Not long," she lied.

His smile at her turned into sadness as he asked, "Any word on the boys?"

"Not yet," she whispered.

"I would give all that I own if I could get our two boys home safely."

"I know you would."

Alonzo Sandoval had been wealthy from the day he was born. Much of the Sandoval estate had been in the family for many generations. There had been other attempts to strip him of his wealth but none so devastating as the kidnapping of Pablo and Jorge. Well, that wasn't really true, as the worst had been the killing of Pablo's wife. When that happened, he knew his enemies had crossed the line. There would be no stopping them until they were destroyed. Recognizing the anger in Pablo's heart and his tenacity, Alonzo decided his son was the logical choice to solve the Sandoval companies' problems, as he was certain in his heart that Janet's death and the attempts to destroy APS were connected.

Alonzo had rejoiced to see his sons bonding after so many years apart. He delighted in Jorge's admiration of his older brother.

Alonzo's enemies had gone too far in kidnapping both sons. Just when Alonzo felt he needed to take over his companies and the search for his sons, his cancer flared up. He then hoped that Carlos would do what was needed, however, he seemed to be missing in action.

"I need to get out of this bed and take charge of the Sandoval companies and the search for my sons."

"I know you want to, M*i Amor,* but that isn't possible. Julio Batley is doing everything he can to make sure that Red Security locates and frees our sons."

"I don't know how much I trust Julio Batley and Red Security."

"How can you say that?"

"It was one of the Red Security guards who claimed that Pablo was in charge of the kidnapping. There are real questions about Red's involvement."

"Aren't you using them to work with the police and find the boys?"

"Not really, I'm letting them do what they think they ought to do, but I've called on Pablo's team to do the real research. We're not even sure we want to involve the police. They have too many close ties with Red Security."

"What about the transfer of the *Esperanza* Mine? You're trying to supply the ransom so the boys will be released, aren't you?"

"That's taking place as we speak, but I worry it won't be enough. None of this makes any sense." Alonzo started another coughing fit, and Maria Isabella tried to calm him. She hoped that Pilar and the team were doing all they could to implement the release of their sons.

***

When Jorge had looked down at the rocks below, he had an attack of vertigo. For a second he thought he would fall and held tightly to the window frame. He would've crawled right back inside the window because his fear of falling and getting hurt was worse than the fear of the men who'd kidnapped them, but his fear of being diminished in the eyes of his new-found older brother was even greater than that of falling.

Grasping both sides of the window, he stood on the window sill and looked down. The rocks under the window were jagged and huge. He knew he would have to be very careful, because the drop onto the jagged ledge could easily break a leg or sprain an ankle. If he stumbled, the momentum could carry him over the edge onto the jagged rocks and crashing waves below. Carefully searching, he picked out a place to land. First, he lowered himself so that he was hanging from the bottom of the window sill, looked down again, shuddered and dropped. He landed on a large sheet of rock that angled steeply towards the edge of the cliff. The angle of the ledge was so steep that the momentum of his drop caused him to begin sliding toward the edge. As he was sliding, he quickly turned over to his stomach so he could grab hold of something, anything.

As he slid towards the abyss, he dug his toes into the

rocks. He could feel the sharp rocks cut into his knees and arms as he continued sliding. Just as he was sure he would slide over the edge of the cliff, his toes caught on a piece of a rock sticking up. At the same time, he reached out with his fingers and dug them into a sharp groove. He rested on the rocky ledge for a few seconds to allow the fear and shaking to subside and for his heart rate to slacken. In just a few seconds he was able to regain his composure. He stood looking at the swirling waters below.

Then he remembered the window and Pablo. Looking up, he found the concerned face of his brother frantically waving for him to leave immediately. Jorge doubted that he could abandon Pablo, even though those were the instructions given. *What if he gets stuck in the window? What if the kidnappers catch him trying to escape through the window?* Pablo had been very specific though: bring help.

He looked back up at Pablo who was struggling to pull himself through the window and seemed to be irritated that Jorge was still standing there. Pablo waved for Jorge to leave immediately, pointing in a southerly direction. Looking south, Jorge could see why Pablo was pointing. The ledge on which he was standing gradually climbed the edge of the cliff. If he followed it for a hundred yards or so, he would be able climb to the same level as the house and make his way towards the freeway.

Making his way carefully along the ledge, Jorge was startled to hear shouting. At first, he thought someone was shouting at him. Looking back toward the window, he saw Pablo waving him on as he pulled his head back inside their tiny cell. Jorge knew he didn't have much time before their captors began looking for him. He moved as quickly as he could as the ledge gradually climbed the edge of the cliff.

***

"Stop right now or I'll shoot you where you are," shouted Roberto Contreras.

Esteban raised his SAF to begin firing. Roberto reached out and pushed the pistol down. "Not yet. We don't want the police to find bullet holes when they discover his mangled body at the bottom of the cliff." Esteban smiled at that and relaxed his grip on the automatic weapon. "Now go find the brother. He couldn't have gotten far. See if you can see his body at the bottom of the cliff."

Esteban hesitated and then decided his brother had things under control. He rushed out of the little room and up the stairs. Immediately, he went to the window overlooking the cliff. He couldn't see anyone, but the ledge made it impossible to look all the way to the bottom.

Running outside, he ran to the edge of the cliff. He could see the ledge below and the water swirling beneath that, but he couldn't see anything straight down. He was sure that if the brat had dropped to the ledge, he would have slid right off the edge into the ocean below. He looked north and then south. He could see no sign of his escaped captive. Esteban thought Jorge was probably dead, but he couldn't be sure unless he found the body.

Looking to the south, he saw that the ledge below was close enough to the top of the cliff that he could crawl down. He ran quickly to that spot and stopped to look around. He could see no sign of the youngest Sandoval anywhere. He jumped down to the ledge and looked over the edge. He couldn't see a body anywhere. He walked on the ledge towards the north until he was directly under the window. Again, he walked to the edge and could see nothing. That didn't mean anything because the ocean was swirling violently below. He searched through the white foam and saw nothing.

***

As Paul was retracting himself from the window, his arms and shoulders became stuck. He couldn't move. Roberto shouted at him again "I told you to get back in here."

"I'm stuck," replied Paul half expecting to be shot at any moment.

Roberto tried to pull on Paul's leg with one hand while holding his weapon in the other. When he realized that Paul was indeed stuck, he laid his gun on the mattress so he could pull with both hands.

Paul felt the scraping pressure of the window frame on the undersides of his arms as Roberto pulled. "Stop pulling, it hurts," he shouted. "I can do it better myself if you can hold me up a little."

Roberto had no inclination to help the son of his despised enemy, so he continued to pull. Throwing both arms around both of Paul's thighs, Roberto pulled with all his might. Suddenly, Paul's body was released by the window and both men tumbled to the floor with Paul on top.

When Paul landed on top of Roberto's chest, the wind was knocked from his lungs. In a second, Paul realized his captor was somewhat disabled. He spied the automatic weapon lying on the mattress and rushed towards it. Recovering and realizing he may soon change from captor to captive, Roberto threw himself on top of Paul. They both fell to the mattress with the firearm bruising Paul's hip.

Remembering the maneuvers he had used as a high school wrestler, Paul feigned to the left and then flipped his body to the right with his enemy rolling with him. Both men tried to control the other while trying to reach for the gun.

Roberto reached down with his right hand at the same time that Paul kicked him in the stomach. For the second time in just a few seconds, Roberto found himself with no air in his lungs.

Paul took advantage of that brief lack of air and snatched up the gun. He pretended to know what he was doing and aimed the pistol in the direction of his former captor.

Resigned to his fate, Roberto Contreras slumped to the mattress.

Paul remembered Roberto's face as one of the two he had first seen in the market in Horseshoe Bend, Idaho. Knowing Roberto had been the driver in the muddy pickup truck that pushed his motorcycle off the road into the Payette River, Paul was tempted to pull the trigger. He knew he was fully justified. No one would ever question why he had to kill his captor to escape. His hatred for this man and his brother had been the force behind his anger for many months. This man had taken the life of his dear, sweet Janet. He didn't deserve to live. Who knew what would happen if he turned him over to the police, perhaps nothing.

Roberto Contreras could see the hatred in his former captive's eyes. It was similar to the hatred he'd felt for Alonzo Sandoval. He knew he'd wanted to kill Sr. Sandoval many times. Considering that hatred in the eyes of Pablo Sandoval made Roberto realize he may only have seconds to live. Then out of the corner of his eye he caught the movement of someone else entering the small room.

"I'd put that down if I were you," said a smiling Esteban as he pointed his automatic pistol at Paul.

CHAPTER 39

The thirteen steps out of the basement of the cliff house were difficult for Paul to maneuver with his hands duct taped behind his back. The stairway was steep. He leaned against the wall to keep his balance. He felt the tip of the SAF jammed against the back of his ribs as the Contreras brothers forced him up the stairs and out the front door. He stumbled and fell as he was pushed down the five steps to ground level. He felt blood flooding his face from a cut to the side of his head. Perhaps he could waste some time getting up, which would give Jorge more time, but Roberto quickly jerked him to his feet. Paul knew where they were taking him. He was being taken to the cliff's edge where he'd be thrown to his death on the sharp rocks and the whirling, white waters beneath.

Paul wasn't afraid of death. He welcomed it, because he believed it would soon reunite him with his beloved Janet. However, that would rob him of the joy of watching her killers pay for what they had done to her and that couldn't happen with him dead. He thought perhaps Jorge would be successful in leading the police to this place and completing his job for him.

Too bad Jorge couldn't identify them as he'd only seen

those who'd carried out the kidnapping, because Paul was most interested in apprehending the ones who had killed Janet. He decided to delay his death as long as he possibly could. Every minute he kept the Contreras brothers occupied allowed Jorge to get farther away.

He thought of bolting, but both of the Contreras brothers carried SAF weapons. He assumed that if he ran, he would be shot before they threw him off the cliff. He would wait and hope for a better opportunity.

The two kidnappers and their captive headed southwest of the house towards the cliff. As Paul wondered how he would step down the three-foot drop off with his hands behind his back, Roberto Contreras gave him a shove. Paul fell onto the sharp rocks below banging his head and shoulder. The pain was intense from his left shoulder and his head continued bleeding profusely from a cut over his left ear. Esteban smirked as he looked over the edge at the swirling waters around the protruding, sharp rocks below. He was grinning the same evil way he had as they had forced Paul and Janet into the Payette River.

Paul didn't really want to look down. He worried that if he got too close to the edge, it would make it easier for the brothers to push him over. If his hands weren't duct taped together, he could hold on to one of the killers and take one with him.

Roberto signaled to Esteban, who grabbed Paul's arm and began impelling him toward the edge. Paul felt a jab of pain in his left shoulder as he was dragged along. Roberto took hold of the other arm as they dragged Paul towards his death.

***

As Gus drove, Pilar brought Nelson Retamal up to

speed. After answering her cell phone, she reported, "Adriana says we should be approaching an exit. The place they are holding Pablo and Jorge should be near here, next to the ocean."

"We are approaching an exit in just a few hundred meters," replied Tino.

Pilar looked up as the SUV left the freeway. They could see a winding road leading through jagged boulders towards the ocean with what appeared to be a teenager watching them furtively as he, too, ran in the same direction.

"That looks like ... it is," screamed Pilar. "That's Jorge." She lowered the window and shouted, "Jorge!"

Jorge stopped, turned in shock and then smiled broadly as he recognized Pilar. "I got away. Pablo sent me for help. They still have him."

"We should call the *Carabineros* so they can rescue him," suggested Tino.

"We don't have time," wailed Jorge. "They'll kill him. We have to help him now." He started to run down the frontage road toward the cliff house.

"Wait, Jorge," shouted Pilar. "We'll help you."

The cliff house was not visible from their location. The road weaved in and out of huge, sharp, protruding boulders. Jorge informed them of its proximity, only a couple hundred meters away. As they moved stealthily along, he described the setting of the house perched on the edge of the cliff. He explained that, on foot, they could get close to the house without being seen so they parked their vehicle.

Movement was difficult because the boulders were sharp with many crevices. Jorge, who was leading the group, signaled for them to stop. Carefully, they positioned themselves so they could see the entrance to the house.

Gus studied the layout of the land and asked, "OK, what

is our plan?"

"How many are holding Pablo?" Nelson wanted to know.

"There are only two right now but both are armed with FAMAE SAFs."

Before they could formulate any plan, the front door opened and three men descended the front steps. Pilar gasped as Pablo fell to the ground and then covered her mouth with her hands. Jorge noticed the tears in her eyes.

Quietly, the foursome maneuvered closer, keeping out of sight as Pablo and his kidnappers moved toward the cliff. Again, Pilar had a difficult time not screaming as Pablo was shoved over the edge of the cliff onto the ledge. They could see the blood streaming down his face as the kidnappers dragged him towards his death, which was only a few feet away.

Pilar couldn't contain herself any longer, so she flung the nearest rock at the kidnappers as she rushed towards them screaming. The rock bounced off Roberto's back. Both brothers swung around to face the woman rushing towards them. Roberto was raising his weapon towards her when Pablo hit him in the back with his right shoulder. Esteban fired his weapon toward the oncoming foursome. Retamal returned fire hitting Esteban in the left shoulder.

Neither brother saw the two-by-four crashing down on Esteban's head knocking him unconscious as his weapon slid off into the deep. Roberto stumbled backwards until he lost his footing on the uneven rocks. Fearing he would fall off the cliff, Roberto fell away from the edge. He aimed his automatic weapon at Paul, but Jorge swung the two-by-four again into the wrist holding the gun. The gun dropped from his hand, and Paul kicked it out of reach. Tino picked it up.

Still unconscious, Esteban started to squirm and Roberto

screamed as he held on to his damaged wrist. Nelson and Tino kept the Contreras brothers covered with their weapons while Jorge quickly undid Paul's duct-tape handcuffs. Gus took hold of each of the evil brothers by the back of their collars.

Paul was very happy to see his younger brother. "I thought you'd gone for help."

"Aren't you glad I didn't?"

"Now I am, but I wouldn't have been if you'd been pushed over the edge into the ocean with me."

"Well, that didn't happen. Besides, I did bring help."

Paul turned toward Pilar. He saw her collapse to the ground holding her stomach. Blood was oozing through her fingers. He rushed to her side as he bellowed, "Pilar, you've been shot."

"I know, I'm sorry. I couldn't let them kill you."

"Now you've been shot. Oh Pilar, Sweet Pilar, not you too."

Tino ran for the SUV while Nelson and Gus kept their weapons aimed at the Contreras brothers. Carefully, Paul and Jorge lifted Pilar into the back seat. Paul was confused, not knowing which direction to go. He wanted to make sure the killers didn't escape; however, he couldn't leave Pilar's side.

Nelson took charge. "We'll hold these two until we're able to turn them over to the police. Pablo, you get Pilar to the hospital."

Relieved, Paul crawled into the back seat with Pilar and rested her head in his lap. Tino jumped into the driver's seat and they drove off to find a hospital. Pilar was conscious, but she'd lost a considerable amount of blood.

Knowing she was in shock, Paul found a jacket that had been lying on the seat and placed it over her shoulders. He lightly stroked her hair as they almost flew down the freeway towards the South.

"How are you feeling?"

"I think I feel thirsty."

Paul found a bottle of water in the holder and pressed it to her lips. "Just sip enough to wet your lips."

Her mouth felt like cotton and the cool wetness felt wonderful as she sipped the water. Again, she said, "I couldn't let them kill you."

"You didn't let them kill me. You saved me. I was so eager to catch the men that killed Janet that I didn't realize I was putting others, you and Jorge, in danger. Oh Pilar, please don't die. I couldn't stand to lose you, too."

She looked up into his tear-stained eyes as hers also filled with moisture. Even though it hurt to do so, she reached her hand up and placed it behind his neck. He bent down and softly kissed her.

***

Nelson, Jorge and Gus forced Roberto and Esteban back to the cliff house, where they used the same roll of duct tape to secure their captives' hands behind their backs.

"Now what do we do?" asked Jorge.

Gus replied, "We need to turn these two over to the *Carabineros,* but first we need to let your family know that you're safe."

Knowing the *Carabineros* would soon take the Contreras brothers into custody, Nelson had some questions he wanted answered first. Jorge explained he'd overheard the Contreras brothers admitting they had killed Janet and wanted to kill him and Pablo the same way.

Both Esteban and Roberto were reluctant to answer any questions about the kidnapping, about the event on the Payette River, the bombing of Alonzo's car or the crash caused to Guillermo Gallardo, but Jorge got a reaction when he mentioned the *Esperanza* Mine.

"That mine belongs to us," screamed Esteban.

"Be quiet," Roberto shouted as he glared at his brother.

"It is ours or it was until your father, the great Alonzo Sandoval, stole it from us."

"I told you to shut up," roared Roberto.

"That mine has been owned by the Sandoval family for decades. What makes you think it is yours?" questioned Gus.

Finally, Roberto answered, "We've seen the deed. The *Esperanza* was owned by our father."

Gus interrupted. "Rodrigo Contreras was the general manager of the *Esperanza* in the sixties and early seventies. He never owned it."

"That's not true, we have the deed."

"That deed couldn't be valid. We've researched the ownership in preparation to transfer it to you. It was always owned by the Sandoval family," corrected Gus.

Slowly, the information surfaced that Pedro Velasquez had provided the deed. He'd contacted the Contreras brothers and convinced them that they were the rightful owners of the *Esperanza* Mine. He promised to help them get the mine back. He had persuaded them to try to kill Paul and Alonzo so they could retrieve the mine.

They explained that Pedro Velasquez represented an organization, *Tierras Restauradas,* which helped restore properties to their rightful owners. It was instrumental in restoring properties that were confiscated when Allende nationalized companies for the use of the Chilean government. When those properties were privatized and returned to the rightful owners, many were stolen by rich friends of Pinochet. Instead of the *Esperanza* being returned to Rodrigo Contreras after it was nationalized, it was instead given to Alonzo Sandoval.

Gus responded. "The *Esperanza* was never nationalized. Only foreign-owned mines were nationalized."

"It sounds like you two were duped by this Pedro Velasquez fellow," smirked Nelson Retamal.

Roberto and Esteban began to wonder if they had been deceived. Everything had been so convincing. They'd been positive they were the rightful owners of the *Esperanza* Mine. They'd been positive that Pedro Velasquez had a reason for sending them to the United States to kill Pablo Sandoval. They truly believed that once they carried out the orders of Velasquez, they would be rich men. Now they realized they would go to prison, probably for the rest of their lives.

Roberto was reluctant at first, partly because he was afraid of Velasquez and partly because of his hatred for the Sandoval family. He began to suspect that his hatred was misplaced. Perhaps his hatred should be toward the man who had misled them for so many months.

No longer wanting to protect Pedro, Roberto explained that their contacts with Pedro was over the internet. He explained that Velasquez would be calling soon to get their report. They agreed to have a conversation with him using their webcam. Nelson, Jorge and Gus would stay in the background.

After waiting more than a half hour, the team began to wonder if the Contreras brothers were just delaying the inevitable. They were almost ready to give up when a light ring sounded on the computer with a pop-up asking if they wanted to accept the call. Retamal nodded to Roberto.

"How did it go, boys?" Pedro asked.

"Not well," replied Roberto

Jorge was shocked at the voice he heard. He

maneuvered around so he could see the face on the screen. "Oh no," he exclaimed. Then realizing he'd said it out loud, put his hand over his mouth in shock.

Pedro shouted, "Is there someone there with you?" The screen went blank.

CHAPTER 40

The mother, grandmother and daughter were all in the kitchen putting together the evening meal. Vanessa looked up when she heard the phone ring. Marcela answered, gasped, listened for a moment and then hung up. All the blood had drained from her face.

"What is it?" questioned the grandmother, Freya, with great fear in her eyes.

"It's Pilar. She's been shot. She's being life flighted to the new military hospital as we speak.

"What's wrong with Auntie Pilar?" asked a worried niece, Vanessa.

Freya automatically began removing her apron as she started to gather her things.

Marcela put out her hand to stop her mother. "I'll drive you, Mother. Give me a minute to call Orlando to watch the children."

"I want to go with you," wailed Vanessa.

"Not right now, sweetie. When Auntie Pilar is feeling better, I'll take you to see her."

The operating room had already been prepared and Pilar was rushed there directly when she arrived at the hospital. Marcela and Freya only had time to squeeze her hand, kiss her forehead and tell her they loved her as she was rushed past them.

The nurses tried to give the sister and mother encouragement, however, both could see the apprehension in their eyes. Marcela and Freya were guided to a waiting room where a young couple was waiting for news regarding their young son who had been hit by an automobile.

The waiting room was pleasant enough with couches and chairs around the outside edge. At one end was a table with a half-completed jigsaw puzzle. At the other end was a television set, mounted high on the wall displaying a soccer game with the sound off.

At first, Marcela and Freya talked and worried about Pilar. They tried to rest but were too preoccupied. One of the nurses brought them each a soft drink, but both were too nervous to drink more than a couple sips. Finally, their empty hands, longing for something to do, drifted to the jigsaw puzzle.

Almost two hours later, after much hand wringing, worrying and praying, the surgeon entered the waiting room asking for Señora Donoso. Trembling, Freya stood up and replied, "I'm Señora Donoso."

"It was touch and go for a while," the doctor informed them. "But your daughter is a strong woman, and the surgery was a success. The bullet entered her stomach low and missed the vital organs. She lost much blood, so she's been given a transfusion. She's in recovery right now and in a few minutes will be moved to ICU. You can see her there, but she will need much rest for a few days."

***

"We didn't expect you today," commented Osman, of *La Clínica de Reposo de Las Amapolas de Los Andes*. "You usually come on Sundays."

"I know. I'll be out of town on Sunday," replied a downcast Carlos. "I wanted to visit my mother before leaving."

"You are such a dedicated son, even when she doesn't recognize you. I admire you." When Osman noticed the hint of sadness in Carlos' eyes, he was sorry he'd mentioned that Maria Luiza Mendocina didn't often recognize her son.

"How is she today?"

"She's been sleeping a lot. I hope she wakes up for your visit." Osman noticed that Carlos wasn't carrying the traditional bouquet of flowers or box of candy. He decided not to mention it.

Carlos found his mother lying awake in her bed. She turned and saw him enter but gave no sign of recognition. Carlos stepped over to her bed and took her hand in his.

"Hello, Mother. I couldn't wait until Sunday to pay you a visit."

She glanced at him vacantly and reverted her eyes back to the television.

Carlos gazed around the room. It was very plain and sparingly decorated. The flowers from the previous Sunday were still in the vase on the table by her bed. He glanced back at his mother who now was intently watching a *novela* on the TV screen.

Squeezing her hand, he said, "I'm going away for a while, Mother. I won't be able to bring you flowers and candy."

She gave no acknowledgement that he was talking. "I'm sure you'll be fine here," he continued. "They take such good care of you."

He sat quietly, holding her hand for almost an hour. He didn't even look up when the *Carabineros* entered the room.

***

Jorge and Paul entered the huge bedroom to find their father propped up in his vast, cannonball bed. An ignited fireplace was the focal point of the sitting area with a couple of overstuffed love seats. Maria Isabella immediately arose from a chair next to the bedside of her husband and rushed to hug her son.

"Jorge, Pablo," she gushed, "you cannot know how happy I am to see you. We were so worried. Did they hurt you?"

Jorge responded, "No, Mother, we were fine. Pablo took good care of me."

Paul gave Jorge a quizzical look. "I didn't take care of you. It was because of me you were kidnapped."

Jorge looked directly at his mother. "The only way we could escape was through a window so small Pablo knew he couldn't get through. Still he helped me get out knowing he'd still be there with the kidnappers."

Maria Isabella turned to Paul and gave him a motherly hug. "Thank you so much for protecting him."

Paul protested, "It was Pilar and Jorge who saved me. The kidnappers were trying to push me off the cliff into the ocean when Jorge attacked them with a two-by-four. He's the real hero."

Alonzo lay on his bed with a huge smile on his face. He loved to see the rapport that had developed between his sons. He could sense the love they felt for each other. He wasn't yearning for death, but knew he could die in peace, knowing his two sons had each other.

Noticing his father smiling from his bed, Paul walked over and reached down to take his hand. Alonzo grasped Paul's hand with both of his. "I'm so sorry my invitation for you to come to Chile almost cost you your life. I'm so happy you boys are safe."

"If you remember right," Paul corrected, "my life was endangered long before coming to Chile."

"I believe that was my fault also. My enemies went to extremes to destroy me. Damaging my companies and my employees was not enough. They had to attack my son and his lovely wife all the way up in Idaho."

"Yes, we're positive now that the same ones who were holding us and trying to kill Jorge and me were also responsible for Janet's death. They've been apprehended now. Justice will be served."

"I understand that Pilar was shot. How did that happen?"

Smiling brightly, Jorge offered his explanation. "She was amazing. When she saw the Contreras brothers try to throw Pablo off the cliff, she went after them screaming. She distracted them long enough for the rest of us to save Pablo. Since she was the one making the most noise and running towards them, they shot her."

"The report is that she is recovering well," suggested Maria Isabella.

"She is," replied Paul. "She'll need to rest in the hospital for a week or so, but we hope for a complete recovery."

Alonzo smiled mischievously as he remarked, "She better recover quickly, as we definitely need her."

"I know I need her," acknowledged Paul stifling a tear.

Maria Isabella joined the two of them near her husband's bed. "Can we dare to hope that we are now safe?"

"Well, the Contreras brothers have been captured. We believe there was someone who was issuing the orders, someone who was the mastermind behind Janet's killing, our kidnapping, as well as the sabotage of the Sandoval companies."

"Do we know who that is?"

"We have an idea, but as of just a few minutes ago, he still hadn't been apprehended."

"What were these people trying to accomplish?" asked Maria Isabella.

"Didn't they want the *Esperanza* Mine?" asked Alonzo.

"That was the intention of Roberto and Esteban Contreras. They really believed the mine had been stolen from their father and was rightfully theirs. They'd been convinced that if enough pressure was put on you, you'd give up the mine to save our lives"

"I would have. I would have given up the entire Sandoval empire to save your lives. Riches mean nothing to me if I can't have my family safe."

"How did they get the idea that the mine belonged to them?" asked Maria Isabella.

"They were approached by a man, Pedro Velasquez, who had a document supposedly proving the *Esperanza* Mine had been stolen from Rodrigo Contreras in the seventies."

"Is that the same Rodrigo Contreras who served me as the general manager of the *Esperanza*?"

"We think so."

"He disappeared in 1973 along with many others who wouldn't support the junta of Pinochet."

"Yes, and the Contreras brothers were convinced that you had been instrumental in their father's disappearance."

"I may have been the cause of his disappearance but not because of connections with Pinochet. It could have been a message from Pinochet's cohorts to keep me in line though."

"This Pedro Velasquez convinced Roberto and Esteban Contreras that if they'd kill me and severely damage your companies, you'd have no choice but to turn the mine over to them."

"Didn't they realize the police would know exactly where to look for the kidnappers if we turned the mine over to them?"

"No, they were so sure you'd stolen the mine that you wouldn't dare have the government look into the kidnapping."

"Then why did this Pedro Velasquez have them ask for the mine as ransom?"

"We're beginning to think that may have been a smoke screen. That was the bait he held over the heads of the Contreras brothers to use them to destroy you and your business empire."

"Who is this Pedro Velasquez? What does he have against me?"

Paul didn't want to get ahead of himself. "We aren't sure about that yet. We hope to get that information when he is captured."

Jorge could hardly contain himself. "Father, we saw who the mastermind is."

"You saw him?" gasped his mother.

Jorge continued, "The Contreras brothers communicated with Pedro Velasquez over the internet. Nelson Retamal made them agree to talk to him one last time so we could see his face. We stayed out of sight so the mastermind could only see the two of them. When he came online, we heard him and recognized his voice."

Paul tried to get Jorge's attention without Alonzo or Maria Isabella seeing. He was quietly shaking his head for Jorge to stop. Jorge was so excited by this time that there was no stopping him. "Yes, I recognized his voice. Gus did too. Then I saw his face. We saw who it was."

"Who was it?" both Maria Isabella and Alonzo questioned.

Paul's cell phone interrupted them before Jorge could answer their questions. Paul listened intently, thanked the caller and returned his attention to Alonzo and Maria Isabella. "That was Julio Batley. The *Carabineros* have just captured the man Roberto and Esteban Contreras knew as Pedro Velasquez. We know him as Carlos Mendocina."

CHAPTER 41

Vanessa talked rapidly all the way from their home to the hospital. "Is she really okay? Do you think she will like my dress? I thought she would die when I heard she had been shot. Why did those bad men shoot her?" The questions and comments kept coming, but she didn't give time for her mother or grandmother to respond. Marcela realized that Vanessa was very nervous. The more nervous she got, the faster she talked.

Marcela had tried to renege on her promise to take Vanessa to visit her aunt in the hospital, but Vanessa was tenacious. "Isn't Auntie Pilar getting better?"

"Yes, she is much better."

"Didn't you say you would take me to see her when she feels better?"

"Yes, I did say that."

"So, when are we going?"

Even though Vanessa was only seven years old, she could be very persuasive. Marcela chuckled when she thought, *She and Pilar are very much alike.* So, Vanessa won and accompanied her mother and grandmother to the hospital.

Vanessa quit talking the second they passed through the

massive doors of the modern military hospital which, in actuality, was open to everyone. They passed through the vast lobby and entered the elevator to the right. "Which number should I press?" asked Vanessa. Noticing the numbers on each room she asked, "Which room?" With that information, she quickly oriented the group in the correct direction.

Vanessa's eyes began opening wider and wider as they moved from the front door of the hospital, through the lobby, up the elevator and down the hall. They opened the widest as she entered her aunt's room and saw all the flowers. She had planned to ask her Auntie Pilar how she felt. However, her seven-year-old age took over. She blurted out, "Where did you get all these flowers?"

There were bouquets on the window sill, on the bedside table and more on the floor. Even Marcela was startled to see so many flowers. She too asked, "Who sent these flowers?"

Pilar chuckled as she responded. "Except for those on the window sill, which came from my team, all the rest came from one person."

"Oh," responded Marcela as she began to catch on, "that one person is?"

Pilar blushed as she responded, "Pablo."

"Oh my!" her mother exclaimed.

Marcela smiled, "Wow! I'm impressed. Are you? Because I think he wants you to be impressed."

"Oh, I think he just feels guilty that I got shot."

"So, if he sends enough flowers, that will compensate for the damage he caused you?"

Defensively, Pilar replied, "He didn't cause me damage. It was my own fault that I got shot."

"How was it your fault? How did you get shot?"

"That day is a little fuzzy."

Marcela also was concerned. "Are you serious?"

"Yes, some things that happened that day are very clear and others seem hazy."

"How are you feeling? How is the pain?"

"Really, Marcela, while I'm lying here quietly in bed, I don't feel any pain at all, but it returns when I have to reposition myself in bed or when they make me take a walk."

Her mother got up and started for the door. "Now wait, Mother, don't chastise the nurses. It is my physical therapist who comes twice a day and part of the therapy is to get me up and have me walk up and down the hall. It's to help me heal faster."

Freya wasn't sure if she was convinced or not, but she sat back down.

"Besides," continued Pilar, "I enjoy the walks, the opportunity to get out of this room, and I can tell it's helping."

"Good, now tell us how you got shot," asked her inquisitive sister.

Freya looked from one daughter to the other and then back at Vanessa. "Are you sure this conversation is appropriate for some ears?"

Marcela regretted pressing the subject then she looked back at Pilar and realized she wanted to talk. They both glanced at Vanessa and then at their mother, Freya.

Vanessa looked up at her grandmother, who had gotten out of her chair and was moving toward the door again, and rolled her eyes. "I know, I know, 'Vanessa, would you like to take a walk around the hospital?'"

Freya looked back at her daughter, Pilar, thinking, *I want to hear this too,* but she asked, "Vanessa, I saw a delightful art exhibit on the main floor lobby, would like to go look at it?"

Rolling her eyes again, she replied, "Of course, Grandmother."

Marcela and Pilar both laughed as Freya and Vanessa walked out the door. They could hear their mother remarking as they walked down the hall, "We may just try some of that delicious *postre* they have in the cafeteria."

Marcela paused just a moment to make sure her daughter and mother were out of earshot. "OK, now about the day you were shot. What do you remember, and what is hazy?"

Pilar started at the beginning explaining how Adriana had discovered a physical address for the location in which Pablo and Jorge were being held. Since they couldn't know whom to trust, they didn't notify either Red Security or the *Carabineros*.

"So, you thought the three of you, without experience or weapons, could secure the release of Pablo and Jorge?"

"We did have Sr. Retamal from Rodriguez Investigative Services. He had a weapon and has abundant military training. Pablo had given me his number in case he got into trouble."

"Even so, why didn't you just turn it over to him? For you and two members of your team to confront kidnappers who had already committed murder, what on earth were you thinking?"

Tears welled up in Pilar's eyes. "I thought I would lose Pablo. Marcela, if felt like I would die if they hurt or killed him."

Marcela moved to the edge of Pilar's bed. She took her sister in her arms and held her close. Neither said a word for a number of minutes. Finally, Pilar turned to her sister and continued her narrative. "We turned off the freeway and found Jorge. I was so relieved to see him, and yet, my worry increased that we were too late for Pablo."

"Why was Jorge there?"

"Pablo helped him to escape and sent him for help. Jorge explained that Pablo was still being held by the kidnappers. We had to hurry because they were going to kill him. He heard them say it."

"What did you do?"

"We crept along behind the rocks until we could see the house. We saw two men drag Pablo, with his hands tied behind his back, down the front steps. When he fell, I almost screamed. I had to put my hand over my mouth."

"Was he hurt?"

"Oh Marcela, it was horrible. I could see blood streaming down his face. They were kicking him to make him stand up, and there was nothing I could do. The kidnappers laughed like it was a big joke. They persisted in dragging him to the cliff's edge. We continued to creep closer and closer keeping out of their sight."

"Then what happened?" Marcela was bright eyed and attentive.

"They dragged Pablo to what I thought was the edge of the cliff and forced him over the edge. Oh Marcela, I thought I had lost him. I did scream that time, but the crashing waves must have drowned out the sound, because they didn't even look in our direction. They crawled down on the ledge, where they had thrown Pablo, and began shoving him near the edge of the cliff. Jorge shouted, 'They're going to throw him over.' This time I screamed so loud they could hear me, I threw the first rock I could find, and I rushed them."

"You rushed them, all by yourself?"

"Well, there were four men with me. I wasn't alone"

"I can't imagine what you were thinking. Weren't you

afraid you'd be killed?"

"Marcela, I didn't think at all, I reacted. As I've thought about it since, I guess I was thinking that if Pablo were killed, my life wouldn't be worth living. If he were going to be dead, I wanted to be dead too."

"Wow! I knew you had feelings for Pablo, but I didn't realize it had progressed this far."

"I didn't either until I thought of losing him."

Worried about her sister, she asked, "What about his feelings toward you?"

"That's where my memory gets hazy. One of the kidnappers turned and shot. I felt as though I had been slugged in the stomach. I don't remember anything else that happened until Pablo rushed over and held me."

"What is the next thing you remember?"

"All I remember is lying in the backseat of the SUV and my stomach hurt so badly. I felt thirsty. Pablo gave me a sip of water. Then he held my head in his lap. Oh, I don't know whether this part is real or I imagined it."

"Why, what happened?"

"I thought he held my head in his lap. I thought there were tears streaming down his face. Marcela – I thought he kissed me. I must have imagined that."

"I have to admit, I kissed you, and I apologize. I shouldn't have taken advantage of you when you were in shock."

Both Marcela and Pilar turned to see Pablo entering the door of her room carrying an even bigger bouquet of flowers than any of the previous ones.

Pilar held out her hand to him. He replaced Marcela on the edge of the bed.

Marcela thought she should look away, but she couldn't.

"Oh Pablo, I'm so happy that you're safe. I was so

worried."

"I'm safe, and so are you. I can't believe that my tenacity put you and Jorge in jeopardy. I am so sorry. Can you forgive me?"

"There is nothing to forgive. You were right to pursue those who killed your dear Janet. If you hadn't, her killers would never have been captured."

Marcela tried to excuse herself so Pablo and Pilar could talk alone, however, Pablo took her by the hand. "Marcela, you needn't leave."

Marcela smiled and relaxed as Pablo continued. "I thought I was pursuing Janet's killers out of love for her and perhaps, in the beginning, that was true. The longer I continued, the more it turned into the absolute need for their apprehension, pure and simple. My tenacity put people I care about most in jeopardy." He turned to look at Pilar. "Now I realize that I would rather have had the killers go free than to risk your life. One of my strengths became my weakness. My tenacity dulled my senses, clouding what I was beginning to feel for Jorge, for my father and for you. I'm starting to understand why the Lord said, 'Vengeance is mine.'"

Even though Pablo told her she was welcome to stay in the room, Marcela realized that neither he nor Pilar were aware of her presence. She slipped out the door to begin looking for her mother and daughter.

CHAPTER 42

Even though others would have been denied access to the successful APS executive turned criminal, he was, after all, Alonzo Sandoval and Carlos Mendocina had been his second in command. The warden had been reluctant but with appropriate safeguards, Sr. Sandoval was granted permission to visit with his former heir apparent in the conference room next to the warden's office.

This conference room was like no other that CEO Alonzo Sandoval had ever visited. There were no leather chairs and no soft, thick carpet nor a highly polished mahogany table. There were drab metal chairs and a plain grey, metal table over a grey, tile floor. At one end of the room was a chalk board. The one entrance to the room was a reinforced steel door with a small window through which a guard could keep tabs on the inhabitants.

Again, the warden warned Alonzo, but Sr. Sandoval insisted. "I want to speak to him alone."

Pablo, who accompanied Sr. Sandoval to the prison also offered, "I'd be happy to go in there with you, Father. Remember, it's only been a few weeks since you were lying on your death bed."

"I feel much better now, and there are things that Carlos

and I must discuss in private."

"Are you sure he'll even talk to you?"

"I hope so. Yes, I think he will."

He was already seated at the table when a shackled Carlos Mendocina was led into the room with his eyes downcast.

Alonzo began, "Good morning, Carlos."

Carlos didn't answer. With no expression on his face, he glanced up at Sr. Sandoval and then back at his hands.

"Are they treating you well here?"

He looked up and eyed Alonzo Sandoval for a long time before answering. He appeared thinner than before he was arrested, even somewhat gaunt. The confidence in his eyes was replaced with one of defeat mingled with defiance.

Finally, he said, "Yes, they're treating me well. Frankly, I'm treated better than many of the other prisoners. I'm sure your influence is felt even here."

"Yes, I do receive a weekly report of your treatment, either from the warden directly or his assistant."

"Thank you for that."

"I also receive a weekly report on the treatment and condition of your mother. I don't visit her for I'm told she wouldn't recognize me if I did. The staff at the nursing home tell me they miss your visits and how you visited her every week and brought her flowers and her favorite candy."

"She doesn't recognize me either, but I'm sorry I can't take her the flowers and candy. She seemed to light up every time I brought them. She seemed to expect them somehow."

"Perhaps I can help with that. I'll have them delivered to her every Sunday. She won't see you, but she will get her gifts."

Carlos shrugged as he replied, "She hasn't known who I am for a long time. Sometimes, she calls me Joaquin."

Carlos noticed Sr. Sandoval grimace slightly at the mention of that name. He studied Alonzo carefully and finally asked, "Why are you here?"

"I have some questions I want to ask you, Carlos."

Carlos frowned apprehensively as he thought. *Yeah, I'll bet. I've always had some questions I wanted to ask you, but I never did.* "What questions?" he asked.

"When the police searched your apartment, among other things they found a will, supposedly my will. It had my signature and was notarized even though I didn't sign it."

Carlos stared at his hands but said nothing. "Carlos, that will names you as one of my sons."

Still, Carlos said nothing.

"My question is this, Carlos. Do you truly believe you are one of my sons or was this an elaborate scheme to steal my estate?"

Alonzo waited for Carlos to look up and give him an answer, but it didn't happen. In frustration, he gazed at the young man he'd supported since birth, the young man whose education he had supplied, the young man he'd brought along rapidly and prepared to eventually head the family business. In exasperation he blurted out the question,

"Why?"

With fire and hate in his eyes, Carlos exclaimed, "You know why!"

Alonzo's eyes demonstrated hurt and confusion. "How would I know?"

"I worked hard to do everything you ever asked. I directed the APS companies better than they'd ever been run, and yet, you were preparing to turn the Sandoval companies over to someone you hardly knew."

"You mean Pablo? Carlos, he is my son."

"So am I!" Carlos shrieked.

"Your whole life I've treated you like a son, but you are not my flesh and blood. It is not the same."

"I know it's not the same," yelped Carlos, "because you married his mother, and you never married mine, but I am your flesh and blood."

"Carlos, I am a friend of your family. I am not your father."

Carlos looked up, but all the blood had drained from his face. "But, my mother …"

"Did Maria Luiza tell you I'm your father?" questioned Alonzo.

"Not in so many words. She was a proud woman and was ashamed that I was born out of wedlock. She always brightened up at the mention of your name. Even now, when she doesn't recognize me, her face lights up when I mention you."

"Even so, she never said I was your father." It was a statement, not a question.

"No, she didn't, but she did acknowledge that it was you who provided for us. Later, when I learned of your mistress and perhaps an illegitimate child, it wasn't difficult to put two and two together. I knew who that illegitimate child must be. Why else would you support my mother all these years, pay for my education, and make me your second in command at APS?"

"There never was a mistress or a child," Alonzo confessed solemnly. "I never had that kind of relationship with your mother."

"I don't believe that. Everyone knew. Almost everyone assumed I was your illegitimate son."

"I'm sorry you had that misunderstanding Carlos, but you are not my son. You are the son of my good friend, cousin and associate, Joaquin."

Carlos thought his head would explode. "Who did you say?"

"Joaquin Montalva. He was not only my dear friend, but he was my father's executive assistant. He did for my father what you did for me. He was married to the daughter of a powerful man in Chile. Even so, he and your mother, Maria Luiza, were very much in love. When Joaquin was killed in an automobile accident, your mother was already expecting you. My father committed to supporting your mother and you for the rest of your lives if she promised to never acknowledge who your father was."

Tears welled up in Carlos' eyes, and then the hatred returned. "You lie. You would say anything to keep me from receiving my share of the inheritance. When I told my mother that you had written us into your will and acknowledged me as a son, she was happy you were finally accepting me as your son."

'I'm sorry, Carlos. Think about it. Why would she call you Joaquin? You resemble your father, Joaquin Montalva."

Carlos' face became livid. "You lie," he shouted, "you lie!" As he attempted to advance toward Alonzo Sandoval, the guard burst into the room and immediately subdued him. He was hauled, screaming from the room.

The warden rushed into the conference room as Carlos was dragged out. "Are you all right, Sr. Sandoval?"

"Yes, I'm fine, Arturo, just a little shaken."

"Can I get you something?"

"No, please let me sit for a moment to catch my breath."

As Alonzo Sandoval rode back to the office with Pablo, he rehearsed what he could remember of his conversation with Carlos recounting his mistaken idea that he was a son. Pablo listened politely even though he was deep in thought.

He didn't tell his father that he, too, had assumed the same thing that Carlos thought.

Alonzo noticed the pensive mood of his oldest son. "Did something ring a chord?" he asked.

"I'm just seeing the irony of the situation. Carlos lived and worked with you and longed to be your son. I wanted nothing to do with you and didn't want to be your son. Now, I'm the son and he's in prison. It's sad."

"It is sad. Do you still not want to be my son?" asked Alonzo Sandoval apprehensively.

"No, I'm proud and pleased to be your son. What I realize is that I have wanted you in my life all along. I wanted you to be there for father and son outings. I wanted you to attend my football games. I wanted you to hear me sing. I resented that you had chosen someone else other than my mother, so I pretended I wanted nothing to do with you. Now, I realize you were trying to protect us and keep us from harm's way."

There were tears in Alonzo's eyes as his son spoke of not having a father. "I longed to be near you and your mother. I was so afraid you'd be killed if you came to Chile. Your mother died anyway. I blame myself for her death. Then when you finally did come down here, you were almost killed. It's as though I created what I feared the most."

"My longing to be close to you, My Father, could never be fulfilled until my Janet was killed. I thought you needed me, but in reality, I needed you."

"I hope we will always be together from this day on, My Son."

"You know, Father, I think my desire to get close to you has a much deeper significance."

Alonzo was so happy to be called 'Father' that he almost lost the meaning of what Pablo was trying to tell him.

"What is that?" he asked.

"I think my desire to get close to you reminded me of my yearning to re-establish my relationship with my Father in Heaven. That relationship had been severely damaged by Janet's death. I quit praying for a long time. I didn't start again until I desperately needed His help to escape from the trunk of that car. Later, Jorge and I needed help to escape before we were killed. Now, I want to maintain both relationships, the one with you and the one with my Father in Heaven."

"You know, Son, I think it's time for me to re-establish my relationship with my Father in Heaven, too. I've been thinking about that ever since Jorge was born."

"There is no time like the present. Perhaps we can help each other."

Later, when Alonzo returned home, he had the opportunity to rehash what had happened in the prison and more important to him, with his son, Pablo.

Maria Isabella was obviously shaken. "I didn't even want you to go to the office, let alone go to that prison. You haven't recovered your health sufficiently yet. You shouldn't have gone in there alone. He might have hurt you."

"It's hard for me to think the Carlos I knew could ever hurt me or anyone else for that matter."

"Alonzo, he was responsible for four deaths, and he tried to have you killed twice."

"All because of a misunderstanding."

"It was more than a misunderstanding. He was filled with jealousy and rage. Even though you supported his mother and him, he wanted more. He built it up in his mind that he was your disinherited son. He not only wanted to be included in the will, he tried to kill those who would have shared the inheritance."

"I know all that in my head, but down here" he pointed to his heart, "I can't know."

"How did he get Rodrigo's sons to help him?"

"As he had forged a new will with very convincing signatures, witnesses and notary, he also forged the deed to the *Esperanza*. He used that forged deed to convince the Contreras brothers that I'd stolen the mine from their father. He convinced them that I would return the mine to them as ransom for our sons. They believed him. In their rage they, too were willing to harm and murder innocent people to accomplish their evil designs."

"What will happen to Carlos and the Contreras brothers?"

"They'll spend a long time in prison."

"Will they be sent to the United States to stand trial for Janet's death?"

"That's probably what Pablo would want, but in all likelihood, it won't happen. Idaho has a death penalty and Chile wouldn't allow extradition if death were a possibility. There are negotiations going on right now that would allow them to be sent to the United States, but the death penalty would have to be off the table."

"Do you think that will happen?"

"Probably not."

"What will Pablo do now?"

"All along, he has said he would be returning to the United States when Janet's killers had been apprehended, but so far, he hasn't taken any steps to do so. I'm not sure he even wants to."

"Is that because you've been ill, and he's trying to do your work as well as that of Carlos?"

"That's probably part of the reason. He also seems to enjoy time with Jorge."

"I know. Isn't that wonderful? Jorge now has all the benefits of an older brother, one he really idolizes."

"I think those feelings are mutual, but it isn't just our family."

"What do you mean?"

"Not only has Pablo found a family that loves him, he may have found a new love."

"You mean Pilar?"

"I think so."

"Oh, I hope so. It has been over a year since Janet's death. It's time for Pablo to move on with his life, and I would love to have another woman, especially Pilar, in the Sandoval family."

ABOUT THE AUTHOR

I am a husband, father of 8, grandfather of 32 and great-grandfather of 7 so far. Raised on a farm near Eagle, Idaho, my degrees are a BS at Brigham Young University and a CLU from American College and still, I don't have a clue. I served two missions for the Church of Jesus Christ of Latter-day Saints in Brazil and Chile. I spent my working years farming and selling. During those years, I've given hundreds of estate planning seminars and facilitated many personal relationship workshops.

My career in financial services was cut short, after 35 years, when inclusion body myositis robbed all my muscles of strength, finally giving me the time I always wanted to write. Since being confined to my wheelchair, I use my time to write in a blog (papamarshall.blogspot.com), poems, short stories, novels, and nonfiction. Writing serves not only as great therapy, it keeps me out my wife's way.

67644465R00204

Made in the USA
San Bernardino, CA
26 January 2018